# CITY OF NIGHTMARES

Stepping into the darkness of the bedroom, she reached for the light. Without
a sound, the man lunged from behind before her hand found the switch. Bobbi
went stiff with an electric jolt of fear. A
musty, foul-tasting glove covered her
mouth and nose.

"Hello, Bobbi," a voice said. "You've
been looking for me, haven't you? Well,
guess who's here . . ."

# CITY OF
# PASSION

## DALLAS BARNES

AVON BOOKS ◆ NEW YORK

CITY OF PASSION is an original publication of Avon Books. This work has never before appeared in book form. This work is a novel. Any similarity to actual persons or events is purely coincidental.


AVON BOOKS
A division of
The Hearst Corporation
105 Madison Avenue
New York, New York 10016

Copyright © 1988 by Dallas Barnes
Published by arrangement with the author
Library of Congress Catalog Card Number: 88-91583
ISBN: 0-380-75504-1

First Avon Books Printing: December 1988

AVON TRADEMARK REG. U.S. PAT. OFF. AND IN OTHER COUNTRIES, MARCA REGISTRADA, HECHO EN U.S.A.

Printed in the U.S.A.

K-R 10 9 8 7 6 5 4 3 2 1

This book is dedicated to
Bobbi, Randa, and Helen.

They hid their tears and their pain
but never their hearts.

# THE SUNSET QUICKIE

Bobbi Marshal was a shapely brunette in her late twenties. She was walking west on the north side of Sunset Boulevard, wearing a black leather miniskirt, mesh nylons, high heels, and a form-fitting, sleeveless turtleneck sweater. None of the passing motorists jamming the six-lane-wide street for the afternoon rush hour mistook the girl for a tourist or a secretary on her way home from the office. They knew what Bobbi Marshal was, and many of them, especially the married ones, were looking for her.

The waiting families would be told the usual stories—traffic was heavy, there was an accident on the freeway, the car was low on gas. The fifty or hundred dollars spent would be hidden in the office petty cash or an expense account, or the kids could always wait until next month for their trip to the dentist. Seldom were the "Sunset quickies" discovered. But then, sometimes, they were.

Bobbi Marshal watched as the polished dark Chrysler cruised by a second time. The driver, dressed in a conservative suit and tie, stared at Bobbi as the car moved slowly by. Bobbi forced a short, inviting smile. The man was working on his nerve. Bobbi deliberately brushed at imagined lint on her breast, pulling the material of her turtleneck sweater tight. The man switched on a right-hand-turn signal and swung onto Laurel Canyon. Bobbi knew he was going around the block again. "Gotcha." She smiled and chewed faster on her gum. She really hated the man. She also hated what she was doing, but she had no choice. This would be her sixth pickup since coming out onto the street two hours earlier. Business had been brisk, and she was tired. Her ankles were swollen from the damned high heels, and she felt half naked. She looked forward to going home.

Bobbi was almost to the intersection of Laurel Canyon when someone whistled from a passing car. Bobbi paused, glanced back over her shoulder. There was the Chrysler in the curb lane, approaching.

This time the Chrysler pulled to a stop beside Bobbi. The driver, a distinguished-looking man in his mid-forties, ran the right window down and leaned toward it. "You looking for a ride?"

Bobbi stepped to the open car window. The heavy aroma of the man's cologne boiled out to greet her. It seemed men had to put on fresh aftershave before getting laid. Like the ancient rite of the Tangeian warriors, who splashed on human blood before sacking an enemy's village, she suddenly remembered from a psychology class at USC. A horn blared behind the Chrysler. A nearby sign clearly warned that it was a No Stopping zone. "What kind of ride you talking about?" Bobbi smiled seductively at the man.

The horn behind the Chrysler sounded again. The man acted nervous, worried. He glanced over his shoulder at the irritated motorist behind him, then back to Bobbi. He opened the door. "Get in."

Bobbi climbed into the car and closed the door. The man pulled the car in gear and swung onto Laurel Canyon. The inside of the car was clean, and the man was wearing polished brown shoes: a professional of some kind, Bobbi Marshal decided. "Where are we going?" she asked.

Traffic was lighter now on the side street, and the man looked at Bobbi. She could almost feel his hungry eyes roaming her body. "How much?" he asked bluntly.

"How much?" Bobbi repeated innocently. "I don't understand."

"Come on," the man answered. "I'm no Vice cop and

you're sure as hell no Girl Scout. I'm talking about getting naked with those tits hanging in my face." He reached out and cupped Bobbi's left breast in his hand.

The move surprised her, but she quickly pushed his hand away.

"Oh, you mean sex?" Bobbi asked.

"The word is fuck, honey, and I'll pay a hundred dollars for a party at my house."

"In that case," Bobbi said, reaching into her leather shoulder bag, "I better show you my diaphragm." She pulled out a small, wallet-sized case and flipped it open to reveal the silver and gold badge of the Los Angeles Police Department.

The man's jaw fell open.

"Pull over to the curb," Bobbi ordered. "You're under arrest for soliciting for the purposes of prostitution."

A black and white patrol car roared alongside the Chrysler. Its red lights were flashing. The passenger officer gestured for the Chrysler to pull over.

"You bitch, you won't get away with this," the man growled at Bobbi after a quick glance at the patrol car. "I'm a judge and I'll have your ass."

"Careful, your honor," Bobbi answered sarcastically, "that's what got you in trouble in the first place."

"You'll regret this," the man growled, pulling the Chrysler to the curb.

"Could you speak a little louder, judge?" Bobbi said. "I want to make sure we get all this on the tape."

A uniformed officer pulled open the driver's door and took the judge by the arm. "Step out of the car, sir, and keep your hands in plain sight."

"Get your hands off me. I'm a judge."

The officer pulled the judge out of the car and threw him against the side of it. "I don't give a shit if you're one of Santa's helpers."

Bobbi Marshal slid out of the car on the passenger's side as an unmarked police car came to a smooth stop behind the Chrysler. Detective Sergeant Brad Chilcoat, thirty-four years old, climbed from behind the wheel and walked to where Bobbi stood. She was watching the now handcuffed judge being put into the back seat of the patrol car. Brad Chilcoat was smiling—he did that often, finding that it added to the aura of confidence he carried with his six-foot-two athletic frame—but it was a friendly smile. "One more, partner, and you get not only the toaster but a GE microwave oven as well."

"What I'd like to get is out of here," Bobbi answered. "That's number six. How many of these sex-starved idiots can Vice want?"

A tow truck arrived, amber lights flashing, and pulled to a stop in front of the Chrysler, then backed up for the hookup. The tow truck, like Brad Chilcoat and the patrol car, had been standing by two blocks away at the command post staging area at Fairfax and Fountain, headquarters for what Hollywood Vice was calling "Operation Short Sheet." Two months earlier the same effort had been called "Operation Long John." The time before that, "Pillow Talk." The beleaguered Hollywood Vice Unit, unable to cope with the seemingly endless army of prostitutes, had aimed their efforts at an easier target, the johns, the would-be customers. The results, well-publicized and good fare for the local evening news, had made it look as if the police really did have the situation under control. Each campaign had sent shock waves of fear through the would-be johns, and for a few days at least, innocent women could walk Sunset Boulevard without a steady stream of cars pulling over to offer rides, money, and insults.

The bimonthly "sweeps," as the lieutenant in charge of Hollywood Vice enjoyed calling them, had been staffed by policewomen from the city's seventeen police divisions. Each campaign involved eleven Los Angeles policewomen who, in provocative dress, lured the horny into the Vice trap. Bobbi Marshal, a detective from the Wilshire Division Sex Team, reluctantly was one of them. Her partner, Brad Chilcoat, had tagged along. Chilcoat had told her, "I like to be around when you dress kinky," but the truth was that it was a dangerous assignment, and Chilcoat was worried about her. Although each of the decoys was wired for sound and unmarked surveillance vehicles were used, things could still go wrong. This time they hadn't.

"Six is the lucky number." Chilcoat smiled at Bobbi. "Wanna know how we came up with that number?"

"I'd rather not."

"Let me help you with your radio and we'll head for the barn." The radio was taped to her skin between her breasts.

"I'll manage," Bobbi said, moving toward their waiting car.

Brad Chilcoat drove as Bobbi reached under her turtleneck sweater and carefully pulled the heavy tape from her flesh. "Ouch," she complained as the small transmitter and tape came away.

"Want me to kiss it and make it better?" Chilcoat asked with a smile.

Bobbi stuck the ball of tape and radio into her purse. "I'm told by those who have that it doesn't come any better."

"Touché." Brad Chilcoat smiled.

They drove to the operation's command post in a supermarket parking lot, where Bobbi quickly filled out an arrest report. The air was thick with radio traffic. Motor officers and uniformed officers milled around as several TV crews moved about with their portable cameras and floodlamps.

The irate judge arrived and was loaded into a waiting B-wagon, a delivery van reinforced and turned into a jail bus. The eager TV news crew quickly gathered around to add to the judge's embarrassment. He tried to hide his face, a difficult feat for one with his wrists shackled behind his back.

Lieutenant Piefer, a graying man with a neatly trimmed beard, sat at a folding table with a city map, several portable radios, and a plastic overlay marked with grease pencil indicating the locations of the decoys still out on the street. Bobbi approached the lieutenant with her completed arrest report. "I've got my quota for the day, lieutenant," she said, handing the report to him. "Any idea where he works?"

"Superior Court. Department one-oh-three," the lieutenant answered. "One of my men had a weenie waver trial start in his courtroom today." The lieutenant signed the bottom of the report and tossed it into a basket with others. "You're a free woman, Marshal."

"The pleasure's all mine," Bobbi said, digging the small radio transmitter from her purse. She set it on the table.

"You ever want to come to Hollywood Vice," the lieutenant said, studying Bobbi, "we could sure use you."

"I don't doubt that, lieutenant." Bobbi smiled. "But I have this aversion to being used."

Brad Chilcoat was talking with two helmeted motor officers when Bobbi walked up. "Come on, partner," she said to Chilcoat, "let's get back to the real world."

"See you guys," Chilcoat said to the men and walked away with Bobbi.

The two officers watched Bobbi in her miniskirt and heels as she moved away with Chilcoat. "Doesn't seem fair," one of them complained.

"How's that?" his partner questioned.

"The city gives me a Harley Davidson, and Brad Chilcoat gets that."

Bobbi and Brad drove south on busy La Brea Avenue and turned east on Venice Boulevard. "You want to try some follow-up tonight?" Brad Chilcoat said, with a glance at Bobbi.

It was nearly six o'clock, and they normally were end-of-watch at four-thirty. Bobbi had kicked her heels off and was massaging her feet. "I don't think I could walk another step," she complained. "Let's put it off until tomorrow."

"You know, the next time you catch this duty, you might want to try roller skates."

"You're sick."

"Just think of the concept," Chilcoat suggested. "Whores on wheels."

"No wonder they charge so much," Bobbi said, continuing to massage a foot through the dark mesh nylon. "They don't give it to their pimps, they spend it on podiatrists."

"Try to hold on," Chilcoat said as he slowed for a traffic signal. "We're only two blocks from the station. I'd hate to have to give you mouth-to-mouth resuscitation."

"I would, too," Bobbi agreed.

The chance that Bobbi Marshal would be able to go home to soak her feet had disappeared when the man had parked his car across the street from the girl's house on South Rimpau nearly six hours earlier. He knew the young black woman was a nurse and that she worked from midnight to eight a.m. at the California Hospital on South Hope Street. He knew she slept days. He knew a lot about her. He'd been following her for over a week. He'd circled the day in red on his calendar at work that morning. It was his nineteenth red circle, and while drawing it, knowing this was the day, he had become excited.

The twenty-seven-hundred block of South Rimpau was lined with a collection of aging, weathered frame homes and apartment buildings. Although it was deep within the ghetto, it was still an attractive, quiet neighborhood.

Left at home in the daytime were the elderly or the infirm, and if they did watch the street, it wasn't to act as watchmen. The "Neighborhood Watch" was a white man's invention. Here it could mean slashed tires or a bottle of flaming gasoline on your front porch. Here the majority of the nine-one-one calls, when they were made, were anonymous.

The man sat in the car for some time looking at the house and thinking about the woman sleeping inside. He knew she was home. Her car was in the driveway. He knew that her bedroom was in the left rear of the house off the kitchen. He already knew he'd enter through the front door. His heart quickened when he thought about it. He'd never done it in the daylight before. The idea had come to him as soon as he learned she worked nights. He even had himself convinced that she could be lying in there nude.

Twenty-nine-year-old Lisa Cartwright was tired when she got home. The middle of the week usually provided a quiet night at the hospital where she worked as one of three emergency room nurses. Last night had been a staggering exception, and only dawn had brought relief from the five auto accidents, a premature birth, two ODs—one an eight-year-old—a gunshot victim, and an attempted suicide. All this and not even a full moon. Lisa skipped her usual breakfast in the cafeteria with the other nurses, drove home, showered, and fell into bed.

The telephone in the kitchen brought Lisa from her deep, dreamless sleep. She squinted at the bedside clock. It was a little after twelve. Lisa didn't know how long the telephone had been ringing, but it continued as she lay on the fuzzy threshold of consciousness until she was fully awake. Lisa pushed off the bed and hurried, still nude, into the kitchen. "Hello," she said, grabbing the receiver.

"Miss Cartwright, I'm sorry to bother you." It was the hospital. "This is Sharon Parsons in Administration. Cathy Nelson is reporting off sick tonight. I wonder if you could cover for her?"

"You had to call me at noon to ask that? I was sleeping."

"I'm sorry. I'm only following policy."

"Yes, I'll cover for her."

"Thank you," the woman said, and hung up.

Lisa slammed the receiver down. There went her night off. She had been hoping that Tim Hawkins, one of the new interns in the ER, would call. They had dated several times; it was a nice, easy relationship. They had talked last night about a possible day trip to Catalina Island. Maybe he wouldn't mind waiting until tomorrow. Maybe when they got back from Catalina she'd invite Tim home with her. She hoped he'd call.

Lisa left the kitchen and walked down the hall to the bathroom. The house was warm and quiet. The only sound was the gentle tick of the kitchen clock and a distant jet as it rumbled overhead on its final approach to Los Angeles International. With the curtains closed, the house was dim and comfortable. Lisa was glad she had bought it. It was a good investment for a young professional. Yes, moving to Los Angeles had been smart. Stepping into the bathroom, Lisa opened the mirrored cabinet and got out her toothbrush. She turned the water on in the sink and began to brush. A thump in the hallway startled her. She turned the water off to listen. Silence answered her.

The man was already in the house when the telephone rang in the kitchen. He moved quickly to flatten his back against the living room wall. There, while the phone rang, he slipped on his gloves. Then the floor creaked, and he heard her walk into the kitchen. Now she was in the bathroom. He was inching down the hallway when he bumped into the framed picture on the wall, and it thumped to the carpeted floor. He froze.

Lisa was frightened. Her heart was racing, and she held her breath. Living alone had its price, and the price was fear. It was fear of being alone in the house at night that led to her working nights. Sleep came easier during the day. She reached for a terrycloth robe hanging on the back of the bathroom door and slipped it on. Sunlight glowed around the edges of the blinds in the small bathroom window. A bird chirped outside, and the hallway remained quiet. Lisa willed herself calm. It was only fear, she told herself, a fear born in childhood when her mother would leave her alone at night. None of the horrors she had imagined had ever come to pass, but the fear of being alone had continued to haunt her throughout the years. Now it seemed the moment had arrived. She was alone and frightened in her own house; her mother wasn't coming home to ease her fears. Lisa tied the belt on the robe, took a deep breath, and opened the bathroom door slowly.

The hallway was still dim but warm and quiet. Lisa stepped carefully from the bathroom and looked up and down the short hall. She saw the framed picture sitting on the carpet and breathed a sigh of relief. Moving to the picture, she picked it up. The nail on which it hung was bent downward in the soft plaster. Lisa adjusted it and rehung the framed print of a field of flowers. She was pleased with her courage. It was a small victory, but still a victory.

Lisa walked into the living room and peeked out the little window in the front door to check the mailbox. It was still empty. She returned to the kitchen. Fully awake now, she realized she was hungry. She took a Tab from the refrigerator and a bag of chips from the cupboard. If she was going to work tonight she had to get some more rest. Maybe one of the soaps would lull her back to sleep.

She paused briefly in the hallway at the door of the bedroom to consider the idea of a hot soak in the bathtub. She opted for bed and the TV. The bath could come later. She stepped into the room.

The man was waiting behind the door. He lunged and grabbed her from behind. A gloved hand clamped over Lisa's face. "Don't scream," a hot, masculine breath said in her ear. Before she could react, he pushed her toward the bed and came crashing down on her from behind. Lisa groaned as the breath was forced from her. The man was heavy and strong. She heard the can of Tab thump against the floor and fizz as it spilled onto the carpet. Her face was forced into the tangle of sheets and pillows. "Don't make a sound," the voice growled again. The gloved hand was pulled away from her face, but Lisa was paralyzed with fear. Her arms were yanked behind her and bound together. He was quick and strong; she was helpless. He grabbed her by the hair and lifted her head. She briefly glimpsed a white cotton glove as he tied the gag around her head. She fought instinctively. He pushed the bone of an elbow into the back of Lisa's neck and pressed her down hard into the pillow. "Be still," he warned. She kicked with her feet. He struck her hard in the kidney. She gagged and nearly vomited, making raspy, sucking sounds through the nylon that was tied tight around her mouth and head. Shaking the case off a pillow, the man worked it over Lisa's head and sat her up. "Now we're gonna play house," he said, slipping the robe off her shoulders. "You've got gorgeous tits," he said as he pulled off his gloves and touched her.

Lisa shuddered as a bone-deep chill of fear swept through her, and she wet on the sheets.

"Now look at what you've done. You've been a bad girl." The man raised a hand and smacked hard at the pillowcase that covered Lisa's head. She tumbled to the floor like a broken doll. The man stood over her. "You know what happens to bad girls, don't you?" He unzipped his pants. "Let me show you."

Lifting the trembling girl off the floor, the man laid her on the bed on her back and forced her knees apart. "You're gonna love this," he said, climbing onto the bed.

The torture continued for over three hours. The man raped and sodomized her repeatedly, and when he could no longer arouse himself, he violated her with the handle of a hairbrush he found on the dresser top.

When he had finished with her, he washed himself in the bathroom, tore out the telephone in the kitchen, and stuffed three pairs of Lisa's panties into his pockets. Then he knelt beside the gasping, trembling girl on the bed. "I've got to get back to work now, honey," he whispered to her. "But don't worry. I'll come back and see you again sometime." The bed creaked, there was movement in the hallway, and then the front door opened and slammed shut. He was gone.

Lisa's insides were aflame. She lay still for a long time while the pain smoldered agonizingly. She knew she needed help. She rolled to the floor and staggered to her feet. The robe was in a tangle around her bound arms and the pillowcase was still over her head, but she staggered toward the front door, crashing into the walls and over furniture as she moved. Blood ran down the inside of her legs, leaving a crimson trail.

# 2

# PARTNERS

Lieutenant Aaron Stovich, a broad-shouldered, short-necked, dark-haired man, was still at his desk at the head of the Wilshire Division Detectives squad room when Detectives Chilcoat and Marshal entered. Lieutenant Stovich was the officer-in-charge of the Wilshire Detectives Special Investigation Team, SIT. The team was made up of the six-man Homicide squad, a Juvenile coordinator, two Juvenile detectives, and the Sex team—Detectives Chilcoat and Marshal. Lieutenant Stovich's presence in the deserted squad room after end of watch usually meant one of his teams was still in the field.

"Something cooking tonight, lieutenant?" Brad Chilcoat asked.

Stovich took the stub of an unlit, chewed cigar from the corner of his mouth. "Got a Homicide team up on Olympic. Someone stuck an eight-inch screwdriver in a bus driver's back. How'd it go in Hollywood?" he added with a look at Bobbi's heels and miniskirt.

"As Bobbi told her last customer," Chilcoat answered, "I'll let you be the judge."

The lieutenant smiled at Bobbi. "You arrested a judge for soliciting?"

"A woman's gotta do what a woman's gotta do," Bobbi answered.

"This was probably the last john sweep you'll ever work," Lieutenant Stovich said as he thought about it.

"That won't break my heart," Bobbi answered, stepping out of her high-heeled shoes.

"Maybe this will," Stovich said, offering Bobbi a telephone message slip. "Came in ten minutes ago. Seven-Adam-twenty-one got the call. Victim's at West Adams Hospital. They say it looks like Big Foot."

"Big Foot." Brad Chilcoat grimaced, moving closer to Bobbi to look at the message.

"That will make nineteen rape victims, from Simi Valley to San Pedro," Bobbi said, thinking out loud.

"He's never hit during daylight hours before," Chilcoat said. "Maybe it's not him."

"The officers at the hospital said he used the pillowcase and the panty hose gag," the lieutenant added, putting the chewed cigar back into the corner of his mouth. "It's Big Foot, and this is his fifth hit in our division."

"Could be coincidence," Chilcoat said. "I can't see Big Foot switching to daylight."

"Well, whether it was Big Foot or Donald Duck, it's still a rape," the lieutenant said, "and it's still yours."

"We'll let you know," Bobbi said, tucking the message slip into her shoulder bag. Then, with a look at Brad Chilcoat, she added, "I've got to change first. Give me five minutes."

"Take your time. I wouldn't think of going anywhere without you," Chilcoat answered.

Bobbi smiled as she moved away.

Brad Chilcoat and Bobbi Marshal had been partners for over two years. In Wilshire Division they were known as "The Surfer and the Sensuous Centurian." Brad Chilcoat claimed he worked sex crimes because he was an expert in matters pertaining to sex. The real reason was that he was an outstanding detective with a penchant for detail, an important trait in solving sex crimes. The details were the nails in the lid of every conviction. In addition, Chilcoat, although an extrovert with a quick wit, was discreet with the details of the sex crimes he investigated. Sex crimes could be, and often were, the source of lurid stories and bad jokes among the boys in blue. Cops are not known for their sensitivity. Experience had taught most that the cop who opened his heart usually found a knife stuck in it. Detective Brad Chilcoat was an exception.

In addition to being a good detective, Brad Chilcoat prided himself on being a good father. He took immense pride in his eight-year-old, blue-eyed, blond twin daughters.

Exceptional detective, great father, and a real prick as a husband was how Cathy Chilcoat described her husband of ten years. The Chilcoat marriage, like many cop marriages, was in trouble.

Detective Brad Chilcoat, missing a quality relationship at home, was trying to fill the vacuum in his life with quantity. He usually stalked and often seduced every female who crossed his path. Once he had confessed to Bobbi Marshal that he wasn't looking for a serious relationship, just serious gratification.

Bobbi Marshal knew of Brad Chilcoat's reputation when she accepted the Sex team assignment. After two weeks of Brad's suggestive remarks and admiring looks, she had had enough. She took him into one of the small interrogation rooms. "Look, you've never screwed any of your partners in the past, have you?" she asked bluntly.

"No," Chilcoat answered defensively.

"Well, you're not going to screw me, either," Bobbi said. "And unless we agree on that now, I walk out that door and you find someone else to work with."

Chilcoat studied Bobbi for a long moment. "I agree," he answered soberly.

The chill the confrontation caused lasted throughout the afternoon, but by the next morning it was gone. Brad and Bobbi seem relaxed around each other. The jokes and remarks continued—the leopard couldn't change his spots—but the look in Brad's eyes was different. In the months that followed the two partners molded themselves into a polished investigative machine. Their individual talents and strengths complemented each other as they combined efforts to combat the endless army of deviates and rapists that plagued the seven square miles of the City of the Angels that the LAPD held them responsible for.

Bobbi Marshal knew about the battle her partner was fighting at home. She understood his need and his futile search for love, but she also knew she couldn't fill it. She wasn't sure any woman could. She knew instinctively that the slightest yielding on her part to her partner would be disastrous, both personally and professionally.

Brad Chilcoat was a handsome, attractive man, but, more important, he was her partner, and as such he was her confidant and her friend. In his hands he held her career and, many times, her fate. The trust, the bond between the two, was stronger than that between most lovers. Their lives were intermingled, they shared everything, everything but sex, and because of that intimacy, sex was something they both knew they could and would never share.

# 3

# A FOUR-LETTER WORD

It was happy hour in Los Angeles, and across the face of the sprawling city drinks were splashing over ice to ease the day's burdens. It was the transition from day to night. The golden hour. The time to arrive home, to relax, to be with friends or family. But in the midst of the four million souls that called the City of the Angels home, there was one lonely, frightened, battered young woman.

Lisa Cartwright was in room two-twelve on the second floor in the west wing of West Adams Community Hospital. The paramedics who picked her up on South Rimpau had talked about taking her to California Hospital, but even in her dazed hysteria Lisa pleaded with them not to take her there. They must not see her. She wasn't sure she could ever go back there. The paramedics agreed and took her to the smaller West Adams Community Hospital.

The physical pain was gone now. In its place was a heavy numbness that made her arms and legs feel like wet quilts. She knew it was drugs from her heavy eyelids and labored breathing. Her shocked and abused body cried out for healing sleep, but Lisa was afraid to close her eyes. Reason told her she was safe here in the hospital, with three other women in the room, but the residual panic was still strong. She was alone, frightened and defenseless. There was no one to call, no one to offer help. She felt guilty and dirty. She knew that she had caused the rape. If only she hadn't been sleeping nude. If only she hadn't left her husband. If only she hadn't moved to Los Angeles.

The man had invaded more than her home. He had invaded her. He was gone now, but she was different. It was as if he was still there and would never leave. The thought brought tears, and once again, drawing herself up into fetal position on the bed, she began to weep. A small, animallike whimper crept uncontrollably from her lips, from deep inside her.

"Hey, give us a break, will ya?" a harsh female voice called from somewhere beyond the curtain that surrounded her bed. "We're trying to watch 'Wheel of Fortune.' "

Detective Bobbi Marshal scanned the medical treatment form while she and Brad Chilcoat waited for the emergency room doctor to finish suturing a fifteen-year-old who had landed on his chin instead of his feet after a jump from a skateboard. The medical report on Lisa Cartwright was spartan, but Bobbi had read enough of them to understand the painful details behind the sketchy remarks.

Patient suffering vaginal hemorrhaging due to rape trauma.

External exam reveals heavy bruising and tears in soft tissues surrounding vagina.

Internal reveals—tissue damage, bruising.

Anal exam reveals—bruises and slight hemorrhage.

Foreign matter, hair, and unidentified debris removed from vaginal canal. Antiseptic applied.

Stitches applied area of clitoris.

Pain and sedatives administered. Local and general.

B.P. and heart elevated but within limits.

Patient alert but unresponsive to verbal inquiries. Recommend post-treatment therapy. Admit and observe—follow up O/P Clinic—3 days.

C. Kandell, M.D.

"Dr. Kandell can see you now," a nurse at the reception counter said to Bobbi and Chilcoat. They followed the nurse through a set of double doors and then into a scrub room. The black doctor was in his mid-forties, his natural beginning to gray at the temples. He was at a scrub sink running water over his lathered hands. "I've only got a minute," he said. "Got a fifteen-year-old fully dilated and ready to deliver."

"She couldn't make it to her own doctor?" Chilcoat questioned.

"She's never seen one," Dr. Kandell answered, turning off the water with an elbow.

"Doctor," Bobbi said, "I went over your treatment notes on Lisa Cartwright. I saw you couldn't get a vaginal slide. Without evidence of male semen present, rape is difficult to prove. Can you testify that the girl was raped?"

The doctor toweled his hands dry. "Raped? Yes, I can testify to that. Are you going to interview her?" he added.

"We'd like to," Chilcoat answered. "We need a description of the man who did this."

"I pumped her full of sedatives but she's still on the edge," the doctor warned. "You'll probably get more if you wait for the hysteria to pass."

"Thank you, doctor," Bobbi said, "but it's important we try and get a description from her as soon as possible."

"I hope you find this man," the doctor went on. "I've treated a lot of rape victims. This guy's a real bastard."

"Yeah, we know," Brad Chilcoat answered.

Lisa Cartwright tensed and cowered when Detective Bobbi Marshal pushed the curtain aside and moved to the rail at the side of her bed.

"Lisa," Bobbi said. "I'm Detective Bobbi Marshal from the LAPD. I'm here to help you in any way I can. Is there someone I can call for you? Someone who might be worried?"

Lisa Cartwright didn't answer. She didn't want to talk. Bobbi Marshal wasn't surprised by the silence.

"You're safe now, Lisa." Bobbi laid a hand on Lisa's shoulder. "No one's going to hurt you again. We're going to find the man who did this to you. Can you tell me anything about him? What did he look like?"

Lisa took a jerky breath as she allowed her mind to consider the question. "I . . . I couldn't see. He was just there. He . . . he said he'd come back." Her voice was ragged with emotion. She covered her face with her hands and wept.

"I'm sorry this happened to you, Lisa," Bobbi said. "And I can only imagine how you must feel, but it will pass. You're a beautiful young woman. Don't let this man take any more from you than he already has." She patted Lisa's shoulder. Lisa didn't answer.

"Anything?" Brad Chilcoat questioned when Bobbi stepped out of the hospital room.

Bobbi shook her head. "Not tonight. Maybe in the morning."

It was dark when the two detectives left the hospital. They drove west on Adams Boulevard. Lisa Cartwright's home on South Rimpau was less than two miles away.

"Brad," Bobbi said soberly, "you're a man."

"Thanks for noticing." Chilcoat smiled, with a glance at his partner.

"What thrill can a man get out of doing that to a woman?" Bobbi continued.

"Don't confuse being a man with being a rapist," Chilcoat cautioned as he slowed for a red light.

"I've never met a rapist who wasn't a man," Bobbi countered.

"Personally, I don't think I could combine intercourse with violence," Chilcoat conceded. "Hell, even having the TV on bothers me."

"I wonder what it is this man wants?" Bobbi said.

"Same thing all of us want," Chilcoat answered with a tone of authority. "Love."

"The only thing that rape and love have in common," Bobbi disagreed, "is four letters."

"Wrong," Chilcoat said. "From the cradle to prime time we hear people talking about, singing about, plotting about making love. A guy doesn't say he screwed his girlfriend. He says he made love to her. That's what we've all been taught. We use it in music, we see it on TV, and we bullshit about it in locker rooms. Big Foot doesn't think he's out there raping women. He thinks he's out there making love to them."

"That comes very close to saying that all rape victims provoke their own rape," Bobbi warned.

"I'm not saying that," Brad Chilcoat defended, "but I'll bet you a set of satin sheets that all these women know who this guy is. They've met him."

"I've heard enough," Bobbi warned. "You're really beginning to piss me off."

"But you're so cute when you're pissed." Chilcoat chuckled.

Brad Chilcoat had telephoned the Scientific Investigation Division at Parker Center from the hospital to request a photographer, Latent Prints, and a criminalist to meet them at the crime scene on South Rimpau. There were two detective cars and a black-and-white sitting in front of the house when Chilcoat swung the car onto the block. "Looks like the gang's all here," Chilcoat said as he pulled to the curb. A crowd of curious black spectators stood in a tight knot across the street from the police cars.

Two uniformed officers were standing in the small front yard of Lisa Cartwright's home. "You guys get the original call?" Chilcoat said when he and Bobbi reached them.

"Yeah," answered the taller of the two, a slender man with a bushy mustache.

"Front door was open?" Bobbi questioned.

"Just like it is now," the officer answered as his eyes roamed Bobbi's body. She considered saying something but decided not to. She hadn't really resolved how she felt about such looks.

"Did you look inside?" Chilcoat added.

"I'm the only one who went in," the officer answered. "I checked each room. I didn't touch anything."

"And you stayed with the victim?" Bobbi said with a look to the other officer.

The officer nodded. "She was lying out here on the grass, near the curb. Still had the pillowcase over her head and her hands tied behind her back with panty hose. I untied her."

"Did she say anything?" Bobbi questioned.

"She kept saying she was sorry," the officer answered. "She wouldn't say anything else."

"Did you ask her about the suspect?" Chilcoat asked.

"Yeah, but she didn't answer me. She was shaking and crying."

"Where's the pillowcase and the panty hose?" Bobbi questioned.

"In the trunk of our car," the officer with the mustache answered.

"Book them as evidence to be analyzed," Chilcoat said. "And leave a copy of the report in the Detective Bureau for us."

"That's it?" the mustache asked.

"Yeah, you can go."

The criminalist's name was Wade Morris, and Bobbi and Brad worked with him often. He was a chunky, balding, fifty-year-old man in wire-rimmed glasses, a gray suit, and surgical gloves. Morris took his business seriously and he was good at it. He was in Lisa Cartwright's bedroom kneeling beside the disheveled bed when the two detectives stepped into the room. Bobbi fought a reaction when she saw the swath of blood and yellowing stains on the wrinkled sheets. The room was small but tastefully decorated. It was obviously a woman's room. A flattened nurse's cap lay on the cushion of a chair in the corner. At the base of the chair sat a pair of white shoes. A closet door, standing partially open, revealed a white uniform. The girl had not mentioned being a nurse. Bobbi made a mental note of that. She could almost sense the presence of the rapist in the room. She wondered if it was his odor that tainted the air. Only a few hours separated her from him. She was beginning to doubt they'd ever find this man.

"Hello, Wade," Brad Chilcoat said to the kneeling man.

Morris glanced up at the two detectives. "Take a look at this," he said.

Bobbi and Chilcoat moved closer to look over Morris's shoulder. Lying on the floor was a twelve-inch wooden ruler positioned parallel to a wet stain, a Tab soft drink can, and a large shoe print in the soaked plush carpet.

"Big Foot," Bobbi Marshal said, looking down at the impression.

"No doubt about it," Wade Morris agreed. He pushed to his feet with a grunt. "But it's too soft to get any detail with a cast. Got some good pictures of it, though. Hope you didn't mind me starting without you?"

"Not at all. Anything else?" Chilcoat questioned.

"We've got photos and prints of this room. They're working in the kitchen now," Morris advised.

"The kitchen?" Bobbi asked.

"He tore out the telephone," Morris said, pulling off his surgical gloves. "Like always." He tucked the gloves in an outside jacket pocket and dug out a pack of cigarettes. "Do you mind?"

"It's your lungs," Bobbi warned.

Morris lit up, sniffing the air as he did. "What is that you're wearing?" he said to Bobbi. "It's not your usual."

"It's Charlie," Bobbi granted Morris's sensitive nose. She was annoyed with the question.

"You usually wear Chanel," Morris exhaled.

"Not when I'm pretending to be Suzie Quickie on Sunset Boulevard, I don't," Bobbi answered.

"Only a policewoman would know what kind of perfume whores wear," Morris commented.

"Oh, I think I could name a few policemen who would know, too," Bobbi retorted.

"Could we table this until our next Mary Kay party," Brad Chilcoat suggested, "and perhaps talk a little about what happened in this room today?"

"No forced entry," Morris said, pulling out a small notebook. "Front and back doors have dead bolt locks in excellent working condition. No evidence of tampering."

"Maybe the doors weren't locked," Chilcoat suggested with a look at Bobbi.

"What else?" Bobbi said to Morris.

"I've collected several of what appear to be pubic hairs from the surface of the sheet. I also picked up a hairbrush with a bloody handle from the floor next to the bed. I'll let you draw your own conclusions, and I'll take the sheet for blood and semen examination."

"How soon can we have it?" Chilcoat asked.

"Day or two," Morris said, putting away his notebook. "But don't look for anything new, because it isn't here. We've had footprints, blood type, hair color, and approximate age since this bastard's fifth rape. You find out who he is and I'll put him here with enough evidence to convict him nineteen times, but first you got to find him."

"You think we don't know that?" Chilcoat answered.

They searched the inside of the house and then the outside, but found nothing of any evidential value. They drew a sketch of the crime scene and took measurements. Every room was photographed and print dust covered nearly every surface in the house. While Wade Morris folded up the soiled sheets to put them in plastic bags, Bobbi and Brad worked their way up and down the block knocking on doors and asking questions. No one had seen or heard anything. If they had, they weren't interested in talking to the police. Few even admitted ever seeing the girl.

When they left the scene, Chilcoat taped police evidence seals on the front and back doors with the hope it would keep the vultures away. It seldom did.

"You hungry?" Chilcoat questioned as he turned the detective car north on La Brea Avenue.

"How can you think of food driving away from the scene of a rape?" Bobbi said.

"Man cannot live on sex alone." Chilcoat smiled. "Believe it or not, this gorgeous body does require nourishment."

"I'm not hungry. Drop me at the station. I'll brief the lieutenant and get out a teletype."

"You don't mind?"

"If I did, I'd say so."

Bobbi was annoyed with her partner. She knew what he was going after, and it wasn't dinner. This was part of the routine that had evolved. Whenever legitimate overtime took them into the night, which it did often, Brad Chilcoat would use it for his own purposes. He was already late.

"Was it Big Foot?" Lieutenant Stovich called, the moment Bobbi Marshal walked into the detective squad room. He was sitting with two detectives from Homicide near the head of the room.

"Yes," Bobbi answered flatly as she crossed to her desk to drop her shoulder bag onto its surface. The four-inch thirty-eight in the purse thumped against the desktop.

"Shit," she heard Lieutenant Stovich complain. His chair scraped against the tile floor. He pushed from his desk and crossed to where she now sat behind hers. "Where's the surfer?" Stovich said, leaning against a nearby desk.

"He went to get something to eat." Bobbi lifted a yellow tablet from a desk drawer.

"Any description, anything new?" the lieutenant pressed.

"Nothing," Bobbi admitted. "The girl's still in shock, but she claims she never saw him. He was just there. I'll try again in the morning."

"First he terrorizes the night, now the sonofabitch hits during the day. Any doubt it was Big Foot?"

"None," Bobbi assured him. "Same panty hose tie-up and gag. Same knots. He used a foreign object and he tore the telephone out."

"Uh huh. How many other cases you got cooking?"

"Couple stat rapes, an incest, two child abuses. Why?"

"I'm gonna give your caseload to Juvenile. I want you and Chilcoat on this full-time. Do what you have to do, but find this sonofabitch."

"Yes, sir."

The lieutenant walked away. Bobbi picked up a pen and went to work on the teletype.

072188
APS OOL 400 500 600
LAP AREA BROADCAST
2240 HRS
WIL/D LOS ANGELES POLICE DEPARTMENT
CRIME 261 RAPE
DATE/TIME     7/21/88     1200/1300
VICT . . . CARTWRIGHT, LISA
    F/NEG     DOB 1/25/59
LOCATION . . . 2706 S. RIMPAU, L.A.
SUSP . . . M/W, BRN HAIR, EST 200 LBS,
    SIZE 13 SHOE, NFD
WEAPONS . . . BODILY FORCE, HAIRBRUSH
    HANDLE
VEHICLE . . . NVS
M.O. . . . SUSP ENTERED VICTS RESID ABV
DATE & TIME. NO FORCED ENTRY. SUSP AS-
SAULTED VICT & BOUND HANDS BEHIND BACK
WITH NYLON PANTY HOSE. SHEER ELE-
GANCE. NOT PROPERTY OF VICT. VICT GAGGED
WITH SECOND PAIR SIMILAR PANTY HOSE.
SUSP RAPED AND SODOMIZED VICT IN B/RM
OF RESID. SUSP USED HANDLE OF HAIRBRUSH
TO ABUSE VICT SEXUALLY. SUSP TORE TELE-
PHONE FROM WALL. PROMISED TO RETURN.

LARGE FOOTPRINT, SEMEN, PUBIC HAIR RE-
COVERED AT SCENE
AVAILABLE FOR COMPARISON. SIMILAR M.O.
IN 19 SIMILAR CRIMES.

ATT: RAPE DETAILS—ANY INFO TO—

RE: WILSHIRE DETECTIVES/SIT SEX
 B. CHILCOAT, 13982      B. MARSHAL, 14406
 DR. 88-329-248

Bobbi took the teletype and a crime report she had written to the Records Office down the hall from the Detective
Bureau. There the teletype would soon go out over the
network, and the report would be duplicated for distribu-
tion.

She was returning to the Detective Bureau, already
thinking of the hot bath that was waiting at home, when
the station sergeant stepped out of the windowed watch
commander's office and called to her. "Hey, Marshal."

Bobbi paused, looked at the uniformed sergeant. His
name was Carson, and he was an academy classmate.

"Got a minute?" Carson questioned. "Got something
I think you might be interested in."

"Sure," Bobbi said, walking to the watch commander's
office. The windowed office was the nerve center of the
division. It was equipped with a bank of radio monitors
and a tactical radio telephone that could cut into any of
the division's three frequencies. A computer video screen
printed out a constantly updated location and nature of call
on the division's patrol units. Several closed-circuit TV
monitors swept the station's front lobby, the parking lot,
and the detention cells. A graying, uniformed lieutenant
sat at one of the office's two desks, laboring over paperwork. Sergeant Carson returned to his chair behind his
vacant desk when Bobbi stepped into the office. "We've
got a seventeen-year-old whore who walked into the lobby
about twenty minutes ago," Carson explained.

"Sounds more like a Juvenile problem than the Sex team's," Bobbi suggested.

The girl was a busty, braless, dishwater blond with heavy makeup and blue eyes. She wore a low-cut, vee-neck sweater and tight black spandex pants with red heels. Her neck was draped with a collection of cheap chains, and she wore a ring on each finger. Bobbi bet she was closer to fifteen than eighteen. "Sit down," Bobbi said, escorting the girl into one of the squad room's small, windowless interrogation rooms. The girl reeked of cheap perfume and Juicy Fruit gum.

"You're pretty for a cop," the girl said, popping her gum after a once-over look at Bobbi.

"And you're pretty young for a seventeen-year-old," Bobbi countered.

"I got ID. I'm no runaway," the girl answered quickly, digging into her bulging purse.

"I'm sure you have," Bobbi said, waving off her effort. "Just tell me who you are."

"Fawn Tyler."

"The desk officer said you wanted to report a rape. Is that true?"

"Yeah."

"Rape isn't some john refusing to pay, you know?"

"Yeah, I know. I was forced."

"When did this happen?"

"Last Friday night."

"Six days ago! What were you waiting for?"

"My girlfriend to come back. It was a twosome thing. I got scared and ran off. I hitched back to L.A., but Debbi never came back. I think they killed her."

Bobbi glanced at her watch. It was nearly eleven p.m. She was getting tired, and she knew the story wasn't going to be a simple one. Coming from teenage whores they never were. "Okay," Bobbi said, taking in a breath. "Let's start at the beginning." She had a yellow pad and pencil.

Slowly and tediously, Bobbi drew the story from the

girl, who was old beyond her tender years. It had started on La Brea Avenue, several weeks earlier, where the girl normally walked the street at night near the Galaxy Motel. Del, a trick, a muscular man with dark eyes and a pock-marked face, had picked her up and driven her to a motel somewhere in the Valley. "He was kinky," the girl told Bobbi. "He was into golden rain and bondage. We did everything but intercourse. He couldn't. He couldn't get it up."

"But you said you were raped?" Bobbi said, laying her pencil down.

"Yeah, I was," Fawn defended. "After I dated him two times, he asked me to bring another girl. He said he'd pay me two hundred bucks." Bobbi resumed making notes as the girl talked about Debbi. Debbi was younger than Fawn, only fifteen. They both worked out of the Galaxy Motel. Fawn had known Debbi for several months. She knew Debbi needed the money because she was hooked on crack. Debbi was quick to accept what Fawn called "a party invitation."

Again they made a trip to a motel in the Valley. Fawn couldn't remember where. She and Deb were both high. At the motel, Del ordered the two naked girls to fondle each other. When they refused he slapped them around. Del quickly became aroused and mounted Fawn. Debbi tried to retreat to the bathroom but Del lost his erection and his temper. He beat both again, giving Debbi a bloody nose. When the bleeding wouldn't stop, Fawn was ordered to get dressed and walk to a drugstore on the corner to get some cotton. "He told me, 'You don't come back, bitch, I'll kill her.' "

Fawn's voice was edged with fear as she told of walking to the nearby drugstore. "I didn't want to go back, but Debbi was crying when I left. I bought these cotton ball things, and went back to the motel. When I looked into the parking lot I saw Del loading this thing into the trunk of his car. It was wrapped in a sheet and it looked like a body."

"Have you ever seen a body wrapped in a sheet before?" Bobbi questioned.

"No," Fawn admitted.

"Did you see a foot, a hand? Anything?" Bobbi explored.

Fawn shook her head. "No, and when Del started to get in his car I ran. I hitched back downtown."

"And you don't remember where the motel is or what it's called?"

"No."

"And you haven't seen Debbi since then?"

"No, Del killed her."

Bobbi shook her head in disagreement. "Fawn, Debbi's a missing fifteen-year-old prostitute; that doesn't necessarily mean she's dead. Just like you, she may have been so frightened she never came back. It's not so unusual. Maybe she went home. Freaks like Del are an occupational hazard."

Fawn searched Bobbi's face for a moment. "You're not going to do anything about it, are you?"

"Fawn, you and Debbi are on the street by your own choice. So don't be so quick to point the finger when things go wrong. And you've made the situation worse. Why did you wait so long before coming in?" 

"I was scared. I still am. I know Del killed her." There were tears in Fawn's eyes. One spilled over and streaked mascara down her cheek. "Will you help me, please?"

# 4

# INTO THE NIGHT

It was ten minutes after midnight when Bobbi Marshal dropped the teenage prostitute at the Galaxy Motel on South La Brea. She had briefly considered arresting Fawn as a juvenile for violating provisions of the Welfare and Institutions Code and putting her in protective custody, but it was likely the girl would simply deny the story she'd told, be promptly released, and flee. Bobbi had learned that protecting people from themselves was not always an easy job. She gave Fawn her card, twenty-two dollars from her purse and told her to stay off the street. "I'll call you tomorrow. Be here," Bobbi warned.

"Hey, do you think I could get a job as a lady cop?" Fawn smiled into the open door of the 240-Z.

"Good night, Fawn," Bobbi said. She put the car in gear and roared away.

Her condo was on the sixth floor of the Stonehaven Towers on Lindenhurst, just north of Fairfax and Wilshire. Two blocks from the LA County Art Museum and one block off Wilshire Boulevard's famous "Miracle Mile" was a fashionable place to live. Bobbi Marshal enjoyed it. Her father held the second mortgage and the payments took a sizable bite out of her monthly income, but Bobbi owned it, and to her that was important. She'd moved in five months ago.

The six lanes of sprawling Wilshire Boulevard were quiet, basking in chalky cones of night lighting that reached down from the rows of streetlamps flanking the

curbs. The only sound was the rumble of a street sweeper
that moved along the curb with its amber strobe light
flashing, looking much like a giant urban snail. Bobbi
Marshal's headlights appeared from the east. As her
240-Z approached Fairfax, she slowed and swung north.

The gated subterranean garage of Stonehaven Towers
was quiet and cold. Bobbi welcomed the warmth of the
elevator. She leaned against the smooth wall as it climbed
upward. It had been a long day, and in less than six hours
she'd be starting another one. She wondered if this was
how it felt to be old. She couldn't understand how Lieutenant Stovich did it; he was still at the station when she
left. A soak in the tub was going to feel very good. The
elevator chimed as it stopped, and the doors parted on the
carpeted hallway.

Keys in hand, Bobbi moved down the hallway. It felt
good to be home. She wondered if this was how Lisa
Cartwright felt when she walked to the front door of her
home earlier in the day. She expected comfort, security,
privacy, peace—all the things the Constitution guarantees.
Instead she was bound and gagged and raped in her own
bedroom. Big Foot, a faceless, lust-filled man who left a
trail of broken young women across the city, had been
waiting there, hiding in what Lisa had thought was the
comfort and security of her home. The thought made Bobbi's heart race with a vicarious fear—or was it vicarious?
Bobbi paused at her door. The dead bolt lock looked undisturbed, the same as Lisa Cartwright's. Bobbi thought
about the gun in her shoulder bag. She fought an urge to
lift it out. She told herself the fear was not rational, simply
a leftover from the bizarre day. She pushed the key in the
lock and twisted. The lock snapped. Bobbi pushed the
door open.

The interior of the condo was wrapped in darkness. The
sunlight had been bright in the morning when she left for
work, so Bobbi had drawn the curtains. Now she damned
herself for it. She stepped into the darkness and closed the
door. Crossing to an end table, she quickly switched on a

light, and her growing swell of fear subsided. She returned to the door and set the dead bolt. Was it an occupational hazard or the price of living alone? Bobbi wasn't sure, but she did know she hated being afraid. She wondered how many other women were alone and afraid this night. Knowing that many were brought her little comfort.

Cathy Chilcoat tried going to bed after Brad failed to come home, but sleep was not to be hers this night. The memories of their years together kept drifting through her mind. Remembering the good times somehow made the bad times seem even worse. The walks on the beach, the vacation in Mexico, the camping trip to Yosemite, buying the house, the Christmas Brad had brought home the puppy, the flowers he brought when the twins were born. Cathy wept in the stillness of their bedroom, cursing the emptiness beside her, yet praying Brad would come through the door, take her in his arms, and say he was sorry; but he didn't come, and eventually she stopped crying. The pain turned to rage and Cathy got out of bed. It was time for him to pay.

It was nearly two a.m. when the car pulled into the driveway. Its headlamps swept across the dark living room where Cathy Chilcoat waited.

She bolted to her feet. Her face was an angry mask. "You're not coming into this house anymore smelling of other women and lying down in my bed," Cathy warned angrily. "You're not a father, you're not a husband. You're nothing but a male whore."

"Cathy, I worked late," Brad pleaded, in a less than convincing tone.

"You bastard," she growled, picking up a vase of dried flowers. "You don't even have the courage to admit it." She flung the vase at him. It crashed hard against the wall. Shards of pottery rained down on the tile entryway.

"You're a fuckin' psycho," Brad Chilcoat barked as the anger swelled in him. "Just like your mother."

"Mommy!" an eight-year-old, frightened voice called

from the mouth of the hallway. "I'm scared." The little girl was dressed in a nightgown covered with kittens. Her eyes were rimmed with tears.

Brad Chilcoat marched angrily by his eight-year-old daughter. "Ask your mother what she's doing," he snapped as he went down the hallway and into the master bedroom. There he slammed the door behind him.

Cathy moved to take her daughter into her arms. "I'm scared too, honey, but we're gonna be all right."

It was six-ten in the morning when the bedside telephone rang. Bobbi Marshal was awake instantly. The alarm had gone off at five-thirty as always, but the weary Bobbi had reached out and turned it off. Her morning run and exercises could wait. She'd make up for it tomorrow. This morning she needed just a few more minutes of sleep. Bobbi looked at the digital display on the clock. "Oh, no," she groaned, knowing the forty extra minutes of sleep was going to make getting ready on time a real task. She reached for the telephone as it rang a second time. She knew it had to be a call out. Maybe Big Foot had struck again. "Hello," she breathed into the receiver.

"You're sleeping nude, aren't you?" a masculine voice whispered in her ear.

Bobbi tensed and drew the sheets up over her breasts. "Who is this?" she demanded, but her voice echoed the shock she felt.

"A voice from your past," the man answered, and Bobbi recognized the voice.

"Don, you creep." Bobbi smiled, lying back on the pillows. She was flattered he was calling. Don Roberts was a handsome, thirty-four-year-old junior partner in the prestigious law firm of Sheldon, Roberts, and O'Shay. The two had met in an elevator at the Criminal Courts Building several weeks earlier. As a matter of fact, they met that way four times before Bobbi finally accepted Don's invitation to share a coffee in the first-floor cafeteria. The coffee led to a dinner invitation. Bobbi was surprised and impressed when the dinner was served on a forty-two-foot yacht off Newport Beach at sunset.

Don Roberts had inherited his fortune from a father whose millions were made during California's booming sixties. The senior Roberts, an avid pilot, died along with his wife, doing what he loved best—flying. The twenty-year-old Don was to go on to graduate from Harvard with a degree in law. As his father had wished, he joined his uncle's law firm. Having matured into a successful corporate attorney, he was now well on his way to amassing his own fortune.

Don Roberts was pleasantly surprised to find that the detective with the flashing eyes and the sensual smile was from the well-known Marshal banking family in San Marino. "Whatever made you want to be a policewoman?" he had asked.

"Have you ever worked in a bank?" Bobbi quipped.

Don Roberts found the female detective not only attractive but fascinating, while Bobbi welcomed Don's gentleness and charm. Working with an army of men she loved but still considered basically crass, Bobbi found Don Roberts to be a breath of fresh air. After their second date, dinner in Westwood and a musical at the Schubert Theater in Century City, the telephone had been quiet. A week had passed. Bobbi was certain Don had gone back to the bevy of beauties that always seemed to flutter around corporate law offices. A female detective might be a passing interest, but not a relationship one allowed to become serious. Yet he had surprised her again.

"Don't avoid my original question," Don said on the other end of the line. "You were sleeping nude, weren't you?"

"Here," Bobbi teased, purring into the receiver, "I'll raise the sheets and you can look."

"I'll be right over," he said eagerly.

"Where are you?"

"Los Angeles International."

"Coming or going?" she questioned.

"Just in from Manila."

"So that's where you've been."

"Missed me, didn't you?" he said.

"What did you say your name was?" Bobbi teased.

"How about dinner tonight?" he countered.

"I've got a long day ahead of me," Bobbi warned.

"So do I," Don said. "I'm not worried about what time. I'd just like to see you. Why don't you give me a call at my office when you get off and we'll hide somewhere for a quiet dinner?"

"Sounds great," Bobbi agreed.

"So does your voice," Don said. "I missed you. Now I've got to run. Goodbye."

It was a rush, and the condo was left in a mess, but Detective Bobbi Marshal swung her 240-Z into the parking lot of the Wilshire Division Station at seven-forty-five. Parked in front of the station were two minicam vans from local television stations, a station wagon from an all-news radio station, and several other cars. Bobbi assumed another homicide was generating news. She was surprised to see Brad Chilcoat's four-wheel-drive jeep parked among the other civilian cars that lined the private vehicle side of the lot. Usually Brad walked into the detective squad room at eight o'clock sharp. His joke was he didn't want the city taking him for granted by showing up early.

Bobbi found a parking space near the rear of the lot. It was a bright, clear day, and the sun felt good on her shoulders as she headed for the station's rear door. She wondered how much Don Roberts's call had to do with her improved morale. There was little doubt it would make the busy day ahead a little easier. Big Foot's first rape five months earlier had started the long stretch of frustrating days. He raped seemingly at will, ignoring and eluding the small army of detectives that hunted him. He'd struck in eight of the city's eighteen divisions. Five times in Wilshire Division alone. He was averaging a rape every eight days. And after one hundred and fifty days, they were no closer to catching him than they had been the first day.

The painful reality was that the police did not solve every crime. Television had raised public expectation to a level no police officer or department could match. Joe Friday and Kojak were illusions. Big Foot was not. The police needed and prayed for a break. Eventually Big Foot would make a mistake. Most criminals did. The wait was not easy, not for the police and not for the growing list of rape victims.

Seventeen-year-old Fawn Tyler was also on Bobbi Marshal's mind. The bizarre tale of Fawn's missing girlfriend could not be ignored. The rape of a seventeen-year-old prostitute was not something the district attorney was going to get excited over, but Bobbi believed the girl. The law was designed to protect Fawn Tyler as much as any virginal seventeen-year-old. Somehow she had to convince Lieutenant Stovich that she and Brad could handle Big Foot and the teenager's rape as well. First she had to verify some aspect of Fawn's story, to find some fragment of truth which would indicate the whole story was true. Maybe a polygraph examination? No, there wasn't enough evidence to justify that. Maybe Brad would have some ideas. Bobbi was eager to share the story with him.

"Hey, Marshal," a voice called from behind her as she neared the rear door of the station. Bobbi paused and turned. She recognized the voice of Dan Shea. He was a detective sergeant, a good friend of Brad Chilcoat's, and he worked Wilshire's Homicide team. Shea was a dark-haired man with deep brown eyes and a square jaw. Bobbi thought he looked like a recruiting poster. He was the kind of man who looked uncomfortable in a suit and seldom buttoned his collar or wore his tie knotted tight. He had a reputation for being a tough cop and looked capable of being brutal. Bobbi guessed it was camouflage for the difficult assignment the man worked. If you could get into the role, then you didn't weep at the sight of a battered eight-year-old or the lifeless form of a young teenager killed in a gang fight. The facts that Dan Shea was a friend of Brad Chilcoat's and that Homicide, like the Sex team, was part of the Division's Special Investigations Team put the two of them together often. Dan Shea was single but he had never asked Bobbi out. Although the attraction between them was unspoken, it seemed mutual, and Bobbi had done nothing to discourage him. Perhaps, Bobbi concluded, he, like she, decided it wasn't wise to mix romance and the job. It could, and often had, proved to be a deadly mix.

"I ran into Brad last night," Shea said as he reached Bobbi. "He said Big Foot added to his scoreboard yesterday."

Bobbi nodded agreement as a hint of Shea's cologne reached her. "He told you right."

"You got anything new?" Shea questioned as he reached to open the door for Bobbi.

"Nothing," Bobbi admitted, stepping into the station's rear hallway. "We're still up against the wall."

"Talk to the mailman," Shea suggested. "It's worked for me in the past. People in the neighborhood can be indifferent or too frightened to talk. The mailman comes and he goes. He knows his route. If Big Foot's been camping on this girl's street, stalking her, someone's seen him. Mailmen remember what they see."

"Why are you so interested?" Bobbi questioned candidly as they walked toward the detective squad room.

Shea glanced at her and smiled. "Just protecting my own turf. Nineteen rapes. I figure Big Foot's luck is running out. Maybe his next victim will fight, someone will walk in. Something's going to go wrong and he's going to graduate from sex to murder. I got enough to do. Catch him before that happens."

"You're all heart."

"So they tell me."

They reached the door of the squad room. Unlike the evening before when the room had been quiet and deserted, now it was a sea of faces and ringing telephones. Some sixty detectives, working Burglary, Robbery, Autos, Juvenile, and Crimes Against Person crowded the rows of

desks as they sorted through crime reports, read arrest
reports, and offered the seemingly endless stream of victims a sympathetic ear and a word of encouragement.
Bobbi moved through the maze of desks toward the corner
of the squad room reserved for the Special Investigations
Team. There Brad Chilcoat waited at a desk.

To the first-time visitor the busy squad room, with its
constantly ringing telephones and mix of laughter, curses,
and conversation, seemed chaotic. To Bobbi, and the others, it was the office, a place to work and be among your
own. A place that became the focal point of any crime
committed within seven square miles. And this morning,
it was a place where the press waited on the arrival of
Detective Bobbi Marshal.

"You're in early," Bobbi said as she sat down across
from Brad Chilcoat. She noticed he looked tired, worried
maybe.

"Sugar and cream, right?" Brad smiled, sliding a sty-
rofoam cup in front of Bobbi.

"You don't know how much I appreciate this," Bobbi
said, sampling the cup of hot coffee. "I hardly had time
to brush my teeth this morning."

Brad Chilcoat shook his head in disapproval. "I don't
know how you keep up this party-girl pace."

"Yeah, right," Bobbi countered.

"Seriously," Brad warned, as he leaned into the desk
that separated them. "You better tighten your bra straps.
Something's in the wind. Stovich wants to see you."

Bobbi's eyes went immediately to the lieutenant's desk
at the head of the squad room. It was vacant.

"He's in with Captain Westly. They're waiting for you,"
Brad added.

"Me?" Bobbi questioned, suddenly alarmed.

"I don't know why," Brad answered. "The lieutenant
said to send you in as soon as you got here."

"The judge," Bobbi said as the thought of the arrest on
Sunset Boulevard came to mind.

"I'd bet my gavel on it." Brad Chilcoat smiled.

\* \* \*

Captain George Westly prided himself on running a tight ship at Wilshire Division of the LAPD. That didn't mean the crime rate was any lower; as a matter of fact, there had been a significant increase since his arrival at Wilshire Division eighteen months earlier. Nor did it mean the morale of the working detectives was any better. What it did mean was that there was an orderly and uninterrupted flow in the volume of paperwork between Wilshire Division and the seat of ultimate police power downtown at Parker Center. Weekly, biweekly, monthly, quarterly, and semi-annual reports filtered into Parker Center from Wilshire Division complete and with clockwork precision. No one could say Captain George Westly wasn't a good administrator, although many of the detectives at Wilshire Division did say it was unfortunate he had flunked his test to become an RTD bus driver eighteen years earlier. The fact that George Westly's older brother was a U.S. senator from California had not gone unnoticed by the LAPD. Many suspected that the sixteen-million-dollar federal grant to upgrade the department's antiquated Communications Division was George Westly's ticket to the rank of commander, a promotion which was now pending. But now Senator Phillip Westly was dead and younger brother George was on his own. He was glad he was on the eve of promotion and only twenty-four months from retirement. He hoped his ulcerated stomach would stay together that long. The events of the morning were making that possibility seem very remote. If there was something that aggravated George Westly more than sloppy administrative work it was surprises. Two camera crews and six reporters in the station's lobby definitely fell into the category of surprise.

Captain Westly, just arrived at the station, was about to question why the press was in the lobby when his secretary summoned him to the telephone. Commander Hodges from Public Affairs was calling. "What the hell's going on, George?" the commander had demanded. "I'm getting calls from CNN, UPI, and AP. They wanna know about this rapist one of your detectives claims has terrorized the city." The shocked George Westly had no answers. He was embarrassed and angry. "Who the hell's in charge of your division, captain? I want some answers, and so does the deputy chief."

George Westly was still trembling from the first call when the second one came. It was from Raymond Bendicci, the district attorney for the County of Los Angeles. Bendicci was a powerful, influential man, and George Westly knew a call from him didn't mean good news. George slipped an antacid tablet in his mouth before picking up the receiver. "Good morning, Mr. District Attorney," George said with a trembling voice. "I know why you're calling, sir, and I'm working on the details of the latest rape right now. Can I call you back in a few minutes?"

"Rape!" the district attorney said. "I don't know what the hell you're talking about, captain. I'm calling about yesterday's arrest of Judge Unger."

"Oh, yes, the judge's arrest," George answered sheepishly. Lieutenant Stovich had briefed the captain on the judge's arrest when he called him at home the night before with the results of the latest gang murder.

"My prosecutors have listened to the audio tape and read the arrest report, captain," the district attorney said, "and we're of the opinion this case is marginal entrapment."

"Yes, I see," Westly agreed, wishing he knew more about the law. "Well, can't the case simply be rejected?"

"I'm afraid if we do that, captain, we might be accused of offering the judge preferential treatment. You see, he's the brother-in-law of Governor Ryder. You understand these political situations, don't you, captain?"

"Yes, I see," George said, fearing this could influence his promotion.

"I'd consider this a great personal favor, captain, and I'm sure Governor Ryder would, too. Of course, we're not asking you to do anything unethical. If you think the case has merit, then please proceed with it. I'll be glad to pass your decision on to the governor.''

"I . . . I'll see what I can do," George Westly stammered. He wished his brother were alive. "I can say, I tend to agree with you.''

"We'll need a firmer stance than that, captain," the district attorney warned.

"Yes, I know. Let me get back to you on this.''

"We'd like an answer soon, captain. Before the press has it.''

"Yes, of course, soon.''

Seventeen-year-old Fawn Tyler was up earlier than usual. Since the night Debbi had disappeared, she'd been afraid to go back out on the street. Broke and frightened, she'd spent each day in the less than glamorous room at the Galaxy Motel watching television. She'd paid the rent for a month, now only six days from ending, bought two dresses and three pairs of shoes, and had her nails done. The money from Del had seemed like all the money in the world, but now it was gone.

After putting her last dollar and fifty cents in the machines at the motel for a Diet Coke and stale cookies, she knew she had to do something. It was that same night she'd hitched a ride to the police station on Venice Boulevard. She had stood across the street for almost an hour before she got the nerve to go in. Now she was glad she had. Not only was the policewoman Bobbi good-looking and kind, but she had given her twenty-two dollars and a promise to help.

It was daylight and Fawn was hungry, so she decided to walk to the McDonald's which was less than a block away. Maybe if she was lucky she could pick up a trick on the way back. She had put on a tight tee shirt, a pair of red jeans, and white heels. She checked her image in the mirror before leaving the room and was pleased with what she saw.

Leaving her second-floor room, Fawn walked to the stairs at the head of the hallway that led down into the lobby. She was halfway down the stairs when she heard a heavy masculine voice mention her name. It sent a bolt of electric fear surging through her that made the hair bristle on the back of her neck. She knew whose voice it was. Fawn inched quietly down the soiled, carpeted stairs until she could see the reception desk. There, standing with his back to her, was Del, the burly man with the pockmarked face. Fawn shivered as she remembered his foul breath and strong meaty fingers that left bruises on her ribs and breasts. Fawn knew Del was looking for her. She watched in horror as he took money from his wallet and offered it to the black clerk behind the counter. Fawn turned and bolted up the stairs. Her heart was pounding and her mind was filled with panic.

# 5

# SISTERS OF FATE

Captain Westly and Lieutenant Stovich were waiting in the captain's office when Detective Bobbi Marshal was escorted in by the captain's adjutant. Lieutenant Stovich offered a glance of recognition but nothing more. "Sit down, detective," the sober-faced Captain Westly ordered.

Bobbi seated herself in the remaining chair beside Lieutenant Stovich. It faced the captain's desk, so she crossed her nyloned legs and adjusted her skirt. Something in the air was making her very aware of her femininity.

"Detective," Captain Westly began, drumming his fingers on the desktop and looking out over the top of his glasses. "You're aware of the Detective Bureau policy that requires crime teletypes be reviewed by supervisory personnel for approval prior to broadcast, aren't you?"

Bobbi wasn't sure what she was being accused of. Obviously the meeting wasn't about the judge's arrest after all, but the captain's tone left little doubt that he was unhappy with something. "Yes, I'm aware of the policy," Bobbi admitted.

Captain Westly picked up a copy of a teletype that lay on the desk in front of him. "You wrote this teletype last night?"

"If it's about Big Foot's latest rape, yes, I wrote it."

"And did you have it reviewed for approval?" the captain pressed. "Before you decided to announce we had a rapist roaming the face of the city?"

"No, but it seemed time . . ."

"Answer the question," the captain barked.

"No, sir, I did not," Bobbi defended. "It seemed a routine matter, and Lieutenant Stovich was busy with a homicide. I've written hundreds of teletypes, every detective does."

"I'm not talking about other detectives or other teletypes." He held up the teletype. "I'm talking about this piece of inflammatory guesswork that's caused a great deal of alarm and concern at Parker Center."

"Guesswork?" Bobbi questioned.

"Yes, guesswork," the captain shot back at her. "Do you have any hard evidence that a single man has committed these nineteen rapes?"

"It's called 'modus operandi,' captain," Bobbi answered soberly. "It means by method of crime committed. I didn't invent it."

"But you are the one who's declared we have a hot prowl rapist out there who's attacked nearly twenty women!"

"Yes, and I'm prepared to defend it," Bobbi said, gripping the wooden arms of the chair. "SID's working on the evidence to link them together."

"Explain that to the press waiting in the lobby," the captain ordered. "You wanted notoriety, young lady, you're about to earn it."

"All I wanted, captain, is Big Foot captured."

Captain Westly removed his glasses. "You are not to use slang names on this suspect or any other suspect. Is that clear, detective?"

"Yes, sir."

"The violation of the teletype policy cannot, and will not, be ignored. It has caused me and Lieutenant Stovich considerable embarrassment. Yesterday the city paid you to act like a prostitute. Today you're being paid to act like a detective. I expect to see your performance level improve. You'll be notified of my decision. That's all."

Bobbi, smarting with a mix of anger and embarrassment, glanced at Lieutenant Stovich and then pushed to her feet. It was obvious she was alone in this. "What's more important, gentlemen—your embarrassment or the prevention of another rape?"

"We're not talking about embarrassment or prevention," Captain Westly snapped. "We're talking about policy."

"You could have fooled me," Bobbi shot back.

"That's all, detective," the captain warned, pushing on his glasses.

Bobbi moved for the door.

"By the way, detective," the captain added as Bobbi opened the door. She paused to look to him. Westly rocked back in his chair. "Knowing that your arrest of Judge Unger was likely to generate a great deal of controversy, I've reviewed the reports. Frankly, it's my opinion it would be in the best interests of all concerned if the charges were dropped."

"Based on what, captain?" Bobbi questioned.

"I don't have to explain my opinions to you, detective. I've given you the opportunity to reconsider the prosecution. If you don't agree, I'll dispose of it myself."

"Give my regards to the judge," Bobbi said sarcastically as she stepped out and closed the door.

Earlier, when he first awoke, with his wife still beside him in the bed, he had moved close to her and pressed his body to hers and cupped a breast. It had become their unspoken signal. She pretended interest and fondled him. He tried to will himself erect, concentrating on the rape of the girl. He'd climaxed twice during his time with her. That proved he wasn't the problem. When his wife's fondling failed to arouse him he became irritated. He pushed the covers aside and mounted her, hoping that would ready him. He moved his body against hers. She arched her back, eager for him. Her rushed warm breath on his neck assured him that her desire was sincere. It had been a long time for the two of them, but his body again failed him, and his moderate erection faded into a flaccid, unfeeling embarrassment. When he stopped his efforts the woman's breath became still and quiet. He silently damned her. If only she would resist. If only she would fight him. Finally she spoke. "I'll be late for work."

He rolled aside and she climbed out of bed.

There were only two calls on the day's schedule, and neither of them was very interesting, so he had lingered in bed after his wife left. Using the remote control for the television set he was flipping through the channels, taking little interest in anything he found. On the second hour of the "Today Show," Willard Scott looked even heavier. Joan what's-her-name, on "Good Morning, America" was talking to a senator's wife. Who cares? CNN was showing a clip of the latest rioting in South Korea. "Bewitched" was on channel thirteen. Whatever became of the guy that played her husband? He switched again and found "Live" superimposed at the bottom of the screen. It looked like the lobby of a police station and an impromptu press conference. The camera lights were hot on an attractive brunette. Her sober words brought a strong reaction from the man. He pushed the volume button to increase it as he sat up straight in the bed.

Bobbi Marshal could feel the heat from the camera lamps as she spoke into their glare. "We have reason to believe the suspect may have committed as many as nineteen rapes in the past five months."

"Can you tell us what evidence you have that links these crimes together?" a female voice urged from behind the lights.

"Only in general terms," Bobbi answered. "If we give specifics it might lead to false confessions or copycat crimes. We can say the man's targets are young, attractive, single, professional women who live alone."

"You used the word target, Detective Marshal. Is that an indication the man is stalking his victims?" another reporter questioned.

"Yes," Bobbi said to the camera. "We have evidence

that would indicate the suspect is familiar with the victim's life-style, daily routine, work schedule, and so on.''

"Do you have a description of the man?'' a voice off camera called.

Bobbi nodded. "A partial description,'' she said.

The naked man sitting on the bed tensed and pulled the tangle of sheets up over himself as if that would shield him from anything the attractive policewoman might say. He held his breath as she spoke.

"We know he's a big man. A Caucasian with sandy brown hair and a gentle voice, weighing approximately two hundred pounds and wearing a size thirteen shoe.''

"Do you have any firm leads?'' a reporter pressed.

"We're actively pursuing a number of leads,'' Bobbi answered. "And the Scientific Investigation Division as well as a number of Sex teams from other police divisions have joined in the investigation.''

"Do you have any advice for the single women who may be watching?'' a female reporter questioned.

"Yes,'' Bobbi said. "Think defensively. Use common-sense rules about your safety. This man's only raped women alone, and he's never used force to gain entry into their homes.''

"Are you saying these women contributed to their own rapes?'' a reporter quickly asked.

"We'll keep you posted on any progress we make,'' Bobbi countered, ignoring the question. "Thank you.'' She turned and walked away.

The truth was, Detective Bobbi Marshal felt the rape victims had a common bond. She wasn't sure what it was that made them all sisters of fate, but there was something. Maybe it was attitude. Some women, and Bobbi knew she was among them, displayed an aura of confidence. An aura that warned they were not, nor would they ever be, rape victims. While others, somehow, had "victim'' written across their foreheads. It wasn't that they invited their rape. It was more of a general involuntary expression of vulnerability that contributed to it. Bobbi called it "The

Damsel Syndrome,'' an aftershock from the forties and fifties when women were frail, dependent beings who relied on men for protection and provision. Some changed and some didn't. Some were raped and some weren't. Attitude seemed to be a chemistry rapists had learned to read well.

Beth Powers, a sandy-haired, aristocratic-looking thirty-year-old field reporter from KTTV, stepped in front of the camera for the wrap-up. ''That was Detective Bobbi Marshal,'' Beth said to the camera, ''from LAPD's Wilshire Division Sex Team. As you heard, she's one of many detectives assigned to what the police are calling, at least unofficially, the 'Big Foot' rapist. His latest victim . . .'' The screen went black as the man turned off the television set and climbed from the bed. ''Bobbi Marshal,'' he said aloud as he walked naked into the hallway. The policewoman was beautiful, exciting. It was as if she had talked directly to him. What was it she said? ''He's a big man. A gentle voice. Sandy hair. Jesus! She's turned on by all this. A policewoman. He pictured her nude. Flawless skin, tanned perfectly. Body lean and firm, sweating. She was fantastic. The images aroused him. He held himself as he walked toward his desk in the den.

He remembered names. Early in his career that had been important. People were flattered, impressed, when their names were remembered. Later it became a game. Especially remembering the women's. The ones he fantasized about. And then the game evolved into building a mental image of the clients he thought were young, single women. He'd gotten very good at it, and Bobbi Marshal was a name that sounded familiar. He sat down in the cool leather chair at his desk and opened a file drawer. Records were as important as names. He'd learned that lesson too. He thumbed through the file. Madison . . . Markham . . . Marks . . . Marshal. He pulled out the folder. ''Marshal, Bobbi D.'' He smiled, laid the folder on the desk in front of him, and opened it. ''Hello, Bobbi,'' he breathed as he gripped himself. His eyes searched the paperwork.

APPRAISAL REPORT—# 28706

LENDER: GOLDCOAST S & L

SELLER: KEYSTONE DEVELOPERS, INC.

BUYER: MARSHAL, BOBBI, D.—S/fem, 29 yrs—
        Employ/L.A. City

AGENT: J. ADAMS—CENTURY 21

SALES PRICE: $177,900.

Age: New        Type: Condo

Location: 6426 W. Lindenhurst, #608

APPRAISER'S DESCRIPTION OF PROPERTY:

The property is one of seventy-six units in the
newly constructed Stonehaven Towers complex.
It is located on the sixth floor of the building in
the S/W corner. Excellent view from L.R. The
unit consists of six rms. Approx 1600 sq ft. LR/
DR/KIT/BA—1¹/₂/2BDRMS. Master BDRM has
P/W with/pvt BA, SK/TUB. EXCEL flr cover-
ings/elec/heat/air, int/com, microwave, inc.

CONDITION: EXCEL/no flaws

PHOTOS: C-ENC/ 8—SX-70's

BLDG SECURITY: Perimeter, key entry, gated
                parking, key operated elev.
                DEAD BOLTS/excel.

SHOP & SCHOOLS: Close & numerous.

EVALUATION: Price reasonable in comparison to
            local market & recent resales.

APPRAISER: Dick Fredericks, IMAGE MARKET
            APPRAISALS, INC.

DISPOSITION OF KEYS: Returned to buyer's
                     agent—D.F.

The man smiled as he finished reading the report. Taped
to the bottom of the report was a single silver key. He
carefully loosened the tape and pulled the key loose. With
only two calls on his schedule, he'd have plenty of time to
see if the key still fit her lock. He was confident it would.
New home owners seldom changed their locks, although
as many as five or six keys to their homes often went

unaccounted for at the time of sale. The thought of visiting the policewoman's apartment excited him. He squeezed his full erection. The female attorney in North Hollywood could wait. He'd been in her home twice and had been following her for a week now, but Bobbi Marshal was much more exciting. The thought of raping the detective who was hunting him filled him with a passion he'd never known before.

They drove east on Venice Boulevard when they left the station. Bobbi was angry, with a mixture of frustration and disappointment. The responsibility of finding a brutal rapist was pressure enough, but now she was being criticized and pressured by the captain, and a lieutenant she liked and admired had failed to defend her. The fact that her partner hadn't been part of the criticism made it even more personal and stinging. The price of being a female in a predominantly male world of cops, Bobbi concluded. It was a battle she had to fight with each new assignment, each new partner, each new day. Would Captain Westly have been so critical and accusing if it were Dan Shea who had put out the teletype? She knew the answer. It wasn't fair, but it was reality. The answer, she knew, was not in being as good as they were—she was already that—but in being better. She had to prove Captain Westly wrong. She had to prove to Lieutenant Stovich that she was worth defending. She had to find Big Foot. Anything short of that was failure, and failure was not something Detective Bobbi Marshal was ready to accept. What was it her father had said when she joined the police department? "I'll keep a spot open for you at the bank." Like the others, he also expected her to fail. Damn them!

They were stopped at a traffic signal when Brad Chilcoat finally broke the silence. "I called SID while you were playing meet the press."

"Don't make me play twenty questions," Bobbi warned.

"Wade's still working on the evidence, but he had

enough to make it official,'' Chilcoat answered. ''The se-men and the pubic hair match the others. That puts Big Foot's score at nineteen. I passed it on to Stovich.''

''I couldn't believe the way he let me burn in the cap-tain's office,'' Bobbi complained at the mention of the lieutenant's name.

''What the hell did you expect?'' Chilcoat said, rolling the car forward on green. ''He can't approve of one of his people violating policy.''

''He could have said something,'' Bobbi defended.

''Maybe he just didn't think it was time,'' Chilcoat said.

''And maybe he just doesn't care,'' Bobbi suggested.

''He cares,'' Chilcoat answered. ''He wouldn't have us working full-time on Big Foot if he didn't think you could cut it.''

Bobbi stared ahead, not answering.

Chilcoat glanced at her and then went on. ''Wade said he's got cotton fibers from last night's scene. They're dyed black and white. He thinks maybe they're work gloves.''

''Nineteen rapes, and all that five-million-dollar lab can tell us is that the rapist wears works gloves?'' Bobbi quipped sarcastically. ''Three of the victims already told us that.''

Chilcoat evaded her challenge. ''He's also got a make on the shoe prints. Says they're Florsheim.''

''That's about as helpful as knowing he's male.'' Bob-bi's sarcasm continued.

''We've gotta start somewhere.''

''Let's start with Lisa Cartwright at the hospital.''

Chilcoat turned the detective car south on Crenshaw. ''You know, you're not the only one in the world with problems, Marshal.''

''Don't tell me,'' Bobbi said with a glance, ''you went out last night and ran out of Tic Tacs.''

''No, it's more than that,'' Chilcoat answered. ''Cathy wants a divorce.''

Bobbi looked at her partner. He was staring at the rear of a truck they followed. ''What are you going to do?''

"Give her what she wants."

"Maybe you should try putting things back together."

"Shit! Not after last night. She threw all my stuff out of the house. Everything. My clothes. My fishing gear. Even my VCR. Screaming and yelling, acting like some ghetto bitch, woke up half the neighborhood. I'll never go back."

"Where did you go?" Bobbi questioned.

"Holiday Inn on Victory Boulevard. Cost me fifty-two bucks."

"You can't live in a Holiday Inn."

Chilcoat turned the detective car east on Adams Boulevard. "Dan Shea owns a couple duplexes. He's got one vacant."

"Brad," Bobbi warned, "I like Cathy and I like you. I don't want to pick sides. Don't put me in the middle of this thing."

"You're my partner. Not hers," Chilcoat said defensively.

"See what I mean?" Bobbi warned again.

"Okay, okay," Chilcoat agreed.

It was quiet in the car again for a moment as they moved with the traffic. Then Chilcoat looked at Bobby and said, "Is my being single going to change our relationship?"

"Yes," Bobbi answered. "It means no more jokes. No more sexual innuendo. Nothing."

"Okay," Brad Chilcoat agreed, "but that blouse you're wearing really clings, doesn't it?"

"You're a real bastard."

"You've been talking to Cathy, haven't you?"

The black nurse at the reception desk was writing on a chart when Bobbi and Brad reached her. She paused from her work to look up at the two detectives. "May I help you?"

"Yes," Bobbi answered. "We're Detectives Marshal and Chilcoat from the LAPD. We'd like to see a patient by the name of Lisa Cartwright."

"I'm glad you're here," the nurse said. "She walked out about an hour ago."

Lisa used the key she kept hidden under a flowerpot on the front porch. She ignored the evidence seals the police had taped to the door. This was her house. Her boldness faded when the front door swung in and the memories of yesterday's terror reached out to engulf her. She stood silent and stiff, staring into the quiet house for a long time before she gathered the courage to step inside.

Lisa had her car bulging with personal belongings when the detective car pulled to a halt at the curb in front. She paused on the front porch as the two detectives climbed out and moved toward her. She remembered the policewoman from the hospital.

"I'm leaving," Lisa announced.

"Where are you going?" Bobbi questioned.

"Home to Bakersfield."

"I'm sorry, Lisa," Bobbi said sincerely.

"Are you sorry my house is covered with black dust?" Lisa countered soberly.

"That's silver nitrate," Brad Chilcoat answered. "It's used to find fingerprints."

"The man wore gloves," Lisa answered angrily.

"We had to check. I'm sorry if it's a mess."

"You took my sheets and my pillowcases," Lisa complained as the tears welled in her eyes. "Do you know how much they cost?"

"I'm sorry," Chilcoat said.

"How would you like that done to your home?" she demanded.

"I wouldn't like it," Chilcoat admitted.

Bobbi understood the woman's anger and frustration. She'd seen it many times. Lisa Cartwright couldn't be angry or shout at her rapist. She didn't know who he was or where he was, but she could be angry at the man standing in front of her. He was safe to be angry at. He was a cop.

It wasn't coincidental that her anger was directed at the male detective.

"Lisa, before you go," Bobbi said, assuring her they would make no effort to stop her, "is there anything else you can remember about the man? Something you haven't already told us?"

Lisa considered the question carefully before she answered. "When I went in the house this morning I found myself sniffing."

"Sniffing?" Bobbi questioned.

Lisa nodded agreement. "And then I remembered. He smelled. Like real heavy cologne or something, I'm not sure."

Two of the four other Big Foot victims that Bobbi interviewed had reported the same thing. One of them, a buyer from Bullocks, claimed it was the syrupy sweet smell of Brut. "Would you recognize the odor if you smelled it again?" Bobbi asked Lisa Cartwright.

"No," Lisa answered, picking up two of the remaining three suitcases that sat on the front porch.

Brad Chilcoat was quickly to Lisa's side to take one of the suitcases. Bobbi took the third and they moved toward the car parked in the driveway.

"We're going to find this man, Lisa," Bobbi promised as they reached the car.

"I don't believe you," Lisa said as she unlocked the car. "I heard on the news this morning that I'm the nineteenth woman he's raped. Is that true?"

"Yes," Bobbi answered soberly.

"And you still don't know who he is?"

"No."

"Then you have no right to ask me why I'm leaving, or to ask me to stay," Lisa said, loading the suitcases into the back seat. Climbing in, she started the car, backed out, and drove away. Detectives Bobbi Marshal and Brad Chilcoat walked in silence to their waiting car.

"We've got to find this sonofabitch," Brad Chilcoat said as he started the detective car.

* * *

The crime report, taken by the uniformed officers who first interviewed Lisa Cartwright at the hospital, showed her place of employment as the California Hospital on South Hope. Chilcoat and Bobbi arrived there just before ten. They talked to the director of nursing, who had hired Lisa Cartwright. The woman was shocked and saddened to learn of Lisa's rape. The two detectives went through Lisa's personnel file looking for the common denominator that linked her fate to eighteen others in the city. They looked at it, studied it, and then copied it. They found nothing unusual. There was nothing that identified Lisa as a potential victim and nothing that linked her to the others, but they knew it was there.

"You know the reality of this case, don't you?" Brad Chilcoat questioned as they drove away from the hospital.

"What's that?" Bobbi asked as she thumbed through Lisa's résumé and application.

"Short of finding the link between the nineteen victims, all we can do is wait for number twenty."

It was a sobering, chilling thought, but Bobbi Marshal knew it was the truth. The police knew the color of Big Foot's hair, his approximate age, his height and weight, his shoe size, his blood type. The odor of his cologne. The color and texture of his pubic hair. The type of gloves he wore. That likely he had a dominating mother for whom he had a deep-seated resentment, a quiet or absent father, and an unfulfilling love life. A great deal of scientific effort had gone into developing the information and profile the police had on Big Foot, and on the surface it was impressive, but as Lisa Cartwright had so aptly pointed out, "You still don't know who he is." They were no closer to Big Foot's arrest after nineteen rapes than they were after his first rape five months earlier. As Brad Chilcoat suggested, there was little else the police could do but wait for Big Foot's next victim and hope the evidence gathered then would take them a step closer.

"I wonder who she is, don't you?" Chilcoat said as he

weaved the detective car through the traffic on Olympic Boulevard.

"Who who is?" Bobbi questioned.

"Big Foot's next victim," Chilcoat answered. The thought that he might be sitting beside her never entered his mind.

# 6

# THE HUNTED

It was late morning when the two detectives returned to the twenty-seven-hundred block of South Rimpau where Lisa Cartwright lived to "knock doors."

Brad Chilcoat took the east side of the street and Bobbi Marshal took the west. Two and a half hours and thirty-three names and addresses later, the two detectives met on the southwest corner of Rimpau and Jefferson. "Any luck?" Bobbi said to Chilcoat.

"Yeah." Chilcoat smiled. "All bad. I fixed a garbage disposal, got chased by a Doberman, and got propositioned by a drag queen."

"I wonder what people did before daytime television?" Bobbi mused as they walked back to the detective car.

"They worked," Chilcoat quipped sarcastically.

His first call was in Inglewood, a duplex not far from the airport. The tenants, Mexicans who spoke little English, were cooperative but wary as he made his required walk-through. The dim, cluttered room smelled of evaporated milk and soiled diapers. Aliens, he concluded. He stopped at a gas station after leaving and washed his hands.

The second property was in the hills of West L.A. The worksheet showed it was owned by a doctor and was being sold to another doctor for four hundred and sixty-eight thousand dollars. He knew from experience that the sale was likely a deal between friends, with a cash-back agreement outside the sales contract to cover the inflated price, but yet enough to offer the good doctor a much needed tax shelter. Only the disappearing middle class took sales contracts seriously.

Dr. Cohen wasn't home, but a Mexican maid was. "Jess, we expect you," the plump woman said after he showed his appraisal order. It wasn't likely the woman could read English.

"Are you the only one here?" the man asked the maid as he stepped into the polished tile entryway.

"Jess, the señor, he is at the hospital, and the señora, she is at her club."

"I have to inspect every room."

"Jess, I will be in the kitchen," the maid said, and retreated. It always amazed him how quickly he was given complete access to a home. Seldom was he ever asked for identification. Seldom did the home owner accompany him as he inspected bedrooms, bathrooms, closets, attics, garages. The place many claimed as their most private, the place that many protected with bars and elaborate alarm systems, was quickly and with seemingly little regard placed in the hands of a total stranger.

He enjoyed inspecting the insides of homes. There was something exciting about being in a strange bedroom alone. It had started with his mother's bedroom. He was never allowed in there, and he was twelve before he violated her trust the first time. He had searched the drawers, fondling the silky underwear and slips, drinking in the lingering aroma of powders and perfumes. He was to do it often through his teen years, sneaking into the room, running his hands through the drawers. It never failed to excite him. He was fifteen when his mother caught him the first time. She beat him with a wooden spoon from the kitchen, called him sick, and warned him never to go in her room again. Two days later, while she slept in front of the television set, he did it again.

He started in the downstairs of the sprawling house, making notes as he strolled through the sumptuous living room. A curved, railed staircase led to the second floor, where an oil painting in the front hallway of a tall, slim brunette in a low-cut blue gown told him whose room he was entering. The chance that the maid might walk in at any moment added to his excitement as he began searching dresser drawers. The woman had a wide array of undergarments, especially silk panties. He stole two pairs.

It took real effort on his part to fight the compelling urge to masturbate in the master bathroom, but he knew it would diminish the excitement and pleasure that lay ahead in the policewoman's condo. He pushed the stolen panties into his pocket and left the room.

The Detective Bureau at Wilshire Division was not having a normal day. Captain George Westly had cancelled all of his appointments and secluded himself in his office. It had taken most of the day, but with his adjutant's help he finally found a section of the LAPD manual that, at least in his opinion, applied and gave him the authority he was searching for.

SECTION D/67-A1179
LAPD MANUAL & ORDERS

ARREST, DETENTION, CRIMINAL COMPLAINTS
(A) A field officer effecting the lawful arrest of a criminal violator shall seek the immediate approval from the Watch Supervisor to formally book the violator into custody pending the filing of criminal charges with the office of the District Attorney.

BOOKING APPROVAL FORM D5990—LAPD 81
(B) In the event the Watch Supervisor, upon his review of the probable cause to arrest, denies the booking approval, the violator shall be released from custody under the provision of LAPD MA SEC-1007436B.
(C) In the event the Watch Supervisor learns of a

lack of probable cause to arrest after the approval of formal booking, the violator may be released from formal custody, and the case must be presented to the office of the District Attorney for review and disposition.

SEE D/A FILINGS, LAPD MAN SEC 3007963D.

After rereading the manual sections, Captain Westly sent his adjutant from the office and sat down behind his desk to pick up the telephone. He checked the department directory on his desk and then dialed the Hollywood Division Vice Unit.

The extension rang twice before a cheerful male voice answered. "Hollywood Vice, where none of our searches come up fruitless. May I help you?"

"This is Captain Westly, young man. I suggest you work on the way you answer the telephone."

"Ah, yes, yes, sir," the surprised and shaken officer answered.

"Let me talk to your lieutenant."

"Yes, sir."

The line went silent as the captain was placed on hold. As he waited, Captain Westly visualized the call that would be made to the governor's office before the afternoon was over. "Hello, governor, Ray Bendicci in L.A. The problem with your brother-in-law is solved. Yes, a friend of mine, Captain George Westly, took care of it personally. Yes, I'm sure he'd like to meet you too, sir."

George Westly knew the death of his brother, the senior senator from California, two years earlier was going to make his remaining years on the LAPD difficult. When Senator Phillip Westly was alive, George enjoyed the protection his brother's influence offered. Now all that had changed, but it seemed fate was kind, and an opportunity to find the personal favor of Governor Jason Ryder had fallen into his lap. The governor's brother-in-law, Judge Warrick Unger of the Los Angeles Superior Court, had been arrested for soliciting prostitution. The policewoman making the arrest was assigned to Captain Westly's command. It was indeed a golden opportunity, and George Westly wasn't about to let it slip through his fingers.

He also needed to do something with that smartass policewoman. He wasn't about to let some female detective make it look like his division wasn't holding its own against crime.

"This is Lieutenant Piefer," a voice on the line said.

George Westly straightened in his chair. "Yes, lieutenant. This is George Westly from Wilshire Detectives."

"What can I do for you, captain?"

"Yesterday I had a policewoman on loan to your unit. She made an arrest on Sunset that I'm concerned about."

"Judge Unger," the lieutenant said. "Yeah, I've been getting a lot of calls about him. Don't worry about it, captain, the arrest is good."

George Westly cleared his throat. "Well, lieutenant, I'm afraid I can't agree with you. I've looked at the reports, and I think there's a problem with probable cause."

"I understand your concern, captain, but I know the case law on entrapment inside and out, and we're on solid ground here."

"Lieutenant," Westly said, putting an edge of authority and irritation in his voice. "I didn't call you to open up a debate. I'd like the charge dismissed and the five-ten signed off."

"I can't do that, captain," the lieutenant balked.

"Lieutenant," Westly repeated, glancing at the notes he'd made. "Section D sixty-seven of the manual, 'Arrest, Detention, Criminal Complaints,' clearly gives me that authority."

The line was silent for a moment. Then the lieutenant spoke. "Could I have that manual section again, please?"

The captain repeated it.

"Captain, have you discussed this with Detective Marshal?" the lieutenant questioned.

"Yes."

"All right, captain. I'll send you a copy of the five-ten arrest disposition."

"Thank you, lieutenant," the captain said, and hung up. He felt a sudden surge of victory. He checked his directory for the number of the district attorney's office and then dialed the phone.

"Good afternoon, the district attorney's office."

"Captain George Westly calling for the district attorney."

"I'm sorry, captain, the district attorney's in a meeting. May I take a message?"

"He's expecting my call, miss. I suggest you check with him."

"Please hold."

The privacy of Tom Antonopolis's bar gave Bobbi Marshal the chance to fill in her partner on Fawn Tyler and the missing fifteen-year-old, Debbi.

"Jesus," Brad Chilcoat complained when Bobbi finished with the details the seventeen-year-old prostitute had shared. "I don't want anything to do with that."

"Who do we give it to, Juvenile?" Bobbi complained. "They don't have the time or the experience to handle it."

"Neither do we," Chilcoat defended. "Lieutenant Stovich didn't put us on Big Foot full-time so we could go chasing after a fifteen-year-old streetwalker hooked on crack."

"Brad," Bobbi pleaded, "it wasn't a Tupperware party he took her to. He may have killed this little girl."

"Stovich is never going to let us do it," Chilcoat said.

"So we don't say anything to him until we have something solid," Bobbi suggested.

"I don't like it," Chilcoat said, shaking his head.

"Brad," Bobbi said. "The little girl that's missing is only a couple of years older than your twins. Someone's got to care. Someone's got to do something."

The black clerk behind the reception desk at the Galaxy Motel was watching "General Hospital" on a small black and white television set when Bobbi Marshal and Brad Chilcoat walked in. He recognized Brad Chilcoat as a cop immediately. The young black man stiffened as the two reached the counter. He'd already decided he didn't like the white cop. He was also betting the good-looking girl with the cop was a secretary or something and they wanted a room for a nooner. Bobbi Marshal surprised him. "I'm Detective Marshal. This is my partner, Chilcoat," she said soberly. "What room is Fawn Tyler in?"

"She ain't in none of them," the clerk answered as he studied Bobbi. He decided he was not going to look at the white man.

Bobbi leaned on the counter. Her eyes were a clear blue and they held the clerk's. He felt as if he were looking into the eyes of a cat. It was as if she were looking deep inside of him, and it unnerved him. Without even realizing it, he had surrendered to her power and authority. At the academy the instructors called it "command presence." In the ghetto it was called "balls," and more often than not it quickly decided the outcome of confrontations. This one was already over. "We can make this easy or difficult. We don't care which," Bobbi warned. "Fawn Tyler's been staying here for a long time, and I'd like to know what room."

"Been," the clerk said. "Been staying. But she's gone now." If the white male cop had asked the question, the clerk would have lied, but an attractive, blue-eyed brunette demanding the truth got it. It was a phenomenon that Bobbi and Chilcoat had recognized and often used to their advantage. "It's sexist," Brad Chilcoat had once declared during a talk about it. "From the time little boys look down and see they have a dick, they're taught to treat women different. Open doors, let them go first, never hit them. Just because you carry a badge doesn't mean we can forget all that."

"Gone?" Bobbi said as her blue eyes flashed in anger

at the skinny black clerk. "What do you mean, gone? Where did she go?"

"I swear I don't know."

"He's lying," Chilcoat suggested.

"I ain't lying," the clerk defended nervously. Bobbi kept her eyes locked on him.

"Let's run a warrant check on him," Chilcoat urged.

The clerk swallowed hard. His mouth was dry. He wished the woman would look away. She just kept staring at him. "Maybe," the clerk said, "maybe she knew about the guy that came lookin' for her."

"What guy?" Bobbi demanded.

"Big ugly dude," the clerk said. He gestured to his cheek. "Had zit scars all over his face."

"When was he here?" Bobbi questioned.

"This morning. But he didn't find Fawn. He went up to her room, but she wasn't in there."

"How do you know that?"

" 'Cause I opened the door for 'im."

"Nice of you."

"Shit, how's I to know? He could have been her brother or something, ya know?"

"Did you get his name?"

"Why would I ask his name?"

"Do you have any idea where Fawn may have gone?" Bobbi asked.

"Hey, guests come and go. I've learned not to get involved."

"Well, you're involved now," Bobbi warned. She dug in her purse. "I'm going to give you a card, and if you see or hear from Fawn Tyler I expect you to call me. You don't, I'm gonna find out and I'll be back."

"I'll call," the clerk promised as he took the card.

"Was Debbi with Fawn?" Chilcoat questioned.

"Debbi? No. She hasn't been around in a week or so."

Brad Chilcoat waited until they were in the detective car and headed north on La Brea before he said anything. "So much for your missing fifteen-year-old," he suggested with a glance at Bobbi.

"Are you crazy?" Bobbi defended. "Everything the clerk said reinforces what Fawn told me. The man with the pockmarked face, Debbi missing."

"Okay," Chilcoat countered, "you got everything but a victim."

"A victim?" Bobbi questioned. "We've got two of them. One probably dead and the other missing."

"I just wanted to see if you were still interested in it," Chilcoat said.

"Interested! Brad, we've got to find Fawn before this guy Del does."

"How?" Chilcoat questioned.

"We'll ask the Vice units for help. They owe me."

"Okay," Chilcoat agreed, "I'll join you in this, but Big Foot's gotta remain number one. Do we agree?"

"Like they say." Bobbi smiled. "If the shoe fits."

They spent the remainder of the afternoon visiting the seven other police divisions where Big Foot had struck. They gathered reports and talked to the Sex teams that were available. It was an exercise in frustration. Big Foot, an urban terrorist in the truest sense, had always struck with total surprise. Not one of his nineteen victims could describe more than his gloved hand. He was a perverted, faceless hulk with heavy cologne and a gentle voice.

At each division Bobbi visited the Vice office to give them a description of Fawn Tyler. Bobbi wanted her picked up and held.

They returned to the Wilshire Station with a stack of crime reports and the realization that the key to Big Foot's identification lay in the yet unidentified bond between his nineteen victims.

They sat in one of the small interrogation rooms to escape the distraction of the detective squad room and studied the reports.

"You know what's shocking?" Bobbi said after reading

the last report. She tossed it atop the others that lay on the small desk between them.

"Shock me," Chilcoat challenged.

"We've got nineteen rapes in eight different police divisions committed by the same man, but in the midst of this high-tech multimillion-dollar blue army no one's coordinating anything. The only way we know Big Foot has hit in Hollywood, Rampart, Central, or anywhere else is because we read their teletypes and they read ours."

"You got a better way?"

"Someone should be looking at the overview, the big picture," Bobbi suggested.

"It's easy to forget you came to drain the swamp when you're up to your ass in alligators," Chilcoat defended.

"We wouldn't even have copies of all the crime reports if we hadn't gone out and collected them ourselves. There's eight Sex teams, sixteen detectives, working on Big Foot, but we're all working independently of one another and pulling in eight different directions."

"Don't say that like I caused it."

"Can you imagine the results if we all worked together?" Bobbi questioned.

"Where do you think you are, Marshal, in Mister Rogers's neighborhood? This is realityville. You're asking eight detective captains to cooperate with one another. They'd sooner push pencils up their asses. They'd all like the chance to stand in front of the TV cameras and take the credit for protecting the virtue of the women in our fair city, but none of them is going to do a damned thing to see some other captain move an inch closer to becoming a commander. No matter how many rape victims it takes."

"It wouldn't be that way if they were the ones that had to face the victims," Bobbi mused.

"Victims are a faceless, forgotten commodity," Chilcoat warned. "Haven't the courts taught you that? Victims don't have names, hopes, or dreams. Sometimes they make the front page but then they're quickly forgotten. Instead we glamorize the criminals. Manson, the Hillside Strangler, Son of Sam. We read books about them, we watch their movies, their trials. We hire attorneys to protect their rights, and we're careful not to inflict cruel and unusual punishment on them. But victims you can find anywhere. The streets are full of them."

"Thanks for your encouragement," Bobbi scoffed.

Lieutenant Aaron Stovich drove to Hollywood Division in the middle of the afternoon after telephoning the Vice Unit to check on the disposition of the case against Judge Warrick Unger. As Stovich suspected, it had been dismissed.

"Let's talk," the sober Stovich said to Lieutenant Piefer when he walked into the Hollywood Division Vice office. Lieutenant Piefer sent two long-haired, bearded Vice officers from the cluttered office and gestured for Stovich to sit down. "You want a coffee?"

"Got anything better?" Stovich questioned.

"Little Wild Turkey?" Piefer offered, opening the bottom drawer of his desk.

"Given the subject matter, it seems an appropriate brand," Stovich suggested as the younger lieutenant lifted out a quart bottle.

"Seems Wilshire Detectives has an acute interest in Hollywood Vice these days," Piefer said, setting a clear plastic cup in front of Stovich and uncapping the whiskey.

"Tell me about Judge Warrick Unger," Stovich urged as the lieutenant poured the drinks.

"Solid case of solicitation against him," Piefer assured, putting the bottle back in the drawer and picking up his own cup.

Stovich tasted the liquor in his cup. It was smooth and inviting after the long day. "Then why did you kick it out?"

The younger lieutenant rocked back in his chair and studied the stocky Stovich. "You know why I kicked it out or you wouldn't be here talking."

"I need to hear it from you," Stovich said soberly.

"You can hear it from the horse's mouth." Piefer smiled.

"You taped it?" Stovich questioned.

"You work Vice in Hollywood," Piefer answered coyly, "you learn to tape a lot of things."

"Let's have another drink," Stovich suggested with a pleased smile.

After several hours' work on the stack of crime reports, Bobbi Marshal and Brad Chilcoat had what they thought was a composite profile of Big Foot's victims. She was an attractive, single, twenty-eight-year-old female professional who lived alone, usually in a condominium, and she was usually home by eight p.m. five nights a week. She worked less than ten miles from where she lived, earned more than twenty thousand dollars a year, drove a late-model car, and did not smoke. She drank in moderation if at all, was usually a college graduate, was actively dating but not divorced or engaged, averaged one date a week, did not frequent singles bars, and had no idea how she was selected as a rape victim.

"Big Foot not only hates women," Brad Chilcoat suggested when they finished, "he hates yuppie women. He's a yuppie fucker."

Bobbi was disappointed at the results. "All we've got now is a composite victim for our composite rapist."

"We need to talk to the victims again," Chilcoat said, pushing aside the wealth of crime reports. "They've got something in common we haven't found. A dating service, a doctor, a TV repairman, a realtor, an attorney. Big Foot knew each and every one of them. I think he even had a key."

"When do we start?" Bobbi questioned.

"Tomorrow," Chilcoat said with a look around the squad room. The majority of the desks were already vacant. He glanced at his watch. "Jesus, it's almost five. I've got to meet Dan Shea at five-thirty. He's giving me a key to the duplex I'm renting."

"Marshal," the intercom in the squad room called, "line six please."

"Go ahead," Bobbi said to Chilcoat. "I'll take care of this stuff."

"Thanks. See you in the morning," Chilcoat said. He grabbed his jacket and was gone in a rush.

Bobbi picked up the telephone, punching the blinking white light on the console. "This is Detective Marshal," she said into the receiver. "May I help you?"

"Is this Bobbi Marshal?" a male voice questioned in her ear.

"Yes," Bobbi answered.

"You looked really great on television this morning," the man breathed.

"Thank you," Bobbi said in a guarded tone. "Who is this?"

A plastic click sounded and a dial tone sang in Bobbi's ear.

The man was standing in the living room of Bobbi Marshal's condominium. After hanging up the telephone he slowly took off his glove. Her voice had really excited him. He'd never called any of them before. The fact that he was calling from her living room added to the thrill. It gave a new dimension to his excitement. Maybe she'd even guess who he was. Even if she did, there was nothing she could do about it. She was his. He would decide the time and the place. The hunted had become the hunter. He'd been in her condominium for almost an hour now. Looking through pictures, he'd found one of her in a bikini. He smelled her perfumes, searched her closets and dresser drawers. He took two pairs of bikini panties and a pair of panty hose. Her scent was still on them. It intoxicated him. Before leaving, he walked to the bedroom again, pulled back the spread, and picked up a pillow. Unzipping his fly, the man pulled out his erection and rubbed it all over the smooth pillow. He moaned with delight. He did the same with the second pillow. Finished, he replaced the pillows and carefully smoothed the spread. "Sleep

tight, Bobbi.'' He smiled, pushing himself back in his
pants.

Riding the elevator to the subterranean garage, he decided to wait there until she drove in. He wanted to see
her. Maybe, he thought, he'd even search her car after she
went up. Her scent and warmth would still be there. He
willed himself calm. He was close to climaxing. He knew
he wouldn't be able to wait long with this girl. This one
was going to be special.

# 7

# WARNING SIGNS

As Bobbi Marshal wheeled the 240-Z into the gate of the Stonehaven Towers garage, she wished she were coming home to stay. Dinner with Don Roberts had sounded inviting in the morning, but now after a long, less than fruitful day and a brief five hours' sleep the night before, she was tired. The thought of going upstairs and fixing her hair and makeup to go out was less than exciting. She briefly considered forgoing dinner and inviting Don over, but there was a chance he might misread that, and it wasn't an evening she felt like fending off some amorous male. Not that she found Don Roberts unattractive. Quite the contrary—he was very attractive. It just wasn't the time. She wondered when would be the time. She was twenty-nine years old and had never been engaged. Her mother had less than subtle ways of constantly reminding her of that fact. At some point, Bobbi wasn't sure when, she'd decided that thirty-two was an appropriate age to marry. After two years of marriage, she'd have a child and then resume her career. The idea of giving up police work permanently for marriage and children was not an option.

Three years seemed like enough time to find a mate. It wasn't that Bobbi was looking. It was more a time of consideration. Don Roberts could not be ignored from that consideration. Wealth, wit, and charm were important. She silently wished Dan Shea were more like that. The thought provoked a smile on Bobbi's face as she stopped at the key lock for the subterranean garage's automatic door. She inserted the key and twisted it. The iron gate began to roll aside. The thought of Dan Shea had surprised her, but now that she allowed herself to think about him, it seem logical. He had most of the traits she hoped to find in a mate. Shea was handsome, successful, confident. She wasn't sure what else, she had to admit, because she really didn't know him. Then didn't that contradict her logic in selecting him? Yes. Then wasn't it more a basic chemistry that attracted her to him? She rejected that, gunning the 240-Z through the open gate and into the basement. Bobbi had seen too many of the so-called chemistry loves develop into bad marriages and then divorce. No, she wasn't going to be swayed by emotion or animal attraction. Selecting a mate was far too important for that. Logic, common sense, and careful planning were at the base of most successful relationships. Dan Shea was not a logical choice. He lacked warmth and a sense of humor—at least she thought he did. Why was it he'd never asked her out? Maybe Brad could give her some insight into him. She thought about Dan Shea as she swung the car into her assigned parking space. She remembered the scent of his cologne as he opened the door for her. She remembered feeling self-conscious walking down the hall in front of him. Why? It didn't matter. He was probably dating someone else anyway. That was probably why he hadn't asked her out. Bobbi opened the car door.

The man parked two rows away watched as she swung her nylon-clad legs from the car. Her skirt was pushed high in the low-slung car and, believing she was alone, Bobbi didn't adjust it as she climbed out, closed the car door, and walked toward the elevator. Her high heels clicking on the polished cement floor made the only sound in the quiet garage. Bobbi took the elevator to the first floor and picked up her mail, then rode the elevator to the sixth floor.

The moment Bobbi stepped into the living room and closed the door, she sensed it. The small hairs on the back of her neck bristled and she tensed instinctively. The room looked undisturbed, familiar, safe, but something was different. Then she realized what it was. The living room curtains were closed. After coming home late to the black void of darkness the living room was with the curtains closed the night before, she vowed she would leave them open every morning. And she had opened them this morning. Hadn't she? Or did she just think about doing it and then forget? She was rushed. No, she remembered clearly that she opened them. Then someone had been in the condo! Someone had closed the curtains. Someone who might still be hiding in a bedroom, waiting. Bobbi realized she was holding her breath. Her heart was pounding. But there was more than the curtains, there was an odor, a sweet, lingering scent in the air. An aerosol spray, a deodorant, and then she recognized it. It was cologne, aftershave. No! Bobbi willed, trying to master her fears and suspicions. Again it was aftershocks of her visit to Lisa Cartwright's bedroom and then coming home alone to her own darkened living room. It was irrational fear, and worse than that it was weak. The hint of perfume in the air probably meant nothing more than maintenance cleaning the hallway carpets. The closed curtains? Thinking and doing were two different things. Obviously she'd forgotten. Bobbi took in a breath, kicked off her shoes, tossed her purse to the couch, and walked across the room and opened the curtains. Bright afternoon sunshine poured into the room.

Bobbi was nearly naked by the time she reached the bathroom, leaving a trail of discarded clothes in her wake. In bikini briefs and bra she knelt beside the sunken tub and turned on the water. As hot, steamy water splashed into the tub, Bobbi stood up to unhook her bra and pushed down her pants. Raising her chin, as they had taught her in girls' school, she studied her figure in the bathroom's full-length mirror. Soft but square shoulders, breasts full and firm. There was no sagging yet. Bobbi wondered how much longer that would last. Lean ribs and a flat stomach with its dime-sized navel. Hips the same width as her shoulders, and long legs with good muscle tone. She was pleased with her reflection. She turned and stepped to the counter to pin up her hair. The tub was nearly full. She could be bathed and dressed, ready to go, in an hour. The idea of dinner with Don Roberts was now an accepted one. What Bobbi Marshal wouldn't allow herself to accept was the fact that she didn't want to spend the evening alone in the condo.

Fawn Tyler was walking south on Highland Avenue just north of Hollywood Boulevard. She hadn't walked the streets of Hollywood for several months. The competition in downtown Hollywood was tough for young prostitutes. What was it her friend Debbi had said, "Why would guys buy it when most girls in Hollywood are giving it away?" And not only did Fawn have to compete with the freebies, there were also the gays, the impersonators, and the teen-age male whores. Hollywood was a sexual stew. But staying on La Brea was too dangerous. She'd fled, leaving everything behind. Scar-faced Del was looking for her, and she knew why. With Fawn Tyler alive, there was someone who could link him to Debbi's disappearance. Fawn was frightened and desperate. She had hitchhiked to Hollywood. All she needed was three Fort Wayne fucks, tourist johns, who usually paid more than locals, and she'd have enough money for a bus to Las Vegas. Maybe, she daydreamed, after she turned a few tricks in Vegas, she could get a job in one of the chorus lines. She did have big tits. Maybe, the dream went on, she could join the police department in Vegas and become a cop like Bobbi Marshal. A horn sounded and brought Fawn's daydream to an abrupt end. She turned and looked. It was a green Ford with a yellow Hertz sticker on the back of the rear-view mirror. It was a Fort Wayne fuck. The balding fifty-year-old offered a cautious grin. Fawn smiled and walked to the car. "Hi." She smiled. She did not notice the burly, thick-necked man with the pockmarked face who pulled to the curb several car lengths behind.

* * *

Brad Chilcoat prided himself on his ability to spot them, and he'd noticed the straw blond when she first walked into the lounge. She was with two other women. It was likely all three worked in a towering office building on nearby Wilshire Boulevard. They sat down at an oval table not far from where he sat at the bar nursing his second drink of the evening. They had a look about them. He'd never been able to articulate what it was. It was just a look. And the blond had it. Finally their eyes met briefly over the twenty-five feet that separated them. The blond offered a quick, bashful smile and looked away, but Brad Chilcoat knew then that he wasn't going home alone.

Chilcoat ordered another gin tonic before he pushed off the barstool and walked to where the three women sat. "Care to dance?" he said with a disarming smile to the waiting blond.

The blond balked, looked to her smiling companions. "I don't know," she stalled. Closer now, he could see she was older than he first thought. Mid-thirties, he guessed, and she was a few pounds heavy but still attractive. He could look down into the shadow between her breasts.

"I haven't stepped on a toe in years." Chilcoat smiled, raising the three fingers on his right hand in a Boy Scout salute. "Scout's honor."

"Go for it, Ginger." One of the brunettes at the table giggled.

"Ginger?" Chilcoat questioned. "With a name like that I know you can dance." He offered a hand. The blond reached out and took it.

Her perfume was rich in his nostrils and her body was warm and firm against his. She smelled clean, and he looked forward to lying with her. It was important to Brad Chilcoat that he not go home alone this night. This was the first night of his new single life. He wouldn't even have to lie to the blond. Cathy wanted a divorce, she could damned well have it. It was her loss, not his. "You know,"

Brad said into the tangle of warm blond hair against his cheek, "you smell just like a legal secretary."

"How did you know that?" the surprised blond said, twisting her face to his. Full lips glistening with gloss were only inches from his face.

"I'm involved in law, too," Chilcoat answered, not telling the woman he'd seen an envelope in her open purse on the table. There was a law firm's name imprinted on it.

"Are you an attorney?" the blond questioned.

"No, I make work for attorneys. I'm a cop."

"A cop? That must be very exciting."

"Right now it is." He smiled.


The restaurant was Le Charcutier. It was French, intimate, and on Beverly Drive just off Santa Monica Boulevard. The maitre d' knew Don Roberts, and he kissed Bobbi's hand before escorting them to a booth in a secluded corner of the dining room. Don ordered for both in flawless French. They dined and drank vintage wine and talked of travel, airlines, and a vacation they both claimed was overdue. It was a relaxed, easy evening, and both enjoyed each other's company. Bobbi Marshal was very glad she hadn't cancelled the date.


Eleven blocks east, in a very different part of the city, Fawn Tyler directed her fifty-year-old Fort Wayne fuck to pull into the parking lot of the Franklin Mint Motel. One would not find a triple-A rating for the Franklin Mint, nor was it listed by the Auto Club as a place to stay when in Hollywood, and to Hollywood Vice it was known as "The Whore Hive."

"The room is forty-two dollars," Fawn Tyler said to the middle-aged All State agent from DeKalb, Illinois, who sat behind the wheel of the Hertz Ford. The man dug in a pocket and pulled out his wallet. Opening it, he gave Fawn two twenties and a five. She noticed he had much more. They had yet to discuss the price for her services, and Fawn had just decided it was going up. "Be right back," she said with a little-girl smile.

"Okay." The insurance agent leered.

"Need a room for two hours," Fawn said to the bearded man behind the counter in the motel office. He had a small TV on, and the sounds of "The Price Is Right" filled the small, cluttered office.

"You got a note from your mother?" The man smiled, looking up and down Fawn's young, shapely form.

Fawn laid one of the twenty-dollar bills on the worn countertop. "Yes, as a matter of fact I do." She smiled seductively. "Doesn't she look just like Andy Jackson?"

The man reached, and his meaty fingers quickly took the bill away. "You know I can't rent you a room by the hour. It's against the law." He chuckled.

Bobbi stepped back from the counter. "It's also against the fuckin' law to report that your motel's on fire, but I will."

The man's dark eyes became angry slits as he glared down at Fawn. Then he tossed her a key. "One-oh-three," he grated, "and don't dirty the sheets."

"Thanks." Fawn smiled as she pushed the remaining twenty and the five into a rear pocket.

The man with the pockmarked face sat behind the wheel of his car in the darkness across the street from the Franklin Mint Motel. He watched intently as Fawn waltzed out of the motel office, with its blinking neon lights, to return to the waiting rental car. After she climbed in, the car moved slowly down the motel's crowded court and swung into a vacant parking space. Fawn and the trick, in his white shoes and white belt, climbed out and walked toward the rear wing of the motel.

The musty odor of mildew reached out of the room as Fawn opened the door and switched on the dim light. The low-wattage bulbs were less expensive, and they made most of the whores look attractive. The bed with its threadbare green spread was king-sized with a noticeable slump near its center. A nightstand, a lamp, a single chair, and a television set bolted to a wall mount completed the tired decor. Fawn tossed her shoulder bag to the chair, locked the door, and slipped the safety chain into its slot. "You want me to take my clothes off or would you like to do it?" Fawn said matter-of-factly to the man who stood wringing his hands and staring at the waiting bed.

"Ah, I don't have much time, honey," the man said, revealing a wire that held an old partial in his upper mouth. "Maybe we could do something that doesn't require us gettin' undressed."

Fawn had already unbuttoned the front of her blouse. She was braless, and the man wet his lips nervously as his eyes found her breasts. "Jesus," he said breathlessly, "you're beautiful."

"You want head or a hand job?" Fawn asked as she sat down on the edge of the bed in front of the man. She made no effort to button her blouse.

"Ah, how about a little of both?" The man was breathing hard.

"I really like you," Fawn said to the man with practiced teenage innocence, "but I have expenses, you know?"

"Oh, sure," the man said, reaching for his wallet as if he was sorry for the oversight.

"Fifty," Fawn said. She was prepared to take much less.

The man said nothing as he dug in the wallet and offered several bills. Fawn took them and jammed them into the rear pocket of her tight jeans.

Pushing the wallet into his own pocket, the man stepped closer to Fawn. His forehead was glistening with beads of sweat.

"You here on vacation?" Fawn asked as she reached and unzipped his polyester slacks.

"Yeah, we went out to Universal Studios today," the man said in short choppy breaths as she reached inside his pants to find him.

"You're nervous," she said, taking his relaxed penis in hand.

"Ah, maybe . . . a little."

"You got kids?" Fawn questioned as she massaged him.

"Yeah. Two. All grown."

A heavy knock sounded on the locked door, ending the talk. The man jerked away from Fawn in shock. The knock sounded again, rattling the metal door and a nearby curtained window. "Who in the hell's that?" the frightened man blurted as he hurriedly zipped his pants.

Fawn moved quickly to the peephole in the center of the door and looked out. The dark-haired man with the pockmarked face stood outside the door. The lens in the viewer made his thick neck look even shorter. Dressed in a dark suit and tie, he looked like a mortician to Fawn. "Oh, shit," she said in a frightened tone.

"Who is it?" the insurance man demanded frantically.

"Police!" a harsh voice answered from outside. "Open the door."

Fawn darted from the door, moving for the bathroom. "He's lying. He's not the police. He's a killer."

"A killer!" The insurance man gasped. He moved for the telephone. The pounding outside the door continued. "Open up."

Fawn grabbed her shoulder bag, locked the bathroom door behind her and scrambled up on the edge of the bathtub. Reaching up to a small window, she cranked it open, and after several attempts succeeded in pushing out the rusty screen. Behind her she could hear the man from DeKalb shouting for help on the telephone. The heavy thumping continued. Del was trying to break down the door.

Jumping, Fawn grabbed the smooth window ledge and tried to pull herself up. Her fingers slipped on the smooth ledge and she fell crashing into the hard bathtub, tearing down the stained shower curtain.

"The girl's not in here!" Fawn heard the Fort Wayne

fuck shouting at the thumping door. "She went out the bathroom window."

"You sonofabitch," Fawn cried as she climbed back onto the edge of the tub a second time. Tears streaked down her young face, leaving dark gray traces of mascara on her cheeks. She was trembling with fear. She knew if the man caught her he'd kill her, and now with no more thumping at the door it meant he was on his way to the rear of the motel. Fawn bit her lip as a childlike sob made her shudder. She turned and jerked open the bathroom door.

"I'm calling the police, you little tramp," the insurance man warned as Fawn ran by him to the door. She quickly unchained the lock, flung open the door, and bolted into the night.

Horns blared and tires screamed as brakes locked to avoid the figure darting across busy Western Avenue. A crowded RTD bus slammed into the back of a compact car. Glass and chrome rained down onto the pavement. The driver of the car would later tell the police he braked to avoid hitting a girl. When asked what she looked like, all he could remember was that her blouse was open.

The terrified Fawn ran for three blocks without stopping or looking back, cutting through alleys and several backyards to finally take refuge in the unlocked dim entryway of a weathered apartment building. She had no idea where she was, and each time a set of headlamps swept over the tattered curtains that covered the window in the door, she cowered in fright. The hallway smelled of spicy Mexican food and beer. Tinny Spanish music drifted from behind a locked door. Fawn Tyler sat down on the gritty worn floor, drew up her legs, and wept. A large yellow cat with one eye appeared out of the shadows. Spotting Fawn, the cat moved to her and, purring loudly, began rubbing against her legs. Fawn raised her head and took the cat into her arms.

* * *

Brad Chilcoat was pleased. The blond had agreed to drive her own car and follow him to his apartment. He was glad, because afterward he never felt comfortable with them. They always wanted assurances, and all he ever wanted was away from them. He called it "fuck and run." Now with his own place he would control the situation. He knew the unspoken protocol of affairs dictated you spend some time with them afterward, but tonight he was tired and irritable, so it was going to be a quickie. Sleep had been elusive during his night at the Holiday Inn, and earlier, before going to the bar, he had tried calling the twins, but Cathy, that bitch, had the telephone off the hook. What the hell was wrong with that woman? Damned women's lib. He almost missed the turn onto the block where his new apartment was. He glanced into his rearview mirror. The headlamps of the blond's car followed obediently, like a moth to the flame. He smiled at the reflection.

The duplex was in Echo Park, north of towering downtown Los Angeles. It was an older, blue-collar section of the city and becoming predominantly Mexican, but still relatively quiet. Brad pulled his jeep to the curb in front of the address and stopped. The headlamps closed on him from behind and then winked off. He climbed out and walked back to the polished BMW the blond drove. She made no move to get out of her car. The woman ran an automatic window down when Brad reached the car. "How long have you lived here?" the silhouette behind the wheel asked.

"Just moved in. Renting it from an old partner." Brad smiled as he zipped his light windbreaker. The night air was cool and heavy with moisture. The parked cars lining the block were already canopied with bonnets of dew. "Where do you live?"

"Westwood," the blond answered. The BMW and the gold she wore had already told Chilcoat the woman didn't travel coach. "It's a long drive. I think I'd better go," she said.

"Go?" Chilcoat said. Then he moved quickly to the

passenger's side of the car. He heard the automatic door lock snap open. He climbed in, took the woman's face in his hand, and kissed her hard. It was a passionate embrace, and when it ended Chilcoat said, "I want you to come in." Then he kissed her again. This time his hand went under her coat, found the bottom of her blouse and then her warm flesh. She moaned as his hand moved up and beneath the cup of her bra. There was no hint of resistance. Breaking the kiss, Chilcoat whispered, "Let's go inside." He knew she was ready.

The blond pulled her keys from the ignition.

The bulb near the front door was burned out and Chilcoat had an awkward moment finding the unfamiliar lock in the darkness. The blond waited silently behind him. Finally the lock clicked and he pushed the door open. "Come on in."

Chilcoat switched on an overhead light. The room smelled of fresh paint. A single shadeless bulb illuminated the spartan, freshly painted room. There was a blanket-covered mattress and two pillows on the carpeted floor and a small TV set sitting on the top of a small inverted trash can. "This is where you live?" the blond questioned as she eyed the room.

"Yeah, moved in today. You want a beer?" Chilcoat took off his jacket and tossed it to the floor.

"Listen," the blond said as she backed toward the door. "I'm not ready for this. I didn't know what to expect but . . ." She looked at the mattress on the floor. "I didn't expect this."

"Wait," Chilcoat said as he moved to put his arms around her. "I told you I just moved in today." The woman was stiff in his arms.

"Let me go or I'll scream," the blond warned.

"Scream?" Chilcoat laughed, but he released her. The blond turned and bolted out the door, slamming it behind her. The BMW roared to life and pulled away. "Damn," Chilcoat muttered as he walked into the kitchen and took a can of beer from the otherwise empty refrigerator.

Sitting down on the mattress, Chilcoat opened the can of beer and switched on the television set Dan Shea had lent him. David Letterman was interviewing Dr. Ruth. "Come on, doctor," he was saying. "Men want only one thing from women, and we're not talking about clean socks."

The short little doctor chuckled along with the audience before she answered in her distinctive, choppy accent. "You know, David," she said, "men want the same thing women do. Love, warmth, security."

Letterman chuckled. "I suppose that's why men are out every night lifting a different skirt."

"The ones who are doing that are the frightened ones," the doctor answered.

"Is that why I always say hold me, hold me?" David mocked. "We'll be right back to see what women are really frightened of. Don't go . . ." The screen went black as Brad Chilcoat turned the set off. He sat in the silence and drank his can of beer. He was lonely and frightened. He wished he were home, in bed, warm, with Cathy sleeping at his side. Somehow it had all slipped away. What was it his old partner, Mat Cunningham, had once warned? "You might screw around—most cops do—but don't let the home fires go out." Now Brad Chilcoat understood, but it was too late. "Sonofabitch," he said aloud, in the empty room.

Not far away, Cathy Chilcoat lay in the darkness of her bedroom, staring at the faint night light framing the bedroom window. She wondered if she'd ever know a comfortable night's sleep again. She wondered if she'd ever know happiness again. It didn't seem likely, not after the solemn day she'd just experienced. In her attorney's office where an array of legal documents lay waiting, the attorney had offered her a pen. "Sign where I've indicated." He had smiled.

The wife who vowed to love and obey became the *Petitioner* and the husband who had promised to love and cherish became the *Respondent*. A part of Cathy Chilcoat died painfully. Staring into the darkness beyond her bedroom window, she wondered if Brad had any regrets. She supposed not. It wasn't very likely that he was alone.

Don Roberts, as Bobbi expected, said good night at her door on the sixth floor. It wasn't until after their kiss that Bobbi said, ''Would you like to come in?''

They sat close on the couch, listening to soft FM music and enjoying the panorama of the city at night. There was little talk, just the comfort of each other's company. Neither seemed to notice the transition from the couch to the floor, but once there the tempo of their shared passion increased. Bobbi knew where it was leading, and perhaps it was time. Her body was telling her it was.

Don's hungry, warm kisses covered her face, her mouth, her neck, and then her breasts as he unbuttoned her blouse and unsnapped her bra. She sighed audibly and arched her back as he took a nipple into his mouth. Bobbi pressed herself against him as she massaged the back of his neck. She felt his hand touch the back of her knee and then move slowly upward. The hand was warm and smooth against her thigh, and it ignited her. Suddenly he stopped and sat up. Bobbi tried to quiet her heavy breathing before she pulled her blouse over her breasts and sat up beside him. Don slipped an arm around her and drew her close. ''You're beautiful, Bobbi,'' he said, holding her and stroking her hair, ''and it's time for me to go.''

Bobbi snuggled close to him. ''I want us to stay special,'' Don continued. He took her face in his hand. ''I want more than one night with you, Bobbi Marshal. I want them all.'' He kissed her.

After he left, she lay in bed waiting for sleep, trying to calm her eager body. It was then she thought about them, perhaps because she was thinking of making love to Don. The line between making love and having sex for gratification was sometimes thin. But nineteen women in the sleeping, peaceful city knew the brutal difference. Big Foot had been their savage teacher. Bobbi wondered where he was. What was he dreaming of? Would they ever catch him? How would she feel when they did? There was an irony in the jumble of random thoughts that drifted through her relaxed mind. She worked Sex, she talked to rape victims, she spent her days hunting for a rapist. Nearly everything she said or did professionally pertained to sex, but her body ached because there was no sex in her life. Sex! It was a crime, it was a joy, it was a regret. It was many things—sometimes it was all things—but it was never easy. The great God-given paradox, Bobbi thought as she lay on the edge of sleep. The one thing that could bring a woman indescribable shared joy could also bring her indescribable horror.

# 8

# THE SUMMONS

The fifty-two-year-old graying Chief of Police James Peck sat in the back seat of his staff car, reading a lengthy budget proposal and making marginal notes. He was oblivious to the sea of traffic that his driver combatted as the car moved slowly inbound from the San Fernando Valley on the Hollywood Freeway. An electronic beep sounded, and a filtered male voice from the radio said, "Staff One, contact Command Central on the Delta frequency."

The driver picked up the mike. "This is Staff One, roger." Then with a glance into the car's rearview mirror, he added, "Chief, did you catch that?"

"Yes," Chief Peck answered, laying aside his paperwork and picking up a beige radio telephone from its cradle. It was a scrambled private line. Keying the telephone, Peck said, "This is Staff One."

"This is Command Central, Staff One," the familiar voice of the chief's adjutant answered immediately. "Advise you use the private entrance upon arrival at Parker Center."

"Roger," Peck acknowledged, not wanting to question the reason on the air. A secure scrambled frequency was only as good as the latest over-the-counters at Radio Shack.

For some reason his adjutant wanted the chief's arrival at Parker Center to be private. Bomb threats, and even threats against his life, were not that unusual. The chief went back to his work on the budget.

Lieutenant Wayne Collins, a thin thirty-six-year-old in

a gray pinstriped suit, was waiting at the entrance to the stairs on the sixth floor when Chief Peck and his driver finally pushed through the door. Peck was red-faced and breathing hard. "This better be good, lieutenant," the chief warned.

"We've got five TV crews, three radio reporters, and eight print reporters on hold in the press room," the lieutenant warned.

"The mayor get caught in another massage parlor?" the chief joked as they moved down the hallway.

The lieutenant offered the chief several reports. Among them was the daily incident report that summarized the major police incidents and arrests citywide for the past twelve hours. "Worse than that," the young lieutenant cautioned. "Hollywood Vice arrested Governor Ryder's brother-in-law for soliciting."

"That's old news," Peck said. "It was on yesterday's incident report. Who the hell cares? He's nothing but a judge."

"He's more than that now," Lieutenant Collins warned. "Now he's a cause. The charges against him have been dropped."

Chief Peck stopped abruptly at the door to his office. His face quickly clouded with anger. "That sonofabitch Bendicci," he said, referring to the district attorney. "He's gone too far this time. I'll have his ass."

"Sir," the lieutenant cautioned, "I value your opinion of the district attorney's family heritage, but this one belongs in our court."

"What the hell do you mean?" the chief demanded as two secretaries moved by them in the hallway and quickened their pace after passing the two men.

"I've only had time to make preliminary inquiries," Lieutenant Collins answered, "but it seems Captain Westly from Wilshire Detectives is responsible for the judge's five-ten release."

"Westly! Why in the hell's he involved? It was a Hollywood arrest. Being the brother of a senator, doesn't he know it's going to make this look like a political favor?''

"I can't answer for Captain Westly, sir," the lieutenant defended.

"No wonder we've got the press here. It looks like preferential treatment. They smell a rat.''

"I didn't want you walking into the reporters unaware," the lieutenant said.

"Jesus Christ," Peck muttered as he opened the door to his suite of offices. "Get Commander Hull up here." Hull was the commander of Internal Affairs.

"Yes, sir," the lieutenant answered.


Six miles to the west in the city's Wilshire District, Captain George Westly was secluded in his office at Wilshire Detectives. He wasn't taking any calls. His adjutant, Sergeant William Shanks, had informed the group of reporters gathered at the reception desk that the captain would not be making a statement.

"What grounds did the captain use to dismiss the charges against Judge Unger?''

"Why are the other men arrested with the judge still being held?''

"Has the captain talked to the governor? Does he know the Bar Association is looking into the case?''

The shaken sergeant knew it was time to find another assignment.

The detective squad room, usually a beehive of activity early in the day, was strangely quiet. Blood was on the water and the sharks—the reporters in the lobby—were circling for the kill. The principals in the case, Judge Warrick Unger and Detective Bobbi Marshal, seemed, at least for the time being, not to be an issue. The issue was who had the power, or perhaps more importantly, who had used it.

Mayor Gates had been delighted to hear of the arrest of Judge Unger, the governor's brother-in-law. He was even more pleased when he learned the arrest was made by an undercover policewoman and that it was for soliciting prostitution. His joy was short-lived. Soon the rumor mill at City Hall brought word that the charges had been dropped. The mayor was livid. He knew that District Attorney Raymond Bendicci was behind it. The DA was a political ally of the governor's. But it wasn't the district attorney; it wasn't the governor. It was an LAPD police captain. It was too late to shut out the press. The embarrassed mayor promised a complete investigation.

Detective Bobbi Marshal knew she was caught up in something big. She also knew it was rare that a police career remained intact after being drawn into the limelight by the press. The reporters waiting in the lobby worried her and she wanted to leave the station, but Brad Chilcoat was waiting for a telephone call from his attorney. The process he used to select one dismayed Bobbi. Chilcoat had seen an ad on television. "Your marriage in trouble? Call Dial-a-Divorce. D-I-V-O-R-C-E. No divorce over three hundred dollars." When Brad Chilcoat called, an answering machine asked him to leave a message. Now he awaited the return call.

While they waited, Bobbi made a list of the addresses of Big Foot's victims. They would begin the reinterviews as soon as Chilcoat heard from Dial-a-Divorce.

Bobbi sensed trouble the moment the uniformed county marshal walked into the detective squad room. She watched as he spoke with a detective from Burglary. The detective nodded and looked toward Bobbi and Chilcoat. Bobbi tensed. "Brad," she said.

Chilcoat sat across the desk from her, working intently on his checkbook. A yellow pad crammed with columns of numbers and notes was at his elbow. "Damn," he muttered, shaking his head and looking at the yellow tablet. "After Cathy's house payment, her car payment, my car payment, the payment on the boat, my rent, and child support, I'm two hundred and forty dollars in the hole every month."

"You're forgetting alimony," Bobbi suggested.

"She won't ask for alimony," Chilcoat said with an air of confidence.

"I think we've got company," Bobbi warned as the marshal was almost to their desk.

"Oh, yeah?" Chilcoat said. He looked up just as the broad-shouldered marshal reached them. He was a sober-looking thirty-year-old with a mustache. "Detectives Chilcoat and Marshal?"

"Lemme guess." Chilcoat smiled with his practiced charm. "We've just won the Publishers Clearing House Sweepstakes?"

The marshal offered a smile, but he also offered each a folded legal document. Bobbi knew it related to the arrest of Judge Unger. She was both frightened and angry. The lewd sonofabitch. "As an officer of the court of Los Angeles County I serve you these summonses. I suggest you contact an attorney, and don't take it personal. I'm just doing my job."

"Funny." Chilcoat smiled. "That's what my partner said to Judge Unger just the other day."

Bobbi unfolded the summons and read. She was shocked.

*You are hereby ordered to appear in DEPARTMENT 100 of the Superior Court of Los Angeles County at 210 North Hill Street, Los Angeles, on MAY 16.*

*LOS ANGELES SUPERIOR COURT*
*CASE NO.: D 120799*

*In RE:*

*PETITIONER:*
*CATHERINE DEVON CHILCOAT*

*RESPONDENT(S):*
*BRADLEY ADAMS CHILCOAT*
*THE CITY OF LOS ANGELES*
*MAYOR LESTER GATES*
*CHIEF OF POLICE JAMES PECK*
*CAPT. OF POLICE GEORGE WESTLY*
*LT. OF POLICE AARON STOVICH*
*DETECTIVE BOBBI MARSHAL*

*At such time and place THE PETITIONER will seek an INTERLOCUTORY JUDGMENT and DISSOLUTION OF MARRIAGE from Respondent (1) BRADLEY ADAMS CHILCOAT with appropriate child support, alimony, and property divisions.*

*The PETITIONER also seeks damages for ALIENA-TION OF AFFECTION from RESPONDENTS (2) through (7) for willfully and knowingly joining in a CONSPIRACY to deprive the Petitioner of the common company and care of Respondent (1) BRADLEY ADAMS CHILCOAT and in so doing has caused the Petitioner and her minor children great mental and physical anguish and suffering for which the Petitioner seeks DAMAGES in the sum of $974,000.00 each from Respondents (2) through (7).*

*The PETITIONER will present evidence that shows the City of Los Angeles, under the administrative and execu-tive direction of MAYOR LESTER GATES, did direct duly sworn CHIEF OF POLICE JAMES PECK, who supervises CAPTAIN GEORGE WESTLY, who supervises LIEUTEN-ANT AARON STOVICH, who did assign DETECTIVE BOBBI MARSHAL, a FEMALE, as a police partner to RESPONDENT BRADLEY ADAMS CHILCOAT.*

*In so doing RESPONDENTS (2) through (6) had knowl-edge that RESPONDENT BOBBI MARSHAL was a FE-MALE of considerable physical attraction.*

*This willful act resulted in RESPONDENT BRADLEY ADAMS CHILCOAT developing an ABNORMAL and UN-USUAL appetite for sex, and members of the opposite sex, which did cause the DECLINE and subsequent COL-LAPSE of NORMAL RELATIONS with the PETITIONER.*

"Oh, Christ," Brad Chilcoat muttered weakly as he finished reading the summons. He felt physically ill. His police career was over. His life was in shambles. He'd been defeated with one swift blow below the belt. He may not have been screwed the night before but he was now. He knew by now other marshals were serving similar sum-mons to the mayor's office and the chief of police. He looked up into Bobbi Marshal's angry eyes. "I'm sorry," he said meekly.

"Chilcoat," the squad room intercom speaker announced, "Dial-a-Divorce returning your call, line six."

The squad room roared with laughter. The shaken Brad Chilcoat punched the blinking light on the telephone console and picked up the receiver. While he talked in muted sober tones, Lieutenant Stovich approached the desk. He had his summons in hand. "Got a minute, Marshal?" he said to Bobbi. It was the first words spoken between the two since the meeting in Captain Westly's office.

"Sure," Bobbi answered, pushing out of her chair.

Aaron Stovich was the old guard. He was an experienced professional with twenty-six years in the department. He'd earned his job as the OIC of the Special Investigations Team and he'd earned the respect of the detectives working for him. He wasn't a coach who sent players in from the sidelines. When his men worked, he worked. The relationship he and Bobbi shared had always been warm and filled with loyalty and trust. At least until the meeting with Captain Westly. The lieutenant's silence had both surprised and disappointed Bobbi. The resulting chill still hung in the air between them.

Stovich looked at the summons in his hand and then across the table to Bobbi. "When your partner decides to get a divorce he does it in style, doesn't he?"

"Is that what this is about?" Bobbi questioned soberly. She wasn't going to let him gloss over yesterday's meeting.

"No," Lieutenant Stovich said, sticking the summons into an inside pocket of his jacket. "I wanted to talk about yesterday's meeting with the captain."

"All right," Bobbi said, coolly examining her painted nails.

"I agreed with the captain on the teletype so I could nail him on the Unger case," Stovich said to her.

"You knew he was going to ask me to withdraw the charges?" Bobbi questioned as her eyes went to the lieutenant's.

"Yes, he wanted me to ask you to do it," Stovich explained, "but I told him I didn't think you'd cooperate. He said he'd order it. If I'd come to your defense on the teletype he might have backed down."

"Would that have been so bad?" Bobbi questioned.

Stovich spread his palms on the tabletop. "You and I, and a couple others around here, are detectives because that's what we want to be. It's not something we do part-time or when we feel like it. We do it because we're professionals. Then we have Westly who calls himself a cop just because he passed a Civil Service exam. The man's an embarrassment to the department. He's unethical, dishonest, and a discredit to the LAPD. I've put up with him for nearly two years. He's unfit for command. He's not even fit to man a radio car. It worries me that he has a right to carry a gun. He gave no thought to Judge Unger's guilt or innocence, only what it meant to him. You know why he did it?"

"No."

"Because the DA asked him to."

"Even though it was unlawful?" Bobbi probed.

"He thinks he can get away with using an obscure manual section, and he just might, unless you're willing to help."

"Help with what?" Bobbi questioned cautiously.

"Help stop him," Stovich explained. "Help get rid of him. You're the arresting officer. If you don't complain, then he's likely to walk away from this, clean."

"You want me to go to Internal Affairs?" Bobbi asked.

"Yes," Stovich answered firmly. "Westly's guilty of obstructing justice, but without you there's no case."

"And what do I get for meeting a captain head on?" Bobbi said, shifting in her chair. The pressure the lieutenant was applying made her uncomfortable. "A merit badge?"

"The thanks of the good cops in this division."

Bobbi pushed out of the chair. "And a reputation as a snitch, a cop who runs to IA. It's tough enough being a woman and a detective, lieutenant. Do you know anybody else who's being sued for nine-hundred and seventy-four thousand dollars by their partner's wife? I don't have to go looking for trouble, I've already got all I need.''

''I didn't say it was going to be easy,'' Lieutenant Stovich said.

# 9

# THE LINK

The day didn't improve any when Bobbi and Brad Chilcoat left the station. Usually they could immerse themselves in police work and forget the troubles of the day, but now the problems were an integral part of their job and their relationship. There was no forgetting it, no escaping it. Bobbi silently blamed her partner's marital infidelity for adding fuel to the fire. The rape investigation and the controversy over Judge Unger's arrest were enough to contend with, but now it was all being amplified by an angry wife who was accusing her of the decline and collapse of the Chilcoat marriage. The inflammatory lawsuit was certain to generate additional interest from the press.

Brad Chilcoat was having similar thoughts. Something about the summons had jolted his sleeping conscience. Maybe Cathy's argument had merit. Maybe working with Bobbi Marshal had affected him. He glanced at Bobbi as she drove the detective car east on Venice Boulevard. There was no doubting her beauty. Raven hair, high cheekbones, a flawless complexion. A model's figure wrapped in fashionable clothes. Chilcoat had to admit he knew this woman better than he did his own wife—he spent more time with her. He ate with her, he worked with her, he laughed with her. If asked, under oath, if he loved Bobbi Marshal, he knew the answer couldn't be anything other than yes. But he quickly reminded himself it was not a romantic love. It wasn't a sexual love. He loved this woman because she was his partner. Would anyone who wasn't a cop understand that? Could they? The marriage vow declared a man was "to love, honor, and cherish." The unspoken vow between Bobbi Marshal and Brad Chilcoat declared they were ready to die for each other. How could that be explained to a judge or a jealous wife?

The tide of events that was sweeping over him was powerful and frightening, but to surrender, to accept defeat, was also to accept the destruction of all the things Brad Chilcoat loved—his family, his partnership, and his job. He didn't know how, he wasn't sure he could, but he knew he had to try. Brad took in a deep breath as he straightened in his seat and looked to Bobbi. "I said I was sorry back at the station," he began.

"I heard you," Bobbi said with a glance at him as she drove. She saw the serious look on Chilcoat's face.

"I just want you to know I'm sincere," he added. "You're the best partner I've ever had, and I hope when this is all over we're still friends."

"I needed to hear that," Bobbi said, offering a grateful smile. "And I may not like what you've done, but I like you."

"You think they'll split us up?" Chilcoat questioned.

"The mayor and the chief have their summons by now. What do you think?" Bobbi answered.

"Then let's go out in style," Chilcoat suggested. "Let's find Big Foot."

"You got it," Bobbi agreed.

Mayor Gates telephoned the city attorney shortly after receiving his summons. On the eve of announcing his formal candidacy for the governor's office, he couldn't afford to be drawn into a nuisance lawsuit. The city attorney did little to quiet the mayor's fears. "The case is unique," the city attorney warned. "Wounded wife against the establishment. It's going to generate press."

"Goddamned cops can't keep their peckers in their pants," the mayor complained as he dialed the chief of police.

Twenty minutes after the mayor's call, Chief of Police James Peck had Deputy Chief Rolland Tate, the commander of the Detective Bureau; Commander Warren Hull of Internal Affairs; Commander William Hodges from Public Affairs; and Captain Stewart Thomas, the department legal liaison officer, all sitting in his office on the sixth floor of Parker Center. Peck briefed the four men on the receipt of the summons and the call from the mayor. The chief passed around the summons for the four men to inspect. "This is the second time today the department's been caught with its pants down, gentlemen, and frankly," Peck warned, tapping a pen on his desktop to emphasize the point, "I'm getting a little tired of it."

"Bobbi Marshal!" Commander Hull from Internal Affairs said with alarm when he scanned the summons and found the name. "She's the one who arrested Judge Unger."

"Why in the hell do you think I called you in here?" Peck answered.

"I pulled her personal package after we started getting calls yesterday," Commander Hodges from Public Affairs offered. "She's been on the job eight years. In the Detective Bureau for the past three. Straight upper ten ratings since leaving the academy. It appears on paper that she's a good cop."

"I'll call Captain Westly," the balding Rolland Tate said, "get him to reassign both of them immediately."

"With all due respect, commander," Captain Thomas cautioned as he adjusted his dark horn-rimmed glasses, "I think if you do that it's going to be read as a reaction to the summons and a near admission of error or liability."

"What do you recommend, captain?" Chief Peck pressed.

"I think we have to be careful and not overreact. A finger pointed at the department is nothing new, but if we start a series of denials and reassign these two people, we're apt to get our noses bloodied."

"These aren't the only male-female partners in the Detective Bureau, you know,'' Commander Tate defended. "We've got ten or fifteen of them, and then there's patrol, they've probably got more than I have.''

"Goddamned civilians love a sex scandal,'' Commander Hull warned. "This is an area where we can't let it get out of control.''

"There's no hint of misconduct here, is there?'' Chief Peck probed.

"This summons hints that there is,'' Hodges said, waving it. "And it's now a public document.''

"All right,'' the chief said, raising a hand to quiet the others. "Before this gains any more momentum, Warren,'' he said to Commander Hull of Internal Affairs, "take a look into the relationship between these two detectives. Do it covertly. If they're playing kissy-huggy in the back seat we need to know about it. I don't want to defend them and then be embarrassed by the fact that they're guilty, but if they're not, if this is just some pissed-off wife wanting to twist the knife in her husband's back, I don't want to run scared.''

"I'll get right on it,'' Commander Hull promised.

"How much time do you need?''

"Without interviewing them? Four, five days' surveillance.''

Chief Peck looked to Commander Hodges. "Bill, how long before the press will have this?''

"That depends on Cathy Chilcoat's attorney,'' he answered. "But I can buy us some time there, only . . .'' His voice trailed away.

"Only what?'' Peck demanded.

"The fact that this policewoman is involved in her partner's divorce and the Unger case, too, muddies the issues. They're both related to sex. Add the fact that she's a looker and it spells trouble.''

"What are you saying?''

"Just that I'm worried.''

"I imagine she is, too,'' Chief Peck said grimly.

\* \* \*

The fading sign on the exterior of the weathered brick warehouse in East Los Angeles read GLOVES INCORPORATED. Brad Chilcoat showed his badge to a gray-haired woman behind a service counter. "For you or the wife?" the sagging face questioned with a glance at Bobbi.

"I'm not his wife. I'm his partner," Bobbi corrected.

"Uh huh, you want a pair too?"

"We'd like to see the manager," Chilcoat said.

"Uh huh, he's with a client right now."

"We'll wait."

"Uh huh." The gray head turned toward a windowed office. "Jerry," the woman called loudly. "Cops wanna see you."

They sat in plastic chairs and waited. Chilcoat thumbed through a tattered copy of *Sports Afield*. Bobbi watched the steady stream of customers. "Who do you suppose is buying all these gloves?" she said.

Chilcoat looked up from his magazine. "Figure there's twelve million people in Southern California. That's one hundred and twenty million fingers. Or if you divide five into that you get . . . or easier, two times twelve million people gives you twenty-four million hands. Now if you sell to only one out of a thousand . . . No, let's say one out of every five thousand."

"I get the picture," Bobbi said.

"It adds up." Chilcoat smiled.

"You wanted to see me?" a balding man in a vest said from the service counter. Bobbi noticed he was wearing ivory-colored gloves.

The two detectives moved to the counter. "I'm Detective Sergeant Chilcoat. This is my partner, Detective Marshal."

"Jerry Levitt," the man answered. "Is this about my brother-in-law?"

"It's about gloves."

"Come on in."

"How can I help you?" the gloved man asked as Bobbi crossed her legs and adjusted her skirt.

"Seems you take your glove business very seriously," Brad Chilcoat said with a glance at the man's gloved hands.

"Might say I've got a hand in it." He smiled, rubbing his hands together. "It's just a little sales gimmick. Makes people remember me."

"We're looking for black and white cotton work gloves," Bobbi explained. "Do you carry them?"

Levitt nodded. "Five different brands. One from Mexico. Two from Taiwan. One from China. One from Brazil. Very popular lines. Cheap, durable. All under a dollar if you buy 'em by the gross, and we require a minimum two-gross order."

"You don't sell directly to the public?" Chilcoat asked.

"Retail?" Levitt shook his head. "Too hazardous. Takes personality, effort."

Chilcoat nodded. "I could see where that might be a problem. Do you have a list of customers who buy these black and white gloves?"

"No, but I could go through the files. Make one up. Might take a couple of days."

"How many customers are we talking about?" Bobbi probed.

The man shrugged. "Four hundred, four hundred and fifty maybe."

Bobbi and Chilcoat exchanged a look. It wasn't an encouraging revelation.

"Any other major glove dealers in L.A.?" Chilcoat questioned.

"We're the biggest. Costella Brothers on Vernon are probably second. Then there's Belman's, and a couple others. We all sell the same stuff. Only so many manufacturers, you know. What are you looking for?"

"A rapist who wears gloves," Chilcoat answered.

"It makes people remember him," Bobbi added sarcastically as she held the man's look.

* * *

The West Coast corporate offices for Florsheim Shoes was on the eleventh floor of the Lincoln Towers on South Flower. Bobbi and Chilcoat met with the director of sales.

"Jesus, I hope you're not going to release this to the public?" the shaken executive questioned after listening to the story of the nineteen rapes and how the man had come to be known as "Big Foot."

"You mean the fact that he's wearing Florsheim shoes?" Chilcoat asked.

"Yes, we're already up to our knee-highs in Oriental sneakers. If you announce that a man like this is wearing our low-cut leather, our product image will be down there competing with New Coke."

"Don't worry," Bobbi assured. "We won't go public. If we did, the man would simply change his shoes."

"Is there any way of tracking down someone who may have bought a pair of size thirteen shoes from one of your stores?" Chilcoat questioned.

The executive considered the question carefully. "Only if they were paid for by credit card or check, and it would require checking with seventy-six stores in Southern California. And how far back do you want to go? Our shoes usually last from three to five years. It would be a major task."

"Can it be done?" Chilcoat pressed.

"Not without great expense and effort. It would be much like looking for a needle in the haystack."

"Well, thanks for seeing us," Chilcoat said to the man as he pushed out of his chair. Bobbi followed his lead.

"I hope you find this man," the executive said.

"We do, too," Bobbi answered.

The reinterviews of the rape victims took three days. They were haunting representations of the composite victim the two detectives had compiled. Nearly all of them had moved, a typical post-rape reaction, and it required time-consuming effort to track them down. The majority of the women were now hostile witnesses, reluctant to talk to the police. Bobbi knew that what they were asking of them was picking at the wounds. It was a painful process, but there were no other options.

The victims, one by one, told their stories. It became a predictable tale of perverted torment. They had all been surprised in their homes; they were bound, gagged; a pillowcase was pulled over their heads. They were raped repeatedly by the man, and then with Coke bottles, hairbrushes, a shoe, and a flashlight. None of the victims had seen Big Foot's face.

Bobbi searched for details that weren't in the crime reports. She wanted to know who had been in their homes. Friends, plumbers, TV repairmen, telephone installers, painters?

They thought they had a break when they found that victims six and nine, who lived within three miles of each other, used the same cable TV company, but a follow-up visit to the installation office revealed the service man was a short, fifty-two-year-old black man who wore a size seven shoe.

The sixteenth and seventeenth rape victims' addresses proved disappointing. Both had moved. One, a twenty-six-year-old elementary school teacher, had sold her condominium and moved back to Detroit. The other, a thirty-one-year-old dental hygienist, had simply vanished. Her three-bedroom house on South Nicolet stood vacant and ransacked. It too had been raped, Bobbi thought as they drove away.

The eighteenth victim, Dianna Janson, was a loan officer at a branch of the Security National Bank on Washington Boulevard. She was shaken by the arrival of the two detectives. She quickly escorted them into a private office. "I've never told anyone," she said in a voice edged with emotion. "I don't have to, do I?"

"That's your choice," Bobbi assured the worried girl, "but we would like you to answer a few more questions."

"I was three months from my wedding," the girl said as tears welled in her frightened eyes. "I told Phil I couldn't go to bed with him because I was a virgin. I wanted to wait until our wedding night. I don't know what to tell him now.''

Bobbi glanced at her partner, and he understood. Chilcoat stepped silently from the room. Bobbi looked at the worried twenty-five-year-old. ''Dianna, you need to tell your boyfriend. If he loves you, you'll get through this. If he doesn't, you need to know that, too. Before the wedding.''

Dianna bowed her head into her hands as the tears spilled.

Bobbi spent another twenty minutes with the girl, letting her regain her composure, offering encouragement, and asking careful questions. The only new bit of information she got was the girl remembering that the realtor who sold her the condo a month before she was raped had flirted with her. Dianna remembered the man as slender and in his forties. Bobbi dismissed it as irrelevant, but the mention of the realtor excited Bobbi. She waited until she was back in the detective car before she said anything to her partner. ''Brad, each of Big Foot's victims owned their own place. None of them were renting.''

''We already tried realtors,'' Chilcoat cautioned. ''They have keys and lock boxes, but not to houses all over the city.''

Bobbi wasn't discouraged. ''Listen to me,'' she urged. ''I just bought my place a couple of months ago. In addition to the realtor, there's an appraiser. He comes in and inspects. He's got to use a key, and his reports go to the escrow companies.''

''How do we check it?'' Chilcoat said. She had his interest.

They drove to the office of Westside Escrow Company on South Fairfax, where months earlier Dianna Janson's escrow had been handled. The office manager was less than pleased with police interest in his files, and when he balked at letting them examine the files, Bobbi looked to Chilcoat and said, ''I'll wait here. You go back to the station and go to work on the search warrant.''

They used the office manager's office after he experienced a sudden change of heart. The search didn't take long. Bobbi found the appraiser's worksheet. He had inspected Dianna Janson's condominium seven weeks before escrow closed. Five weeks after moving in, she was raped. The appraiser, from a company called Image Market Appraisals, had signed his name at the bottom of the worksheet . . . Dick Fredericks.

After talking to one of the other rape victims a second time, they visited the escrow company that had handled her purchase. To Bobbi's delight the agent was a woman and cooperative. Bobbi had to struggle to hold her excitement after they found the appraiser's report. It was signed by the same man, Dick Fredericks.

"Two times could be nothing but a coincidence," Chilcoat warned after Bobbi made a telephone call to the fifth rape victim. "We need three to ice it."

The Golden Coast Escrow office on Beverly Boulevard at the northern end of the division was plush and manned by a small army of agents. "Looks like Beverly Hills detectives," Chilcoat whispered to Bobbi as they crossed the busy office to the manager's desk.

Five minutes later, the file was delivered to them in a quiet conference room. The blond delivering the folder exchanged a smile with Chilcoat and stepped out. "Let me know if you need anything else," she purred.

Bobbi was quickly into the file. She felt a surge of excitement when she found the appraiser's worksheet. The letterhead was Image Market Appraisals. Her eyes went to the bottom of the sheet. It was signed "Dick Fredericks."

"It's him," Bobbi said. Her hand was trembling.

# 10

# A FAWN FAREWELL

The two detectives reached the office of Image Market Appraisals in the fifty-three-hundred block of West Pico Boulevard at five-twenty p.m. A CLOSED sign hung in the window. They were wary of the unmarked car being seen near the office, so they parked at a supermarket a quarter of a block away. Brad Chilcoat walked to check out the office and parking lot.

"No one in the office and no cars in the parking lot," Chilcoat said when he returned. "But there's a space in the parking lot with the name 'D. Fredericks' on it."

The name was proving to be more of a frustration than a lead. Records and Identification had criminal records on thirty-two men by the name of Dick or Richard Fredericks and another fourteen that used it as an AKA.

The license number from the man's car would provide them with an address, enabling them to get a valid date of birth from the Department of Motor Vehicle files. That would separate him from all of the other Frederickses for a positive identification, but first they needed the license number.

"I'll come by here in the morning in my jeep," Chilcoat said. "Let's not spook him with this so-called unmarked car." Bobbi agreed.

The risk seemed minimal. Big Foot's average had been a rape every eight days. Only five days had passed since Lisa Cartwright's attack. Time was on their side.

Detective Bobbi Marshal slept little during the long

night. She was too excited. Big Foot now had a name. It was only a matter of time until they would have him, until they would question him. Rapists usually confessed. It was more often disguised bragging than a sincere confession of guilt. Rapists, Bobbi had learned, seldom felt guilt. Their acts of violence were blamed on their victims, their sometimes dominating mothers, absent fathers, or society. Anyone but themselves.

At one point during the night Bobbi, restless, got out of bed and walked to her bedroom window. Below her the city lay wrapped in darkness, sleeping, but out there, she knew, nineteen women were not sleeping, or if they were it was with the fear that the nightmares or the man himself might return. Bobbi knew they had to capture him quickly. She was eager for the moment, but for some deep primal reason she couldn't quite grasp, she feared it, too.

Seventeen-year-old Fawn Tyler was also having a long night. The girl next to her in the crowded van kept crying in her sleep. There were seven of them in the rusty Chevy van. The long-haired driver's name was Tim, and although the license plate on the van was from Utah, the teenage Tim claimed to be from New Jersey. Fawn suspected the van might be stolen, but the protocol of the street didn't allow such questions. At least it was warmer than the street.

Turning over, Fawn pulled the flap of an army field jacket up over a cold shoulder. Light from an overhead streetlamp glistened through the cloud of condensation fogging the dirty rear window. The moist air in the van smelled of potato chips and sweat. They were parked in the parking lot of an all-night market on Santa Monica Boulevard. Of the six other sleeping forms that lay in a jumble on the floor of the van, Fawn knew only Tim, the driver, and one of the girls, Mandy, an eleven-year-old runaway from Texas, yet the others weren't strangers. They shared a common bond that gave them a sense of family. Ironically, most had no family. Few families were losing sleep worrying over the whereabouts of the seven sleeping souls in the muddy van. Their average age was fifteen. Only two had been reported missing, and that had been four months earlier. In Hollywood they were known as "The Children of the Night." No one was certain of their true number, but the police knew it was in the thousands.

Fawn Tyler had been among their ranks for three years. She was old beyond her tender seventeen years, and she was tired and frightened. The infection that had hospitalized her early last year was back. She'd been to the free clinic, but the medicine wasn't helping much and it was getting worse.

Prostitution had its price. The infection combined with the scar-faced man hunting her meant her days on the street in Los Angeles were over. With the money from three tricks tucked in her panties, she planned to return to the Galaxy Motel in the morning. After being chased in Hollywood, it wasn't likely Scar Face would be looking for her back at the Galaxy. She'd pick up her dresses and shoes and be on a bus by noon. The bus would be warm and comfortable as it rolled into California's high desert toward Las Vegas. She'd never be cold again, Fawn hoped. Vegas would be warm and fun. Maybe a Marine would sit beside her on the bus. He'd be a young man with friendly brown eyes from Kansas City or St. Louis where all Marines were from, and he'd talk about going home on leave. Maybe he'd buy her a Coke when they stopped in Barstow . . . and then she was asleep.

The gun always felt heavy in her hand but Bobbi had learned to use that to her advantage. The weight could be used against the concussion of the recoil to hold a better sight picture when firing. Her index finger was on the trigger. There were five blunt-nose bullets waiting in the chamber of the blue steel Smith & Wesson held at her side. The man was a mere seven yards away. He was armed, and he stood at a right angle to the tense and ready Bobbi Marshal. When he turned, and she knew he would,

Bobbi would raise her gun and fire. She would aim at his upper chest and neck. Head shots were television bullshit. A buzzer sounded. The man swung toward her. Bobbi raised her gun and fired. In three swift seconds a succession of quick sharp blasts emptied her gun as it bucked in her hand. Lowering the pistol, Bobbi pushed the cylinder release with her thumb and quickly dumped the empty smoking cartridges to the pavement. Her left hand gathered five more blunt-nose cartridges from her jacket pocket, and she pushed them into the hot, blackened cylinder. She snapped it closed, raised the gun, and fired again.

Above the roar of the collective pistol fire the electronic buzzer sounded a second time and the dark, bullet-riddled silhouette targets swung away. The amplified voice of the range safety officer commanded in the sudden ringing silence, "Cease fire, clear, reload, and holster all weapons before policing brass."

Brad Chilcoat was waiting outside the wall of the combat range with a small army of uniformed and plainclothes cops. The LAPD required every officer on the job under the rank of captain to requalify monthly. It was a duty most did not argue with.

"How did you do?" Chilcoat questioned as Bobbi reached him.

"He never had a chance," Bobbi said, patting her purse and the now gritty pistol hidden in it.

"You'll do fine as long as it's not a quick draw," Chilcoat teased.

"Did you go by Image Appraisals?" Bobbi asked as they walked to the detective car she'd driven to the Police Academy.

"Yeah. Fredericks drives a brand-new Thunderbird. It's registered to him at an address in Burbank. Let's stop by R and I downtown on the way to the station."

"Yeah, I've got some business to take care of there, too," Bobbi said soberly as she cranked the Plymouth to life.

The innocuous sign on the gray door read INTERNAL AFFAIRS. Bobbi took a breath to calm herself and opened the door. The girl at the reception desk was young and busty. A nameplate on her desk proclaimed it was the domain of Sergeant Janet Houston. The girl's achievement intimidated Bobbi. She was already sorry she'd come. Damn Stovich.

"May I help you?" Janet Houston said with a look up at Bobbi. The woman deliberately turned the report she'd been reading facedown. Her look was one of evaluation, but it was void of any hint of conclusion.

Bobbi had carefully made sure her choice of dress for the day was properly demure. She wore a light gray skirt and a matching jacket over a high-necked blouse with a lace tie for an added touch of femininity. "Yes, I'd like to talk to Commander Hull about a complaint against a member of the department."

"Wife or girlfriend?" the female sergeant questioned without expression.

"I don't understand," Bobbi answered.

"Are you a wife or a girlfriend of the officer?" the sergeant repeated, with a hint of haughtiness in her voice.

Bobbi, already irritated with being pushed into coming, although she had been considering it herself before the meeting with Stovich, decided she didn't like the woman's attitude.

"Neither. I'm Bobbi Marshal. I'm a detective from Wilshire Division, and I'd like to talk to the commander."

Sergeant Janet Houston seemed surprised—very surprised —and it made Bobbi suspicious. It was as if they'd been talking about her and suddenly she'd walked in and caught them. It was a look of guilt Bobbi had learned to recognize. The sergeant stood up to cover her awkwardness. "Please sit down, Detective Marshal. I'll tell the commander you're here."

The arrest of Judge Warrick Unger was big news in Los Angeles, so it seemed logical to Bobbi that Internal Affairs would be aware of her name. It also seemed likely, given

Captain Westly's conduct, that, as the arresting officer, she
might show up in their office. There was no other explanation for the sergeant's reaction in Bobbi's mind.

In the busy Records and Identification Division on the
fourth floor of Parker Center, Detective Brad Chilcoat sat
at one of the review tables. The wide room was a sea of
thousands and thousands of catalogued criminal records.
A small army of clerks, primarily young women, manned
the array of computers and telephones, responding to the
steady stream of calls pouring in from officers on patrol
as well as from the detectives in the city's eighteen police
divisions.

Chilcoat's search was fruitful but also disappointing.
Richard Fredericks, DOB eleven-eighteen-fifty-one, indeed had a record with the LAPD. It consisted of three
violations of the motor vehicle code over a period of five
years—two speeding violations and one unsafe lane
change. Chilcoat growled as he angrily pushed the single
three-by-five card aside.

"Bobbi Marshal's here!" the surprised Commander Hull
repeated as police Sergeant Janet Houston stood in front
of his desk.

"Yes, sir," the sergeant answered.

"She say what she wants?"

"No, sir."

"Damn," the commander said. "I wonder if she made
the surveillance?"

"I don't know, sir."

"All right," Commander Hull said, pushing back in his
high-backed chair. "Clear the outer office and then bring
her in. We don't want to give her faces to recognize later."

"Yes, sir."

"Oh, and alert Higgins. I want my conversation with
this woman recorded."

"Yes, sir."

* * *

It was a bright, sun-filled morning, and the skies over Los Angeles were a cloudless blue. Fawn Tyler stepped off of southbound RTD bus number forty-two on La Brea Avenue half a block from the Galaxy Motel. The sun was warm on her hair and shoulders. It felt good. She was glad she'd be leaving Los Angeles on a pretty day. That was the way she wanted to remember it.

A horn sounded from a passing car. It boosted Fawn's confidence. The fear that had driven her away from the motel was gone now, washed away by the bright sunshine and hope. She'd seen a bumper sticker on a car while riding the bus: "This is the first day of the rest of your life." Fawn decided that was her new motto. She smiled as she strutted toward the motel office. She didn't notice the dark sedan parked near the telephone booth at the Arco Station across the street from the motel. The man sitting behind the wheel had a short, squat neck and a pock-marked face. He dug at an ear with a toothpick as he watched the girl disappear into the motel office. He smiled. His hunch had paid off. Seventeen-year-olds weren't very smart. Especially seventeen-year-old whores. She just couldn't leave her things behind. She had to come back for them. He knew she would. He opened the car door and climbed out.

"Hey, Leroy," Fawn called to the gaunt black clerk behind the counter as she waltzed into the office. "Any messages?"

"Yeah," Leroy answered with a glance. "The police is looking for your white ass."

"The police?" Fawn questioned as she leaned on the counter.

"Uh huh, a foxy detective by the name of Marshal from up at Wilshire on Venice."

"Oh, her," Fawn said. "She's just a friend."

"Yeah, right," the clerk mocked. "And me and Don Johnson are asshole buddies, too. This detective, she says to me, I'm to call when I see you again, and I don't want no trouble with her. So this is your notice."   —

"Okay," Fawn said. "Just give me twenty minutes and I'll be gone. It's checkout time. I don't suppose you could give me tomorrow's rent back?"

"Hey, you know I would if I could, baby, but it's against policy."

"Pay in advance and no refunds," Fawn complained.

"Capitalism! It's a bitch, ain't it?" The clerk smiled, baring horse teeth and red gums. "Where are you going?"

"Away." Fawn smiled.

"Yeah. Dude with scars and the police looking for you. I didn't think you'd even come back for your shit."

"You didn't let them in my room?" Fawn said in an accusing tone.

"Hey, do I look like I run that kind of place?"

"Have they been back since I left? The ugly dude or the cops?"

"I ain't seen nobody. But like I said, I don't want trouble with the police. I'm gonna call her."

"You don't have to call right away. It ain't like I'm dangerous or some shit."

"Couple hours at the most. That's the best I can do."

Fawn pushed from the counter. "When you talk to Bobbi Marshal, tell her I'll give her a call in a day or two."

"Hey, I ain't your pimp, honey."

"Yeah, I know." Fawn smiled as she headed for the stairs. "But I told her you were."

"Bitch," the clerk yelled after her as Fawn bounded up the stairs.

The second-story hallway was dim and it reeked of a mix of cheap perfume and barbecue sauce. The sounds of a "Happy Days" rerun drifted from behind a thin door. Fawn moved down the hallway, digging in her purse for the key. Two suitcases to pack and carry. She wondered what a cab to the bus terminal would cost. Maybe she could hitch a ride. She found the key with its diamond-shaped plastic tail and pushed it into the lock.

The motel room's blackout curtains were closed and the

room was dark. Fawn reached and flipped the wall switch. "Shit," she muttered when the light failed to come on. It was nothing new. Leroy seldom kept more than one good bulb per room. She stepped in and closed the door. The man was waiting in the darkness behind the door. Fawn tensed and opened her mouth to scream the moment he touched her, but it was too late. He was quick and powerful. Taking her chin in his left palm and gripping the back of her head with his right, he pushed down and jerked hard to the right as if opening a safety cap on a prescription bottle. A bone cracked and he felt the girl slump. Her neck was broken.

Commander Hull listened intently as Detective Bobbi Marshal laid out her case against Captain George Westly. She was careful to make it unemotional and matter-of-fact in tone. The fact that she was a woman was not relevant to any of the issues involved. Captain Westly, in her opinion, was clearly obstructing justice.

"Have you discussed this with your lieutenant?" Commander Hull questioned when she finished.

"Yes," Bobbi answered.

"And your partner?" the commander continued.

"Only in general terms," Bobbi said candidly. "He's not really involved."

"What is it you want out of this, detective?" Commander Hull pressed.

"Justice," Bobbi answered soberly.

Chilcoat telephoned Lieutenant Stovich from Parker Center. It was time to brief the lieutenant on the development with Big Foot. "Lieutenant, it's Chilcoat. I've got some good news and some bad news."

"Give me the good news," Stovich said flatly.

"We've got Big Foot identified," Chilcoat answered.

"And the bad news?" Stovich questioned.

"I don't think we can do anything about it."

"Who knows about this?" Stovich asked.

"So far you, me, and Bobbi."

"Keep it that way. Word gets out we've got him made, he's going to rabbit."

"We're gonna need some manpower," Chilcoat warned.

"I'll call in the Sex teams from the neighboring divisions. How soon can you get back here?"

"Twenty minutes."

"I'll be waiting. We've got some work to do."

It took nearly an hour to get them all assembled. They met in the Wilshire Division roll call room. Bobbi and Chilcoat had stopped by the Scientific Investigation Division on Parker Center's third floor to inform criminalist Wade Morris of the meeting. He arrived at Wilshire Station before they did. Lieutenant Stovich had called the Sex teams from West Los Angeles, Hollywood, and Rampart. All were carrying unsolved rape cases attributed to Big Foot. There were eight detectives, four men and four women, including Bobbi and Chilcoat. They swapped stories, complained about excessive overtime, and asked Brad Chilcoat questions about his wife's multimillion dollar lawsuit against the city and the department. The rumor mill had quickly carried word of it across the city. "I heard she's got F. Lee Bailey as an attorney. Is it true the city attorney wants to give you a mental evaluation? I heard two more cop wives are filing a class action suit. They say yesterday the city offered her a million to settle out of court."

Finally Lieutenant Stovich arrived. "Have a seat, please," he said, striding into the room.

The Sex teams moved into the rows of seats behind the long roll call desks and sat down.

Lieutenant Stovich leaned on a desk at the head of the room. It was on a step platform. He took his chewed cigar from the corner of his mouth. "I've just talked to all your captains," he began, "and until further notice you're on loan to Wilshire Detectives."

"Does that mean Chilcoat's ol' lady is gonna sue us,

too?'' a dark-haired detective from Rampart Division questioned. A splattering of laughter rippled over the group.

"I hope not." Lieutenant Stovich smiled, folding his arms. "But you'll have to talk to Chilcoat and Dial-a-Divorce about that."

They laughed again.

"Seriously," the lieutenant continued. "What I'm about to tell you has to stay in this room. You can discuss it, but until further notice, only with the people who are here right now."

Looks were exchanged among the group.

"If we don't keep the lid on this we run the risk of blowing a major case and losing the chance to prosecute a very deserving rapist," Stovich warned.

"Big Foot," a blond policewoman from Hollywood Detectives said.

"Right," Stovich agreed. "Big Foot. We feel confident we've got him identified." He looked to Brad Chilcoat.

Chilcoat took the cue and stood up, notebook in hand. Pens and pencils were pulled from pockets and purses as the detectives prepared to take notes. Chilcoat looked to his own notes as he spoke. "The suspect's name is Fredericks, Richard Paul. He's a male Caucasian, DOB, eleven-eighteen-fifty-one. For you math majors, that's age thirty-six. He has brown hair, brown eyes. He is six-foot-two-inches tall and he weighs two hundred and ten pounds."

He paused for a moment until the pens stopped and then he continued. "He's married. His wife's name is Clair. They have a residence address of fourteen-oh-six Lakespur Drive, Burbank. Fredericks drives a blue eighty-eight Ford Thunderbird, California license, two-Charles-William-Robert, one-three-seven. He has a business address of fifty-three-oh-seven West Pico Boulevard. That's the office of Image Market Appraisals. Fredericks has no criminal record in L.A. We're checking CII and NCIC. My partner will tell you what we know about Dickie Fredericks." Chilcoat looked to Bobbi and sat down.

Bobbi pushed to her feet and looked to the faces of the waiting detectives. "Since Big Foot has never made a forced entry—"

"Say through a door," Chilcoat said in a stage whisper.

The waiting detectives laughed. Bobbi flashed Chilcoat a hostile look. "Maybe when I'm done here, I could call your wife," she said to Chilcoat.

"I'll be quiet," Chilcoat promised humbly.

"In each of Big Foot's cases," Bobbi resumed, "it appeared he entered through the front door. We've never found any evidence of forced entry. To my partner and me, and I'm sure to most of you, that meant the suspect was someone who used a key. Accepting that theory, we looked for someone who would have a legitimate reason to have keys to nineteen different homes spread over thirty square miles of the city, leading us to discover that each of the nineteen victims had recently purchased a home or a condominium. Realtors, obviously, had to be among the suspects. Yet realtors, using a key to lock boxes, are for the most part limited to much smaller territories, and we could find no link between one realtor and the nineteen victims. But there is another required service in the purchase of property that requires the use of a key," Bobbi explained. "And that's an appraisal. The lender hires a firm to appraise every property being purchased. In each of the five rapes in Wilshire Division, we found the victim's property had been appraised by Dick Fredericks from Image Market Appraisals."

An eager murmur went through the group of detectives.

Chilcoat pushed to his feet beside Bobbi. "I picked another three of Big Foot's cases at random this morning. One from North Hollywood, one from Rampart, and one from West L.A. I called the escrow companies the rape victims used. The records showed it was good ol' Dickie Fredericks from Image Market Appraisals."

"Why isn't the sonofabitch in jail?" a detective from West L.A. questioned.

"I think that falls into my category," the balding Wade

Morris said as he stood and adjusted his wire-rimmed bifocals. Bobbi and Chilcoat sat down. "As you know, we've got vaginal slides from eleven of the nineteen rapes we think Big Foot is responsible for." He began to pace back and forth at the head of the room like a teacher. "We've also collected blood and semen from eight of the crime scenes. Sheets, towels, pillowcases, and so on. We've matched these specimens in the lab. I can tell you they're all from the same individual."

Morris stopped pacing for a moment to study his audience. "I can also tell you we've recovered pubic hair from nine of the crime scenes. We've established that the specimens are all from the same individual and that he is male, fairly young, and Caucasian." He resumed his walk. "We have also confirmed that the suspect wears a size thirteen shoe. To be more precise, he wears a smooth-soled leather Florsheim shoe with a one-inch heel. I have pictures of the print from the crime scenes and a good cast from one of them."

Morris was quiet for a moment as he paced, inventorying his thoughts. "Fibers that we've collected from several crime scenes would also indicate the suspect uses cotton work gloves. Black and white in color, a brand available at most hardware stores. What I can't tell you is that all of our evidence came from suspect Fredericks. If I had a sample of his blood or his pubic hair, or his gloves, I could, using circumstantial evidence, put him at each of the crime scenes. The word is if. We're not there yet."

"Thanks, Wade," Lieutenant Stovich said as Morris moved to sit down. "What we've got," he went on, addressing the group, "is a preponderance of circumstantial evidence. Fredericks had access to the victims, and other circumstantial evidence can put him there, but is it enough probable cause to arrest, search, and try him? I don't want to *think* it is. I want to *know* it is, and, like Wade, I don't think we're there yet."

"So what's next?" a voice questioned from the group of detectives.

"It's been six days since Big Foot's last rape. He's hit every seven to ten days," Stovich explained. "We're gonna live with him until he gives us enough to arrest him."

"Surveillance?" one of the women in the group guessed aloud.

Stovich nodded agreement. "Around the clock. There's four teams. We'll go with three-hour shifts. That means three on, nine off. The Robbery team here at Wilshire will back up the team on the point when the suspect is mobile. We can't afford to crowd him or lose him. It could be fatal to someone's health. We'll start at ten o'clock this morning. Any questions?"

"You care how we bring him in?" a Hollywood detective questioned.

"The shooting policy requires you be in fear of your life, or the life and well-being of a citizen," the lieutenant answered soberly.

"Lock and load," another chuckled.

"Okay, here's the lineup," Stovich said, picking up a list. "Byrd and Castle, you're Team One. You're up first. Webster and Lasski, Team Two. You're on at—" Stovich fell silent as the door to the roll call room opened.

Zaddie, a big, broad-shouldered detective from the Homicide squad, stepped in. "Pardon me, lieutenant, but Shea and Weldon are out at the homicide on La Brea."

"Yeah," Stovich said with a glance at the man. "Tell 'em I'll be out as soon as I finish up here."

"It's not you they want, lieutenant," Zaddie explained. "They found an LAPD business card on the body." He looked to Bobbi. "It's your card, Marshal."

## 11

# MEMORIES AND GUILT

Bobbi Marshal knew Fawn Tyler was dead the moment the Homicide detective told them the body was at the Galaxy Motel on La Brea. She'd followed Brad Chilcoat silently down the stairs from the second-story roll call room at Wilshire Station and out into the parking lot. Now Chilcoat was speeding west on Venice Boulevard. Bobbi felt ill. The frightened seventeen-year-old who came to her seeking help was dead. She remembered her impulse to arrest Fawn and put her in protective custody. What was the language of the Welfare and Institutions Code? "A juvenile may be detained when it has been determined that the minor is a threat to the safety and welfare of the community and/or the safety and welfare of the minor."

Fawn Tyler had clearly been a threat to her own safety. Because it had been late and Bobbi tired, she'd let it slide. She took a chance, and now Fawn Tyler was dead. Tears welled in Bobbi's eyes as she damned herself.

Brad Chilcoat glanced at his partner as he swung the car south on La Brea. He saw the storm of emotion welling in Bobbi. "Maybe it's the clerk," he said. "You gave him a card, too."

Bobbi wanted to grab the hope her partner offered but intuition warned her it was false. It would only add to the pain. She didn't bother to answer.

The Galaxy Motel was now a short half block ahead on the right. Two patrol cars and two detective cars sat in the small parking lot. Bobbi's eyes were locked on the motel's office searching for the clerk, hoping grimly that it was he who was dead. Then she saw the lanky, gaunt clerk through the window, standing behind his counter.

Bobbi quickly led Chilcoat up the stairs to the second floor. She was in an insane rush, she knew—hurrying to a dead body made no sense. The body would be there, but something in her, some duty, some unfulfilled promise, made her rush. "Will you help me?" She heard Fawn Tyler's plea echoing in her ears. There were two uniformed officers and a patrol sergeant in the hallway near the open doorway of the room. An officer with a clipboard stepped to block Bobbi's path. "I'm sorry, lady. You can't go in there."

"It's okay, Brant," the patrol sergeant assured. "She's a detective."

"Sorry, ma'am, but I'm still going to need your name and serial number."

Dan Shea stepped into the doorway from inside the room. He was devoid of any emotion. His tie was loose at the collar. He looked relaxed but very much in command. A camera flash inside the room sent fleeting stark shadows into the dim hallway. It made Bobbi squint. Shea looked at her. "Female, dishwater blond," he said. "Sixteen to eighteen years. She doesn't have any ID. We found your card in her purse. You know her?"

"I haven't seen her yet," Bobbi answered, drawing on all of her reserves in an attempt to mirror Shea's coolness.

"Bobbi," Brad Chilcoat said quietly at her shoulder. He stood just behind her. "Why don't you let me ID her?"

Bobbi was still holding Dan Shea's sober gaze. "What do you want?" she said. "A note from my mother?"

Shea nodded. "Okay," and stepped inside the room. Bobbi followed.

An SID photographer and Cliff Weldon, Shea's graying partner, paused from shooting thirty-five-millimeter close-ups of the body when Bobbi and Shea stepped to the bottom of the bed. Bobbi stood rigid at Dan Shea's shoulder, staring at the form on the bed. She bit her bottom lip as her breath rushed through her nostrils.

The body lay spread-eagle on the bed, dressed in tight jeans and high heels. Bobbi remembered the dirty spike heels. The eyes and mouth of the corpse were open as if in a final silent scream of protest.

The warm, slaty taste in Bobbi's mouth was reaching a point where she knew her stomach would soon convulse. She struggled for control.

"Do you know the girl?" Shea questioned.

Bobbi turned and walked out of the room on shaky legs, fighting the impulse to run. The uniformed officers standing at the door moved aside. Dan Shea followed close behind.

In the hallway Bobbi sucked in a deep breath of the relatively fresh air. "Let's talk in here," Dan Shea said, taking her by the shoulder and guiding her into a room across the hall. With a glance at Brad Chilcoat he added, "Chilcoat, give my partner a hand in there, would you?"

"Sure."

Bobbi crossed the dim motel room, pushed the curtains aside, and unlocked the dirty window to slide it open. The sunlight and fresh air helped push back the waves of nausea. Bobbi stared out over busy La Brea Avenue, trying to empty her mind of the images.

Dan Shea closed the door to the room and sat down in a cushioned chair. It creaked as he settled his frame into it. "You know the girl?" he asked as he lit a cigarette.

"Yes," Bobbi answered without turning to him. "Her name's Fawn Tyler." Bobbi turned to look at him. She was more in control now. "I only saw her once. At the station. She came in the night Lisa Cartwright was raped. She and a girlfriend got involved with a kinky trick. Fawn thought he killed her girlfriend."

"Maybe he did," Shea said, drawing on a cigarette.

"Brad and I were out here the other morning," Bobbi continued. "Fawn was gone. The clerk said Del, the scar-faced man, was here ahead of us."

"Was that the clerk that looks like a number-two pencil?" Shea questioned.

"Yes."

Shea knocked an ash from his cigarette into an ashtray on the chipped and battered dresser. "Welcome to the wonderful world of Homicide, Marshal."

Warren Hull, the graying, sober-faced commander of Internal Affairs, was on his way to the chief's office with briefcase in hand. The internal investigation into the five-ten release of the charges against Judge Warrick Unger was complete. Commander Hull had conducted the interviews himself. He had been both shocked and pleased when Detective Bobbi Marshal came in seeking a complaint against her commanding officer, Captain George Westly. Internal investigations, the commander knew from experience, no matter how messy, always looked better when they were initiated by good cops on the inside instead of by some head-hunting expedition led by a deputy from the mayor's office, like the one already in progress. Hull would soon jerk the political rug out from under their feet by announcing to the press the results of his own investigation. Only one thing remained, the approval of the chief of police. "Is the chief in?" the commander said to the brunette receptionist as he strode into the reception office.

"Yes, sir. He's with Deputy Chief Tate." The girl picked up the telephone as the commander marched toward the door to the chief's office. "Let me—"

"Don't bother," Hull said as he rapped on the door and then opened it.

Chief of Police James Peck was behind his desk, jacket off, relaxed in his high-backed executive chair. Deputy Chief Tate, the commander of the Detective Bureau, was sitting in one of two chairs facing the chief's desk. "Glad you're here, Rolland," Commander Hull said to the deputy chief as he crossed to Peck's desk and set his briefcase on it. "Sorry to interrupt, Jim." He glanced at the chief.

"But I knew you'd want this as soon as possible. We've finished with the Unger investigation."

The chief straightened in his chair and moved to rest his elbow on his desktop. "You're right."

"God," Deputy Chief Rolland Tate said with a look at the ceiling, "please don't let it be Hollywood Division again."

"It's not," Commander Hull said, stabbing a report at the deputy chief. It was stamped "Confidential" in red. He offered another to the chief. "I'll give you both the bottom line and my recommendation. I'd like to act on this today. Cut the cancer as quick as possible."

"I'm listening," Chief Peck said.

"The responsibility rests clearly with Captain Westly," Commander Hull began. "He's guilty of conduct unbecoming an officer, lying to a superior in the course of an investigation, obstructing justice, interfering with an officer in the course of his duty, and a half dozen other minor charges. He claims his only interest in the Unger case was possible embarrassment to the department because of obvious entrapment. He used an obscure, inappropriate section of the manual as well as intimidation on the OIC of Hollywood Vice to effect the five-ten release. His adjutant, Sergeant Shanks, claims the captain received a telephone call from the district attorney the same morning the charges were dismissed. But Westly won't admit that. I think the hope it would benefit him politically by finding him favor with the DA and the governor was Westly's primary motive."

"Is the case against Unger solid?" the chief questioned.

"The policewoman was wired. It's all on tape."

"Anybody else tainted by this?" Deputy Chief Tate asked.

"No," Hull answered him. "I personally interviewed everyone involved."

"What's your recommendation?" Chief Peck pressed. He'd heard enough.

"I'd like to call Westly in and ask for his resignation."

"Why not fire the sonofabitch and file criminal charges against him?" Deputy Chief Tate suggested.

"Because I don't think the district attorney will do it, and a trial is only going to keep the controversy alive. I think we need to put this behind us as soon as possible. Don't forget," the commander warned, "Bobbi Marshal is involved in the Chilcoat lawsuit as well. The public, or a jury, might buy that's she's innocent once, but twice?"

"I agree," Peck said, rocking back in his chair. "Get Westly's resignation."

"My pleasure," Commander Hull said, pushing out of his chair. He snapped his briefcase shut.

"Speaking of the Chilcoat lawsuit," Chief Peck said, picking up a pen to play with, "has your surveillance showed anything yet?"

"No." Hull chuckled. "They were surprised when they followed her to my office." He picked up his briefcase. "But keep in mind the summons will have put them on guard too. Time will tell."

"You talked to her, Warren," Peck said. "What was your impression?"

The commander considered the question carefully before he answered. "She's a very attractive woman. I'm sure if you spent eight to twelve hours a day with her it could lead to trouble . . . if she let it. I just don't know."

"Keep me informed," Peck urged.

Hull nodded and moved for the door.


Brad Chilcoat stayed with Cliff Weldon in Fawn's room to help with the investigation at the scene of the murder while Bobbi and Dan Shea remained in the empty room across the hall. While Dan Shea smoked, Bobbi paced and briefed him on her relationship with Fawn Tyler. It was as if she were purging her memory of Fawn to escape the guilt she felt. Shea listened intently to the story.

"Did you believe her?" Shea asked when Bobbi finished.

"Yes," Bobbi answered. "The morning I came out to the motel to see her, the desk clerk mentioned Debbi."

Shea nodded. Bobbi walked to the window and looked outside. She didn't want to remember what she'd seen in the other room.

"I thought you and Chilcoat were working exclusively on Big Foot?" Shea asked as he crushed out his cigarette.

"That's what the lieutenant wanted," Bobbi admitted with a look at Shea, "but I wanted to help this girl." Her face went back to the window. "All I did was get her killed."

"You keep eating guilt like that, Marshal, and you'll last about another three months on this job," Shea warned. "Maybe if the girl had called you instead of running she'd still be alive. Maybe not. It doesn't make any difference now. She was dead the first time she ran away from home. It was only a matter of when and where. The only thing we can do is try to find the bastard that's responsible." Shea was quiet for a moment, then he added, "Sometimes I wish we were better at preventing crimes. Somehow it got all turned around. Protect the innocent. Innocent until proven guilty. Shit, we're so damned busy protecting the rights of the guilty that there's hardly any time left to protect the innocent." Bobbi heard the door open and close behind her. She didn't bother to turn.

Bobbi silently decided Sergeant Dan Shea would have tried to help the girl, too. She stared at the window for a long time. Life on the street, with its high and low dramas, compressed life into mere days and weeks. Maybe, Bobbi thought, that's why so many cops died young. Maybe they had lived their entire lives. If so, if that was it, Bobbi Marshal was disappointed. She wanted more. She'd come to police work with ideals, a sense of justice, a clear understanding of what was right and wrong. Time had changed all that. Reality had changed that. The whites and the blacks she'd once seen so clearly were now a dull gray. The satisfaction she'd expected had never been realized and the joy she hoped to find now seemed nonexistent.

The bitter truth was, police work was a tough, thankless job. Maybe her father was right. Maybe the day would come when she'd say she'd had enough and walk away. It was painful for Bobbi to admit, but the bitter lesson was that truth and justice did not always prevail.

# 12

# A QUESTION OF JUSTICE

The wariness was more a game to him than it was real caution. Especially since watching Detective Bobbi Marshal on television. Her appearance made him realize that the hunt was a reality, but he didn't really think the police were very smart. He never really expected them to find him. He fantasized about calling Donahue after the fiftieth rape and turning himself in on the air. He was certain Donahue could explain his motives. He saw women for what they really were. He'd understand it was their fault. Maybe some of the women he'd raped would want to be on the show. He could see Donahue driving home the question, ''But isn't it true you've had fantasies about being raped?'' The women could wear hoods or sit in the shadows, but why? Being raped made them a celebrity. Maybe he could write a book? Maybe a miniseries would follow? Perhaps he could play himself? He knew the case was too big for the courts. Fifty beautiful women waiting to testify. Many crying on his behalf. The courtroom would be packed with spectators. Women wanting to see him, touch him. A deal would be made, and maybe he'd spend a year or two in a mental hospital. Time to do the book—and they'd have plenty of nurses there. The random thoughts ended abruptly as he wheeled his car into the parking lot of Image Market Appraisals on West Pico Boulevard. He caught sight of the green Plymouth in the rearview mirror as the car swept by. His heart jumped with a combination of fear and excitement. He twisted in his seat to look. There it was, almost to the corner. No whitewalls. No chrome. There was a man driving. A blond woman was beside him. They were cops. Had they been following him? Was it coincidence? He pulled into his assigned parking space and climbed out. The traffic light at the corner changed. The detective car turned right and disappeared from sight. Fredericks dropped his keys into his pocket and headed for the office.

If they were following him they had a disappointing morning, he thought. Two older homes in Echo Park and a small apartment building in West L.A. He was glad he didn't do what he usually did when the schedule was light and visit the Pussycat Theater on Santa Monica.

"Hi, Dick." The petite blond receptionist smiled as Fredericks stepped into the office.

"Hi, Sandy. Any messages?"

"Not a thing."

"Okay, I'm gonna duck out the back and go down to the drugstore on the corner. I'll be back in about ten minutes."

"I've got you covered," the blond said as she resumed her typing.

The alley behind the appraisal office ran east and west behind the solid wall of brick and stucco buildings. Fredericks paused after stepping out the door. He tried to act casual as his eyes searched the alley in both directions. A truck was unloading produce at a nearby restaurant and a dog was sniffing trash cans. He stuck a hand in his pocket to finger some loose change and walked east, whistling as he moved.

He walked the half block to the mouth of the alley. There he moved in close to the back of a video store and carefully looked out into the street toward the intersection of Pico. His heart leaped. "Jesus Christ!" he muttered. The fantasy was one thing. The cold reality of it, another. The green Plymouth was parked on the corner, and the man and the woman in it were looking toward the office parking lot. Fredericks turned and hurried away. He was trembling.

District Attorney Raymond Bendicci sat at his desk in the eighteenth-floor executive office atop the Criminal Courts Building in downtown Los Angeles. As district attorney, he wielded power not only in Los Angeles County but in the entire state. It was a power Ray Bendicci enjoyed, and he was determined not to lose it.

Bendicci was determined to deal with the troubling statistical report on recent filings and convictions. The heads of the Criminals Complaints Division and the Trials Division were seated in his office listening to Bendicci's demand for improvement. The buzzer of the intercom cut the district attorney short. He shot the phone an annoyed look but he reached, punched a button, and picked up the receiver.

"I'm sorry to interrupt," the voice of his secretary said from the outer office, "but Captain Westly from Wilshire Division is on the line." The woman sounded irritated. "It's the sixth time he's called. He's becoming very abusive, and he said if you don't take his call you'll regret it. I'm sorry, I just don't know what to do."

"Tell him to hold for a minute," the district attorney said. "I'll take the call."

"Thank you, sir."

Bendicci moved the receiver from his ear and looked at his aides. "I'm going to have to take this call. Would you excuse me for a moment? This is District Attorney Bendicci," he said in an official tone after his aides had left the office.

"This is George Westly," the desperate voice said in his ear. "And there's trouble."

"What's the problem, captain?" the district attorney asked impersonally, as if the captain were sitting on the witness stand.

"The problem is Commander Hull. The sonofabitch is charging me with obstructing justice."

"Captain," the district attorney explained, "the internal affairs of the LAPD are not judicial in nature. They're administrative. It's an area where this office has no jurisdiction." He was choosing his words carefully.

"You won't help me?" Westly asked. He listened briefly. "You bastard," Westly growled. "You said if I got the charges dropped against Judge Unger the governor would appreciate it."

"Captain," the district attorney warned sternly, "I keep very careful notes of each of my calls regarding matters like this, and I said nothing of the kind."

"You can't do this. I'll tell them everything," Westly threatened.

"Just keep in mind, captain, that it is the district attorney's office that decides whether or not a criminal charge is filed against you."

Captain George Westly didn't answer.

"I think that may have some influence on your pension too, doesn't it, captain?"

Again George Westly's answer was silence. The district attorney reached and punched the intercom button. "Dianne, send Ed and Rose Ann back in, would you? I'm finished with the other matter."

Brad Chilcoat's hunch had paid off. The maid who had been working on the motel's first floor had seen a chunky white man come in the door at the south end of the building from the street level. She had paid little attention to the man. To the Spanish maid he was just another trick. He'd gone to the second-floor stairway. Some twenty minutes later she saw him leaving,

It wasn't much, but Chilcoat knew a white man wouldn't walk far in this neighborhood, and since he had avoided using the motel's parking lot Chilcoat looked for the nearest alternative. He found it—the gas station across the street from the Galaxy.

The owner/operator of the gas station was a short Vietnamese man named Ho. He had dark eyes and a silver tooth. Chilcoat talked to Ho as he pumped gas, cleaned windshields, and made change. Ho's English wasn't much better than his dentist. "Yes, I see car. He park there." He pointed to a pay telephone booth. "No buy gas. No use phone. I tell him he has to go. No parking. He say to me, 'Fuck off.' He big, ugly man. I fuck off."

"Did you see him go to the motel?" Chilcoat questioned.

"I see him go. I see him come back. I got customers. I don't know where."

"What kind of car?"

"Lue. A lue Ford."

"You mean blue or new?"

He nodded. "Yes, a lue Ford. A lue nu Ford."

"A new blue Ford. How about the license number?"

Ho shrugged. "I dunno all numbers but some, two-tree-foo."

"Two-three-four?" Chilcoat verified.

"Uh huh, two-tree-foo," Ho agreed. "Two-tree-foo. Same on plate."

"Would you recognize the man if you saw him again?"

Ho nodded. "I see him. I know him." He gestured to his cheeks. "Scars all over. Like face of moon."

The four detectives had more than they did on most murder investigations when they returned to Wilshire Detectives. Shea, using the description of the suspect's car and the partial license number, sent a teletype to the Department of Motor Vehicles in Sacramento to request all late-model Fords with the numbers two-three-four in their plate numbers. The printout that returned was eight feet long. "Jesus Christ," Weldon muttered in frustration. "That's not a fuckin' clue. It's an ulcer."

Bobbi and Chilcoat were at the Homicide table when Shea and Weldon returned.

"These are the possible license numbers from DMV.

All twenty-seven hundred of them," Shea said, laying the printout on the desk.

"Glad you narrowed it down," Chilcoat said sarcastically.

Lieutenant Stovich approached the group. "Got the murder solved yet?"

"Yeah," Chilcoat answered, gesturing to the printout. "He's hiding in there."

"You two got a minute?" Stovich said, looking at Bobbi and Chilcoat.

Chilcoat pushed from the table. "Sure. I've got these guys off to a good start."

"Watch it, Chilcoat. I may be a witness for your old lady," Weldon threatened.

"Let's compare notes at the end of the day," Shea said to Bobbi.

"All right," Bobbi agreed. She was seeing more in Dan Shea's interest than the case. The seemingly cool, aloof man had a warm side, too. She'd just never seen it before. She turned and followed after Lieutenant Stovich and Chilcoat.

"How is it, working with her?" Cliff Weldon questioned with a look at his partner.

"She smells a lot better than you do," Shea answered as he watched Bobbi walk away.

Stovich led Bobbi and Chilcoat across the squad room to his desk. "Things were a little busy earlier but now that I've got a moment, I wanted to compliment you two on what you've done with Big Foot. Looks like it's only a matter of time now."

"Thanks." Bobbi smiled. "Any word from the surveillance team?"

"Nothing much. Fredericks has been out on what looked like several routine inspections. Last I heard he was back in his office." Stovich looked to Chilcoat. "Give me a moment with Bobbi, would you?"

"This isn't about my divorce, is it?" Chilcoat questioned.

"No, I've got a meeting with the city attorney at three o'clock about that," the lieutenant answered sarcastically. "Now, like your wife said, take a walk."

Chilcoat nodded solemnly and moved away. The lieutenant looked at Bobbi. "Captain Westly was called down to IA late this morning. He's back there again this afternoon. I take it this is in response to your complaint?"

Bobbi didn't answer. She looked toward the captain's office. His adjutant and his secretary were at their desks as usual. Everything looked normal. She returned her eyes to the lieutenant's. "Doing what's right isn't easy, is it?" she said.

"Maybe that's why we're so careful about who we let on the job."

Bobbi didn't answer. She was feeling sorry for Captain George Westly. She suspected that he too had come to the job with ideals and high hopes. He too had wanted to do what was right, what was just. Somehow it had changed, or he had changed. She wondered how much she had changed. She wasn't sure. She was sure she didn't want to be thanked for crushing another cop's career no matter how just the cause. "Maybe," Bobbi said to Aaron Stovich. Then she turned and walked away.

# 13

# AFTERSHOCKS

Lakespur Drive, on the north side of Burbank, was quiet under its blanket of darkness. The big gnarled oak trees that lined the street filtered the light from the streetlamps. An occasional car drifted through the neighborhood. Little else disturbed the tranquil scene. Those enjoying a quiet evening of television had no way of knowing a brutal rapist was in their midst. The Fredericks lived at fourteen-oh-six Lakespur. It was an older one-story, three-bedroom stucco home, and with its fresh coat of paint and new garage door it fit nicely into the upper-middle-class neighborhood. The Fredericsses were a quiet couple. Both worked and had little social contact with even their immediate neighbors. Not an unusual phenomenon in Southern California.

For Clair Fredericks, who was soaking in a hot bath, it was an unusual night. Her husband was home. She knew what the dates circled in red on his calender meant. The lonely nights had already told her. Her husband was having affairs. She didn't really think there was any one woman. There had been no calls. No hidden expenses. No love notes. Just the continuing succession of late nights. He was cruising the singles bars, meeting them at work, looking for love, looking for his manhood. As a nurse, Clair knew her husband's problem was more than physical. When they had first met Dick had been demanding, rough, passionate in his lovemaking. But Clair had grown weary and frightened of his so-called games. She didn't want to be raped, she wanted to be loved, held, caressed. The more she yielded herself, the more distant he became until their lovemaking had stopped all together. That was nearly six months ago.

Dick Fredericks was Clair's second husband. She was eight years older than he, and for a long time she thought that was the problem, but the pats on the ass and the longing looks at the hospital assured her she wasn't completely over the hill at forty-four. Yet she was at an age where she didn't want to start over again. She didn't want to grow old alone. The red circles on the hidden calendar, the collection of panties hidden under the front seat of his car weren't that important. He was home now. Maybe he'd found the answer wasn't out there in a tight sweater. Maybe it was just a phase he was going through. Maybe he was home to stay. Maybe tonight he'd want her. Oh, damn, she hoped so.

The two detectives parked down the street in the 240-Z knew Dick Fredericks had a problem, too, although, unlike Clair, they were disappointed that he was staying home.

"I suppose after nineteen rapes you need a few nights off," Brad Chilcoat said from the passenger side of the car.

"I guess you'd know," Bobbi's dark profile answered from behind the wheel.

Concerned that the unmarked detective car would be easily spotted on the quiet residential street, they had opted to use Bobbi's car. A hand-held radio lying on the center console was on and tuned to tactical frequency two, which was being monitored by Communications Division as well as the standby team waiting in the squad room at Wilshire Detectives. The use of a personal car was a risk for its owner. Should something go wrong and the car be damaged, the insurance company would promptly disallow the claim and cancel the policy. The city was known to be equally generous. Insuring cops was no way to make money.

Bobbi and Chilcoat had been staked on the house for two and a half hours. It was nine-thirty p.m. They had thirty minutes to go until they would be relieved by the next team. Two cars sat side by side in the Fredericks driveway and lights were on inside the house. Nothing had changed since their arrival except Bobbi's opinion of how comfortable the 240's seat was. Bobbi shifted. Her butt was beginning to feel numb. "I wonder what his wife thinks?" she said, staring at the curtain-covered illuminated window of the Fredericks house.

"Maybe she doesn't think anything," Chilcoat offered after a thoughtful moment.

"I can't believe a husband and wife ever get that callous."

"Believe it," Chilcoat urged. "You've never been married. I have."

"Cathy's not suing you because she didn't know what you were doing. She's suing you because she did," Bobbi reminded him.

"Speaking of my dear sweet estranged, I've got an attorney's conference with her tomorrow. They want more child support."

Bobbi looked to Chilcoat. His eyes were hidden in the darkness. "Would you get married again?"

"Is this a proposal?"

"Answer the question, Brad."

"Yeah, I suppose. Most of it was okay."

"What went wrong?" Bobbi questioned.

"I don't know," Chilcoat answered defensively. Bobbi sensed that she was trespassing.

"How about you, Sweet Feet," Chilcoat countered. "You ever going to get married?"

"No one's asked me since eighth grade," Bobbi confessed candidly.

"How about Don Juan or Don what's-his-name?"

"Roberts. We've only known each other a month or so."

"How come you don't date cops?"

"Maybe because most don't ask."

"Did Shea ask you out?"

"No."

"He will."

"How do you know?"

"I know Dan Shea. We were partners for five years in a radio car."

"Why's he single?"

"His wife and daughter were killed by a drunk four years ago."

"Does he date?"

"Hasn't yet, but I think he's about out of it."

"Seven-William-ninety to seven-William-thirty-six," a male voice said on the portable radio.

"Thirty-six," Chilcoat said, "it must be for you."

Bobbi picked up the radio, keyed it. "This is William-thirty-six, go."

"It's almost time for your relief, thirty-six," the radio answered. "Is the chicken still on the roost?"

"Roger. No movement."

"William-ninety, roger. We're leaving the station now."

Brad Chilcoat's feet were itching and his underwear felt stiff and coarse. He'd washed both the night before in the bathroom sink using Irish Spring and cold water—the god-damned water heater was out. As he sat waiting in the conference room of Cathy's attorney's law firm, he was seriously considering asking for custody of the washer and dryer.

After an agonizing twenty-minute wait the lawyer from Dial-a-Divorce arrived for the meeting. "Are you Brad Chilmont?" the tall thin man in glasses asked as he stepped into the room.

"Chilcoat," the surprised Chilcoat corrected. "Who the hell are you?" He'd never seen the man before.

"Murray's car broke down," the harried man said as he searched through a thick file that seemed to bewilder him. "I'm his cousin, Sid."

"His cousin!" Chilcoat blurted. "Are you an attorney?"

"Yes, but I usually handle personal injury. Divorce upsets my stomach."

"Jesus Christ," Chilcoat muttered. He felt physically ill.

The door to the conference room opened a second time and the blond Cathy Chilcoat entered. Her eyes were masked behind blue sunglasses and her lips were set in a sober pout. Cathy's attorney in a smartly tailored three-piece pinstriped suit followed close behind. He looked polished and confident. Cathy and the attorney sat down across the table from Chilcoat and Sid, from Dial-a-Divorce, who was still searching through his papers.

"Are we prepared to proceed?" the attorney at Cathy's side questioned. Chilcoat noticed the man was wearing cufflinks. Gold cufflinks.

"As soon as I find Mr. Chilmont's file," Sid answered, continuing to rummage in his briefcase.

"Chilcoat, goddammit," Chilcoat snapped angrily. "And no, I'm not prepared to proceed. Murray's, I mean, my attorney's car broke down. This guy doesn't even know my name."

"Detective Chilcoat," Cathy's attorney answered coolly, "we of course can't be responsible for the punctuality of your counsel. If we continue this matter, as seems to be your desire, you must assume the liability of the costs."

"What the hell's another couple thousand to me?" Chilcoat said sarcastically.

"Very well," the attorney said. "Let's agree to table this discussion of an increase in child support until the respondent has an opportunity to discuss the matter with counsel."

At first Bobbi sensed it more than she suspected it. It was a haunting, nearly intangible feeling of not being alone. What little sleep she did get had been filled with images of a bloody but alive Fawn Tyler who pleaded for help. And then there was Don Roberts in a passionate embrace with Cathy Chilcoat. She wasn't sure what that meant. Bobbi had never believed dreams were anything more than aftershocks of life experiences, so when she awoke she tried to push the memory of them aside, but the reality of yesterday was no less a reality today. Fawn Tyler was dead. Did Captain Westly realize what he was doing when he got involved in the Unger case? Was she right in what she did? Did Cathy Chilcoat really believe Bobbi was responsible for breaking up her partner's marriage? Would Don Roberts ever call again? When was Big Foot going to strike? The rush of thoughts was with Bobbi when she drove out of the shadowy subterranean garage into the morning sunlight. It was then the feeling grew stronger—the elusive sixth sense that cops often talked about. Whatever it was, Bobbi felt compelled to check her rearview mirror. She searched the reflection but found nothing suspicious. The squad room would offer refuge. There among her own kind the haunting images would fade. She saw the blue Datsun sandwiched among the other cars in the morning traffic, but it was just another car.

They were scheduled for the seven a.m. surveillance of Big Foot. Brad Chilcoat had been waiting at the station when Bobbi arrived. He offered her a copy of the morning *Times* and stabbed a finger at a headline that read *"LAPD CAPTAIN RESIGNS IN WAKE OF JUDGE'S ARREST."* Bobbi took the paper and scanned the text.

*Captain George Westly, an eighteen-year veteran of the LAPD and brother of the late senior senator from California, has resigned after an investigation into his conduct surrounding the dismissal of criminal charges against accused Superior Court Judge Warrick Unger. The judge, arrested by an undercover policewoman from Captain Westly's command at Wilshire Detectives, refused comment after . . .*

Bobbi quit reading. The details weren't important to her. Captain Westly was gone. Justice had been done. Bobbi wondered why it didn't feel that way. Tossing the paper to a desktop she said, "Let's go to work."

It was when they were leaving the station that Bobbi saw the blue Datsun. Was it the same one she'd seen earlier on Wilshire Boulevard? Bobbi considered saying something to Brad, but not wanting to sound paranoid, or like a woman, she said nothing. After they traveled several blocks she glanced over her shoulder a second time. The blue Datsun was gone.

Dick Fredericks left for work at seven-forty a.m. as he did every morning. He saw nothing as he left the block on Lakespur, although he was looking. He checked his mirror periodically as he drove across Barham Boulevard from Burbank into Hollywood. Nothing. Could they have given up? The thought gave him a great sense of victory. He'd beaten them. Somehow they had found him, but his guise of innocence had been so convincing they had moved on to another suspect. Or maybe it was a trap? Maybe they only wanted him to think they were gone? He'd seen that once on "Miami Vice." Well, they weren't dealing with a lightweight. Patience. That was the important thing. He had to be patient. He arrived at his office on West Pico Boulevard at ten minutes to eight. Still he'd seen nothing.

After Dick Fredericks disappeared into the Image Appraisals' office, Brad Chilcoat eased the detective car into the bank parking lot across the street. Along with the backup team they had successfully leapfrogged Big Foot from his home in Burbank to the office on West Pico. Chilcoat pulled in between two other cars and turned the engine off. They had to look through the windows of several other parked cars, but their view of the appraisal office and its parking lot was clear.

"I have a funny thought about Fredericks this morning as I was driving in," Bobbi said as they settled in for the wait.

"A funny thought about a rapist," Chilcoat said with a look at Bobbi. "This should be interesting."

"Well, it's not exactly funny," Bobbi corrected.

"You know, sometimes you sound just like a woman." Chilcoat smiled.

"Promise you won't laugh," Bobbi urged.

"You just told me it was funny. Now you don't want me to laugh. Which is it?"

"Okay, what if it's not him, Brad?" Bobbi questioned. "I mean, what if we're following the wrong man?"

Chilcoat chuckled. "That's called the 'I solved the crime but I only want credit if I'm right' syndrome. Relax," he urged, "this is only day two. What do you expect this guy to do, go around sniffing tires, or what? He'll do his thing and we'll be there when he does it."

"I wish I were as confident," Bobbi said.

"You never will be. You're a woman."

"Don't get on one of your 'Lemme tell you the difference between men and women' kicks," Bobbi warned. "I'm not in the mood."

"See what I mean."

"Watch it, Brad."

"You're right. We're both cops. We've both had the same training. We're equals," he assured her.

"Thank you," Bobbi said.

"But only one of us is wearing panty hose." He laughed.

"You bastard," Bobbi snarled.

Dick Fredericks had started his counteroffensive. At ten minutes after nine he was still at his desk working on the summaries of several recent inspections. "Dick, you still here?" Clark Simms, the office manager, said when he came out of his office.

"I've only got four on the schedule today," Fredericks answered. "Thought I'd get caught up on the summaries from yesterday. Helen is trying to get that forty-unit deal through by the first of the month."

"You're a thoughtful man, Dick," the office manager said and moved on.

Yes. Fredericks smiled to himself. He was thoughtful, and that was why he wasn't going outside this morning, and that was why the two residentials he had been assigned were promptly traded for a major commercial. He was changing tactics. The police were playing a guessing game and he knew it. If they had enough evidence they'd come in and arrest him. They hadn't. They were outside waiting, watching. Well, two could play this game. They would soon tire of watching nothing. He wondered if Bobbi Marshal was among those who'd been watching him. The thought that she may have seen him, followed him, stirred excitement in him. He had the stolen picture of her in the string bikini hidden in his bottom desk drawer. Just thinking of her shortened his breath. He remembered the scent of her in the condo. "Soon, Bobbi, soon," he whispered, squeezing himself under his desk.

At ten o'clock, with Fredericks still in the office, Bobbi and Chilcoat turned over the point to Garner and Dixon from Central Division. Chilcoat drove Bobbi back to the station, dropped her off, and headed downtown for the attorney's conference with his estranged wife.

The detective squad room was strangely quiet when Bobbi walked in. She'd seen it this way once before when a detective from the Robbery team had been killed in a liquor store shootout. The room was occupied by at least half of the fifty detectives assigned there, and the air was electric with tension. Bobbi couldn't decipher the collective look she drew crossing to her desk. She sat down at her desk. The morning *Times* that Chilcoat had handed her earlier was still there, staring up at her. *"LAPD CAPTAIN RESIGNS . . ."* Now Bobbi understood, and she tensed as she looked to the captain's office.

Becky, a pasty, humorless, chunky straw blond who served as the captain's secretary, was stepping out of his office. She was weeping, mopping at an eye with a tissue.

Sergeant Shanks, the captain's adjutant, stood behind his desk packing a box. Bobbi knew that behind the closed door George Westly was doing the same thing. Bobbi turned the newspaper facedown. She ached with a desire to leave, to run, to be anywhere but where she was, but she knew she had to stay. It was as if she had walked onto the stage by accident near the end of the final act. The players were in place. The audience held a collective breath of anticipation. Time had stopped and she was frozen in it. Dan Shea and Cliff Weldon sat at a nearby table. Lieutenant Stovich was at his desk. No one moved. No one spoke. Even the sea of telephones across the squad room seemed to silence themselves for the final scene. Then the door to the captain's office opened. She hardly recognized the man dressed in a plaid shirt and slacks. He looked smaller, his shoulders round and hunched forward as if some great weight pushed on them from behind. He was carrying a cardboard box full of personal effects from the office that was no longer his. He spoke softly to Sergeant Shanks, shook his hand, and then headed across the squad room.

Bobbi had hoped George Westly would opt to go down the front hallway, but that would mean going out the station's front doors and only civilians did that. He was headed for the rear of the squad room and the door for sworn personnel that led to the parking lot. Bobbi Marshal's desk was in his path. Bobbi averted her eyes and hoped he'd pass in silence. She prayed he would. She heard his footfalls stop beside her desk. She forced herself to turn and look up at him. It was obvious the man had not slept. His eyes were bloodshot and puffy. His skin was waxlike and seemed to be slipping from his skull. A muscle twitched at the corner of his mouth. Although he looked broken and defeated, the anger of his glare made Bobbi flush with heat. She felt pity and compassion for him. She wanted to speak, but her mouth was dry and her throat was tight.

"I hope you're satisfied," he said through thin lips.

Then with an accusing jerky look around the silent squad room, he added, "I hope you're all satisfied."

Silence answered him. George Westly adjusted his grip on the cardboard box and then he moved on. Bobbi sat silent, holding her breath, until she heard the door close. A tear spilled and traced its way down her cheek. She didn't bother to wipe it away. She didn't care who saw.

"Come on," Dan Shea said, patting Bobbi on the shoulder. "I'll buy you a cup of coffee."

They walked in silence down the station's rear hallway, passing the windowed watch commander's office. There several sergeants and a uniformed lieutenant were talking and laughing, seemingly unaware of the drama unfolding down the hall. Then again, it wasn't their business. Detectives and uniforms were both cops but it was a different path, a different career, a different mindset. The hallway was busy with a flow of uniformed officers. They looked young. Even at twenty-nine, Bobbi Marshal felt much older on this day.

"Lady's choice," Dan Shea said as they entered the coffee room with its row of vending machines. He walked to a coffee machine with coins in hand.

"I'll have a double on the rocks," Bobbi said, sitting down at one of the three tables.

"That'll have to come later," Shea answered.

"Cream and sugar," Bobbi said halfheartedly.

"How would you like some good news?" Shea said, setting a cup of coffee in front of Bobbi. He eased himself into a chair across from her.

Bobbi sampled her coffee. "Do you have to ask?"

"We've got an ID on Scar Face." Shea smiled, as he tasted his own coffee.

"How?" Bobbi questioned.

"Four hundred and eighteen of the license numbers were registered in the city. Fifty-two of those had criminal records. Weldon and I spent the night pulling mug shots and looking at them. Nine of them had pockmarks. We showed them to our friend Ho this morning. He picked out Delbert Phillips. Positive ID.''

"Did you get an address?" Bobbi asked eagerly.

"Yeah, apartment house over on the fifteen-hundred block of Menlo. Cliff and I went over there this morning at about six. Kicked the door in, terrorized some Mexican woman and her seven kids. Phillips moved six weeks ago.''

"So he's gone?" Bobbi said with disappointment.

"I said it was good news," Shea reminded. "Phillips is on parole for assault with a deadly weapon, so I called his parole officer. He said Phillips was in last week for his monthly progress report. He'd just gotten a job as a laborer with Jacobs Construction.''

"Where are they?"

"Fifth and Hill. They're putting up the new Bradley Building. All twenty-six stories of it.''

"You think Phillips is there?" Bobbi questioned.

"I know he is." Shea smiled. Bobbi could see the excitement in his eyes. "About twenty minutes ago I had his PO call to see if he's at work. He's there.''

"What are we waiting for?" Bobbi said. She was eager to go.

Shea pushed his coffee aside.

"You," he said. "Cliff has to cover a preliminary hearing on a one-eighty-seven. Do you have time to back me up?''

Bobbi was flattered. "Yes," she answered without hesitation. "Brad's at an attorney's conference with his wife.''

"Good." Shea smiled. "Given his mental state it might be dangerous to take him up on a tall building.''

Delbert Phillips was looking forward to the official end of his parole. Released twenty-three months earlier, Delbert was restricted to living in Los Angeles County and required to meet with his parole officer every four weeks. He was tired of pissing in jars for drug tests and being told where he could live and work. But it wouldn't be much longer. Delbert was eager to move back to Las Vegas. He hadn't been there now in almost three years. He missed the dry sizzling heat of the summer. The long warm nights. The lights. The excitement. Life was better there. Full and rich, filled with beautiful women and money. L.A. was a cesspool and he regretted ever coming here.

In Delbert's mind his debt to society had been fulfilled, and in a few short weeks he'd be back in Las Vegas. As Delbert mixed cement on the nineteenth floor of the Bradley Building it never entered his mind that his plans would change abruptly if the police found him. In his mind the murder of the two teenage whores stood among his proudest achievements. It was perfect. There was no way they could ever link it to him.

Delbert liked working high in the skeleton of the new building. He was on the nineteenth floor. The floor and ceiling were in, but the yet wall-less building allowed the gusty wind to whistle through the exposed girders, pipes, and ductwork, and the view was exhilarating. Delbert was working with a five-man follow-up crew. The main work force was busy two stories above. After three weeks' work, he was now entrusted with mixing mortar for the follow-up crew. Often when alone, Delbert would grab a handful of the cool, gray, heavy mud and throw it over the side. Without knowing it, he had succeeded in shattering the windshield of a company pickup truck, damaging a crate of lighting fixtures, and narrowly missing a passing pedestrian.

It was shortly after noon, and Delbert was returning to the freight elevator cage on the ground floor after a visit to the lunch wagon when he saw the detective car pulling into the construction site. He watched as the car drove to the cluster of temporary office trailers. As alarm went off inside Delbert as the screened elevator doors closed and it began a slow, windy, climb up the exterior of the building. A shapely brunette climbed from the passenger's side of the detective car flashing a nylon-clad leg. Several cat-calls and whistles filled the air. The policewoman looked up at the elevator. Although four men shared the car with him, Delbert felt as though he were the only one. He averted his eyes and turned away. "Yeah, up here, baby," one of the others on the elevator called. "I got something you can eat."

Delbert quickly forgot the submarine sandwich he carried. His appetite was gone. When the elevator ground to a bumpy stop at the nineteenth floor he pushed roughly by several others and scrambled off. "Hey, watch it, asshole." Delbert didn't answer.

The panic was quickly overwhelming him, robbing him of his ability to think, to plan. He felt something cold in his hand and looked down. He had squeezed the sandwich through his fingers like play dough. He opened his hand and shook away the paste of meat and bread and wiped his hand on his pants as he moved to the edge of the floor and looked down. Far below he saw the brunette and two men standing on the elevator platform. Above him the bell sounded on the freight car and it started down.

The breeze through the open nineteenth floor seemed colder now, and it made Delbert shiver. Fear found its way to his bladder and filled him with the urge to urinate. How did they find him? How did they know? How?! How?! The "how" no longer mattered. The cables for the elevator stopped vibrating. The car was at the bottom. It would soon be bringing the police up. He had to run. He had to hide but there was no escape. Even the stairs between floors had yet to be installed. He was alone and he was trapped.

Buried deep in all men is the primal instinct of fight or flight. The chance of flight for Delbert Phillips was gone and in its place anger for the coming confrontation rose. The thick greasy cables for the elevator were vibrating again. The car was on its way up. Blood pounded in his ears as adrenaline pulsed through his veins. He growled with rage and moved to the wheeled portable cement mixer that sat nearby. It was still half full of the heavy mortar mixed for the morning's work. Grabbing the cement mixer,

Delbert grunted and pulled the heavy machine to the edge of the elevator platform. The cables crackled as they rushed by under stress. Delbert peered down. The car was six or eight stories below and climbing. He knew he had to hurry. Delbert moved to the rear of the cement mixer and pushed. The rubber wheels grated over the floor and then fell free as the heavy machine toppled over the edge and plummeted downward.

Bobbi stood near the rear of the freight elevator holding her skirt. Sergeant Dan Shea was being a gentleman and pretending he was more interested in the sprawling skyline than he was in the legs he'd already glimpsed. Tom Newcomb, the hard-hatted foreman of the follow-up crew and Delbert's boss, was with the two detectives. "Is Delbert coming back or should I replace him?" Newcomb asked a split second before the top of the elevator car exploded in a shower of twisted steel and gray mud. Newcomb was knocked through the side of the car and he fell, screaming, cartwheeling, sixteen stories to his death atop a bundle of reinforcing rods. The elevator car shuddered under the impact. The stressed cables groaned and stretched under the added burden, but as the crumpled cement mixer rolled off the damaged top and fell, the elevator continued its shaky climb.

Terrified, Bobbi clung to the heavy wire mesh at the back of the car. The shaken Dan Shea, knocked to the floor and splattered with concrete, climbed to his feet. "You okay?" he asked, looking at Bobbi. Blood was running down his forehead from the hairline.

Far below a resounding, shattering thud sounded as the cement mixer impacted, sending up a mushroom of dirt and dust. The hard hats, gathered in groups for lunch, scattered for cover like frightened rabbits. Immediately an emergency whistle began to fill the air.

Nineteen stories above, the twisted elevator car screeched to a halt. Dan Shea stepped off and offered Bobbi a hand. "Be careful," he said. She was quickly to his side. Shea held her hand as his eyes searched. A black telephone sat on a wooden bench near the center of the floor. The only sound was the wind whistling through the stark gray structure. "Stay here," Shea urged. "I'll see if the telephone works."

The foreman's desk, where the telephone sat, was near a partition for a hallway wall. Delbert Phillips stood hidden behind it with a three-foot two-by-four in hand, waiting.

Dan Shea moved quickly to the telephone. He grabbed the receiver and heard a buzzer sounding at the other end of the line. "It works," he said, shooting Bobbi a look. She stood forty feet away.

"Get off the line, we've got an emergency," a gruff male voice ordered in Shea's ear.

"This is Sergeant Shea," he answered. "We're up here and we need help."

"Where are you?" the man asked. "Are you hurt?"

Delbert Phillips stepped around the corner of the partition.

"Dan!" Bobbi shouted when she saw the man. He was holding the club high, ready to strike. Shea turned, raised an arm to fend the blow. Delbert brought the two-by-four down hard. It bounced off Shea's upraised left arm and struck him between the shoulder and neck. His knees buckled and he went down.

Bobbi reached beneath her jacket and pulled the four-inch thirty-eight from her waistband. She took a quick two-handed aim and screamed a warning. "Drop it."

Delbert Phillips turned slowly to Bobbi. His face was an angry mask. He was breathing hard and the club was still tight in his right hand. Dan Shea, semiconscious, lay groaning in pain at his feet. "I don't think you've ever shot anybody," Delbert grated through tight angry teeth.

Bobbi's hands were trembling visibly. "Wanna be first?" she answered. Her voice was edged with fear.

"I don't think you've got the guts." Delbert smiled menacingly. He took several slow, deliberate steps toward her. She was almost within his reach now.

"I don't want to shoot," Bobbi warned as she took a step backward. She was only three feet from the edge. Her hair and skirt danced in the wind.

"I know you don't." Delbert smiled. "Put the gun down. I won't hurt you." He took another two steps.

Bobbi glanced at the fallen Dan Shea. He was now out of her line of fire. "I lied," she snarled, returning her attention to Delbert Phillips. She lowered her aim and fired at his right knee.

Delbert grimaced with the crack of the shot and grabbed his knee. It was shattered. Blood poured through his fingers, but he still stood.

Bobbi took careful aim and fired a second shot into his left knee. Delbert jerked and sank to the floor, his scream of anguish mixed with the wind.

"The first one was from me," Bobbi grated, still holding an aim on the fallen man. "The second one was from Fawn Tyler."

# 14

# CITY OF PASSION

Bobbi was taken from the scene by a uniformed sergeant from Metro Division. The construction site was swarming with police cars and ambulances when the two pulled away. Bobbi was still trembling.

Department policy dictated that the officer or officers involved in a shooting be removed from the scene and isolated as soon as possible and practical by a supervisor the rank of sergeant or above. The reasons varied, but they were all valid. Loitering at the scene exposed the shooter to the press, hostile citizens, family of the victim, and, many times the most insensitive, other cops. When more than one policeman was involved, the isolation prevented the shooters from improving, or improvising, the facts surrounding the shooting incident. In the case of solitary shooters it allowed the concerned officer the opportunity to reflect and calm down.

Bobbi was surprised at how normal things seemed a mere block away as the sergeant drove south on Hill Street. It was as if the life and death struggle that was now only minutes old had never happened. Here it was a calm, normal sunny day. They just didn't know, she told herself. She wondered how many would care if they did. Did the city of Los Angeles care that they had found Fawn Tyler's killer? Bobbi supposed not. They didn't seem interested when Fawn died. Why would they be interested now? Jesus, who did care? What was all this for? The quiet and warmth of the patrol car seemed an insane contrast to the terror and blood on the nineteenth floor of the Bradley Building. Bobbi knew she was on the edge. She drew in a deep breath and let it out slowly. She had to get control. She smoothed her skirt and spotted a run in her nylon. "Shit," she complained.

"You okay?" the sergeant said with a wary look at her as he drove.

"No," Bobbi answered. "I've got a run in my nylon." Her eyes were rimmed with tears.

They drove to Wilshire Station. Word of the shooting had preceded their arrival. Lieutenant Stovich and Brad Chilcoat were waiting. "I just talked to Weldon," Chilcoat said to Bobbi as he walked with her to one of the interrogation rooms in the detective squad room. "He went over to County General. Shea's okay. He's got a broken collarbone. That's all."

"Sorry, but we're going to have to isolate you until the Officer-Involved Shooting Team gets here," Lieutenant Stovich said at the open door of the interrogation room.

"I understand." Bobbi smiled. She was looking forward to the solitude.

"You want a Coke? Something to eat? A magazine?" Chilcoat questioned.

"No, thanks," Bobbi answered.

Chilcoat studied her face. He could see the storm of emotion welling behind her eyes. He stepped to Bobbi and took her in his arms. "I'm sorry I wasn't there, partner," he said, hugging her. Lieutenant Stovich turned and walked away.

"It's okay," Bobbi assured Chilcoat as he released her. She stepped into the room.

"You need anything you let me know," he called as he closed the door.

The small room offered Bobbi comfort and quiet. It was Wilshire Detectives. Bobbi Marshal was home. She was safe here, among her own. A sense of security returned slowly as she relaxed and allowed the blend of shock, anger, and fear to melt into the room. She had survived her first shooting. Eight and a half years of anticipation, preparation, and training, and it was over in six fleeting seconds. The images were already a blur. The towering height. The crash atop the elevator. The hard-hatted foreman disappearing into the sky. Dan being struck. The scar-faced man with the club. The shots. They sounded so toylike, mixed with the wind. A knock sounded outside the door. It had to be Brad again, Bobbi thought. He was acting like a worried older brother. "It's open," she called.

Bobbi recognized the man when he opened the door. It was Lieutenant Brillon from Robbery-Homicide's Officer-Involved Shooting Team. He was a big, broad-shouldered man with a square chin and short-cropped gray hair. "Detective Marshal?" the lieutenant questioned.

The surprised Bobbi glanced at her watch before she pushed to her feet. Forty minutes had passed. It didn't seem possible. "Yes, sir."

"Sit down, Marshal," the lieutenant said, stepping into the room. A second detective, a man with white, wavy hair and a friendly smile, followed the lieutenant. Both carried briefcases. "I'm Lieutenant Brillon and this is Sergeant Oaks." Brillon took off his jacket and hung it over the back of a chair. "We're from the Shooting team. We're not here to pass any judgments, or draw any conclusions. All we want are the facts. We'll ask the questions. You provide the answers. The only requirement we have is that you tell us the truth. Agreed?"

"Agreed," Bobbi answered.

"Then let's go to work," Brillon said, rolling up his sleeves. "We've just come from the scene so we've got a feel for the physical layout. Let's start with your arrival at the construction site."

It was to last for nearly three hours. The two detectives listened to Bobbi's narrative, making notes, asking questions, examining attitudes, opinions. They made scale drawings and they had Bobbi make drawings.

The questions and Bobbi's answers were recorded. The

skilled questions from the experienced investigators brought more and more of the details to the surface. It wasn't that Bobbi was being reluctant. Shock and trauma robbed the mind of important details, but when probed and examined the images returned. When the interview was over, Lieutenant Brillon and Sergeant Oaks knew as much about the shooting as Bobbi Marshal did. After they talked to Dan Shea and the wounded Phillips, they would know more. Then a bottom-line recommendation would be made. Lieutenant Brillon explained it all to Bobbi.

"After our investigation is complete we'll present the facts, along with a recommendation, to the Shooting Review Board. They'll determine whether or not it's within policy."

"I understand," Bobbi answered.

"I have one final question," the lieutenant said as he rolled down his sleeves and put his jacket on.

"Yes," Bobbi said, noticing that they were both getting ready to leave. The portable tapes had been turned off, notes were being gathered and stuffed into briefcases.

"You're familiar with the department's shooting policy that warns that you are to 'shoot only when you're in fear of your own life, or the life of a fellow officer, or the life and safety of a citizen, and that when such criteria have been met the shots fired shall be fired in such a manner as to stop the suspect,' and that it is a violation of that policy to deliberately shoot to wound?"

"Yes, I know the policy," Bobbi said. Her mouth was dry.

"Are you familiar with the term capping?" Sergeant Oaks asked. "Terrorists in Italy used it a lot a couple of years ago. It's when you deliberately shoot someone through the kneecap. Gives them a stiff, crippled leg for life."

"Looks like Phillips may have two of them," Lieutenant Brillon said soberly.

Bobbi searched their grim faces. Both men were standing now. "As I said, gentlemen. He stepped toward me with the club in hand. I warned him I'd shoot. He didn't stop. I fired once. He was still standing. I fired again. Do you want me to apologize for not killing him?''

"Let's hope you don't have to," Brillon said, picking up his briefcase.

"Sometimes living is more of a punishment than dying," Bobbi answered.

Brillon's expression hardened. "Let me tell you something, young lady," he said dryly. "Before you were entrusted to carry a gun you raised your right hand and swore an oath 'to protect and serve.' That oath said nothing about deciding guilt or passing judgment. If we find you used your weapon as a jury I'll personally see that you're fired and sent to prison for assault with a deadly weapon."

"Save your macho lecture for the Police Academy recruits, lieutenant," Bobbi answered quickly. She was tired and irritable. "I was the one nineteen floors above the street. I was the one facing a felon I saw club another cop to the ground. Yes, I'm guilty. Guilty of compassion. Maybe if I were a man I would have emptied my gun into him but I didn't. I didn't because I'm a woman. If you want to pass judgment on me for that go ahead and try, but I'm not going to make it easy for you. I haven't done a damned thing wrong, and I'll be glad to tell my story in court."

The lieutenant held Bobbi's sober look for a moment, then his eyes swept to his partner. "Come on, we're finished here."

Bobbi sat in the interrogation room for some time after they left. The stress of the shooting and the interview left her physically exhausted and mentally drained. Her senses were numb. She couldn't seem to hold a thought. In reality eleven hours had passed since she had come on duty. The only nourishment she'd had, if it qualified as that, was the cup of coffee Dan Shea had bought her. Her heart rate was elevated from shock. She was worried about the outcome of the shooting investigation, and in another hour her third stakeout in less than thirty hours would begin. Finally

Bobbi pushed from the chair and opened the door. She looked weary and drawn when she came out of the interrogation room. Her makeup had faded and her eyes were red with strain. The run in her nylon had found its way farther down her leg. Lieutenant Stovich and Brad Chilcoat were waiting. Chilcoat offered her a Coke. Bobbi drank it in several swallows. "How's Dan?" she asked.

"Probably home in bed by now," Chilcoat answered.

"Which is what I recommend for you," Stovich said, reading Bobbi's condition. "It's been a busy day. Take tonight off."

"What about Big Foot? The stakeout?" Bobbi protested, but her heart wasn't really in it. The thought of going home was an inviting one.

"I've already talked to Randa from Juvenile," Chilcoat said. "She said she'd be glad to fill in for you. You know how hot she's been to work with me."

"Go on," Stovich urged, "get out of here. We'll see you tomorrow morning."

"You want me to drive you?" Chilcoat questioned.

"No thanks." Bobbi forced a weak smile. "I'll be okay."

"Brillon says the shooting looks clean," Stovich said, as Bobbi and Chilcoat moved away. "Too bad you didn't kill him."

Bobbi said nothing.

Driving homeward, Bobbi was negotiating a turn onto the northbound lanes of La Brea Avenue when she glimpsed the car in her rearview mirror. A blue Datsun. It was a half block behind. Was it the same car she'd seen earlier? Logic told her there were many blue Datsuns in L.A., but she raised her foot from the accelerator to allow the 240's speed to drop. The cars behind her quickly closed and passed. The blue Datsun held its distance. Who the hell was this? She was more annoyed than worried, but she understood her feelings from earlier in the day. She was being followed.

Suspicious and determined, Bobbi turned west onto

Olympic Boulevard. She drove several blocks and turned
north onto a smaller residential street. She glanced at the
street sign as she passed it. It read COCHRAN. She pulled
to the curb mid-block and turned her engine off. Her eyes
went to the rearview mirror. A Federal Express van approached and rolled by. Then a station wagon with an
elderly black couple in it, but no blue Datsun. Bobbi
waited. The block, with its duplexes, stucco homes, and
small apartment buildings, was quiet and peaceful. Bobbi
wondered how many rapists lived there. That thought reminded her that just a few blocks farther north was the
stakeout for Dick Fredericks. Yes, this was peaceful, tranquil Los Angeles. The home of Hollywood. The land of
illusions. The cradle of "Leave It to Beaver," "Family
Ties," and *Rambo*. An interesting soup, Bobbi thought.
The same city that produced *Bambi*, also gave the world
*Deep Throat* and a seemingly endless string of bloody *Friday the 13th* sequels. The City of the Angels was in reality
the city of passion. The land of make-believe. Maybe that's
where the Datsun was. Maybe it had followed the yellow
brick road back to Kansas. The thought ended abruptly as
the blue Datsun approached from the north. Confident he
had not been spotted, the driver had driven around the
block for a head-on pass.

Bobbi pretended no interest in the car until it was nearly
to her. Then her eyes went to the front license plate. She
had a felt tip pen in hand from her purse.

"One-Charles-Nelson-Boy, one-three-four," she said
audibly as she jotted the number on the back of a bank
deposit slip.

The driver of the Datsun, a balding, middle-aged man
in aviator sunglasses, never looked at Bobbi as he passed
her, and that was his mistake. Bobbi now had her answer.
She was being followed by a cop. Why? Judge Unger?
Captain Westly? None of it made sense. Then the obvious
explanation cut through her fatigue. Those bastards! It was
because of Cathy Chilcoat's lawsuit. Anger flushed through
Bobbi. She twisted the ignition and the car roared to life.

She jerked the car into gear and the tires screamed as it lunged forward.

Bobbi drove a wild and random course as she raced the 240-Z northbound toward Wilshire Boulevard. When she finally turned onto her block and roared into the subterranean garage, she was certain she wasn't being followed. Let the bastards earn their money.

She felt gritty and soiled and she knew there had to be concrete in her hair, but after letting herself into her condo she collapsed onto the couch in the living room and kicked her shoes off. Ten minutes, she promised herself. Then she'd get up and go bathe. When she awoke more than an hour later her arm was asleep and her neck was stiff. She sat up. The room had been bright with early evening sunshine when she came in but now it was soft with shadows. Bobbi looked to the wall clock. It was seven-forty-five. Pushing off the couch, Bobbi yawned and stretched. She felt hungry but the idea of eating alone was uninviting. She wanted company. She turned on several lights as she walked to the counter to pick up the telephone. It was late but there was still a chance Don might be in his office. She dialed the number. She pictured the corporate law office in Century City vacant as the telephone rang. After the fifth ring Bobbi was about to hang up when Don's familiar voice said, "Law offices."

"Don Roberts, please," Bobbi purred.

"Speaking," he answered, yet to recognize her voice.

"How would you like to get out of that yuppie kingdom and eat your way across a pizza to me?" Bobbi teased.

"Will pepperoni and sausage do?" Don asked.

"Make it a large. I'm starved."

"It'll take me at least an hour and a half. I've got to finish a brief for tomorrow morning."

"That's fine."

"See you then."

"Bye."

Bobbi washed her hair and stood under the hot shower for a long time. Toweling herself dry, she blow-dried her hair, redid her makeup, and put on a green floor-length, low-cut lounge dress. It fit her body like a glove and she wore nothing beneath it except perfume. She didn't stop to consider it, but the emotional highs and lows of the day, combined with the physical danger, had left Bobbi Marshal excited and aroused.

Bobbi met Don at the door. It had been exactly an hour and a half. The pizza box in his hand looked a little silly with his charcoal Brooks Brothers suit. "I think delivery-men usually get a tip, don't they?" Don smiled.

"You can see I don't have any pockets," Bobbi said, gesturing to her wrinkle-free dress. "But wait, maybe this will do." She stepped to Don, slid her arms around his neck, and kissed him. It was a long, passionate embrace, and when she ended it he said, "I may give up law and become a deliveryman."

"Come into my living room, said the spider to the fly." Bobbi smiled, leading him into the room.

They sat at the bar and ate the pizza with Cokes Bobbi had poured. They talked about cars, condos, tax shelters, and a lot of things in between. They talked about every-thing except Bobbi's day. She was deliberately leaving it behind and it felt good.

"I'm planning to sail down to Ensenada this weekend," Don said as they moved from the kitchen bar to a couch in the living room. "Would you like to come along?"

Bobbi knew the significance of his invitation. They had never been anywhere overnight together. "Classmate of mine from the DA's office and a couple from our account-ing firm will be coming, too. I'd like them to meet you," Don added.

Bobbi was flattered. "I'd like that." Her mind was al-ready racing ahead to the reality of the weekend schedule. Three on, nine off. Her fate was in the hands of a sus-pected rapist. She silently damned him, trying to think of a way out of it, but came up short. "But I may have to work."

"That badge must get very difficult to carry some-times," Don suggested.

"Tell me about it," Bobbi agreed.

"Let me know as soon as you can," Don said, running a finger along the smooth line of Bobbi's jaw and down the side of her neck. "Because if you can't go I'll have to invite someone else."

"Don!" Bobbi protested.

"I'm only kidding."

"I'll do my best," Bobbi promised.

"I can only imagine what that's like," Don challenged, searching her eyes.

"Wanna start your weekend a little early?" Bobbi questioned, inching closer to him.

A psychologist could have easily explained Bobbi's compulsion to make love to a man after destroying the career of one man and shooting another, but she didn't stop to consider the psychological motivations behind her desires. They were much more primal than that. Don reached across the short distance separating them to touch Bobbi. It was as if he unleashed her. Bobbi molded herself to him, covering his mouth with hers. The feel of his hair, the taut muscles in his back, the brush of his beard against her cheek and neck, the scent of his skin and shirt fueled Bobbi's desire. She struggled to contain her eagerness as Don warmed to her. He was being cautious and gentle-manly with his approach. His hands were on her back. She wanted them on her breasts She wanted to be naked in his arms. She wanted to be his. Safe and secure. She wanted refuge.

Bobbi responded to Don's advance with subtle, nearly inaudible sighs and the sensual movement of her body against his. She knew it was important that he believe he was seducing her. The heat of Bobbi's passion seemed to find its way into him and he responded.

The now shared passion peeled away the remains of the three-piece suit and the green dress. They were on the carpeted floor in front of the couch. "My God, you're beautiful,'' Don said with a coarse breath as he looked at Bobbi lying nude before him. She answered by raising her open arms to him. Don moved over her, his lips finding hers. Bobbi tensed in anticipation, arching her back. "Oh," she moaned.

Afterward they lay in the embrace for a long while without speaking. Bobbi held him, stroking his back and hair, and when he began to arouse again she whispered, "The bedroom."

The second time seemed to bring even greater relief than the first as they found pleasure with one another. The urgency of their passion subsided and turned to play. They tickled each other, compared toes, bit ears, and had a pillow fight. When it was over they fell exhausted into each other's arms.

Don was lying with his head on Bobbi's bosom when the bedside telephone rang. He had been fondling a breast as desire returned. He paused. "You've been saved by the bell." He smiled.

Bobbi pulled a sheet over her and reached to pick up the receiver. "Hello."

"Bobbi, it's Brad," Chilcoat's familiar voice said in her ear.

"You got Big Foot!" Bobbi blurted as the thought hit her.

"No such luck, babe. I'm sorry to bother you so late but I just wanted to touch base and make sure you're okay."

"I'm fine." Bobbi smiled. "I'm feeling much better."

"You gonna be able to make the stakeout?"

"Sure."

"Good. There's something else you need to know."

"What's that?" Bobbi questioned, almost screaming as Don bit her playfully on the buttock. His head was under the sheets.

"You sure you're all right?" Chilcoat asked.

"Sorry, I had something in my throat." She swung a pillow at the form under the sheets.

"I'm being followed," Chilcoat continued. "I discovered it after the stakeout tonight."

"Who is it?" Bobbi questioned soberly.

"Internal Affairs," Chilcoat answered. "They followed me over to Chinatown tonight. I doubled back and screwed my gun in the guy's ear. He told me everything but what color his wife's panties are."

"What do they want?"

"Who knows? Maybe it's because of Cathy. I don't know. The guy I talked to didn't know. They never tell their surveillance teams why. But if they're following me, guess what?"

"I know," Bobbi answered. "I spotted them coming home tonight. A blue Datsun. I got the license number."

Don, hearing the terse, sober exchange, pulled the sheet from over his head and sat up to listen.

"Good girl," Chilcoat said. "I've trained you well."

"What are we going to do?" Bobbi questioned.

"I don't know," Chilcoat confessed. "Lemme think about it. We'll talk in the morning."

"Brad," Bobbi said, "what did Big Foot do this evening?"

"Nothing. We took him home. The lights went out at ten."

"You still think he's good for it?"

"He's all we've got."

"Good night, Brad."

"See ya, babe."

Bobbi hung up the telephone and looked to Don Roberts.

"Trouble?" he questioned.

Bobbi shook her head. "No. Just business."

## 15

# THE RITUAL

Deputy Chief Warren Hull was in his office on the third floor of Parker Center drinking a cup of coffee and reading the weekly complaint summary. The list seemed to grow longer each week. It was making his stomach knot. The intercom on the commander's desk buzzed to interrupt his reading. He reached and picked up the receiver.

"Yes?"

"Commander, Lieutenant Stovich from Wilshire Detectives is here. He insists on seeing you."

Something had blown at Wilshire Detectives, the commander thought. Aftershocks in the aftermath of such events were not unusual. "All right," Hull said, "send him in."

A moment later the sober Aaron Stovich stepped into the commander's office. Hull didn't get out of his chair. "I've got a busy morning, lieutenant. I'd appreciate it if you were brief."

Stovich walked to the front of the commander's desk. "That was some speech you gave me the other day, commander, when we were talking about Captain Westly. I really believed you. All the concern about the brotherhood of the badge, about trust and truth and justice."

"I don't like your tone, lieutenant," Commander Hull warned, shifting in his chair.

"And I don't like your bullshit," Stovich shot back at him.

"Bullshit!" Hull barked angrily.

"Yes, bullshit," Stovich growled, leaning over the front of the commander's wide desk. "You said when there was a problem in my division you'd come to me. That it was my problem first, and yours only when I couldn't handle it. Isn't that right, commander?"

"What's your point, lieutenant?" Hull said, avoiding a direct answer.

"The point is, you were lying, commander. You knew about the surveillance of Marshal and Chilcoat. You deliberately lied to me in the course of an official investigation."

"I couldn't tell you," Hull defended.

"Couldn't tell me!" Stovich countered. "Tell me what? That you think Chilcoat and Marshal are having an affair? Did you ever stop to think about what you might be doing to this girl? She's already in the pressure cooker with Judge Unger and Captain Westly. And don't forget about the-seventeen-year-old she was working with. Someone broke her neck. And then there's yesterday's shooting. You do hear about these things don't you, commander? Or are you too busy finding the evidence to bag another cop?"

"You're not looking at the big picture, lieutenant."

"Big picture, bullshit," Stovich barked as he pushed away from the desk. "Either you put an immediate end to the chickenshit surveillance of these two detectives or I'll beef you for deliberately lying to a subordinate, and conduct unbecoming an officer."

Hull bolted to his feet. His face was flushed with anger. "Who in the hell do you think you are? You can't threaten me."

"Oh, I know who I am, commander," Stovich answered coolly. "I'm an honest cop trying to do a thankless job and getting shit on from both sides, and you know what? I'm mad as hell and I'm not gonna take it anymore."

"Lieutenant," Hull warned, "if you value your ass at all, you'll leave this office right now."

Stovich held Commander Hull's angry glare. "You've

fucked with the law for so long, you think you are the law. Well, you're not. You're just a cop. At least you were at one time. I'm ready to take a polygraph test. Are you? I'm ready to talk to the *Times* about your tactics of covert harassment. Are you?'' The lieutenant raised a finger to point at Hull. ''Now, you call off the goddamned surveillance or I'll have your ass.''

The commander didn't answer. His face was an angry frustrated mask. A vein throbbed on his forehead. Stovich marched across the office, stepped out, and slammed the door.

Bobbi Marshal was having a difficult time concentrating. Her mind kept drifting back to her night with Don. She was glad the three hours on the point had been quiet. Once again Richard Fredericks had done nothing suspicious as he drove from his home in Burbank to the Image Market Appraisals office. When they turned the stakeout over to the next team, Fredericks was still in the office. ''I hope I never have to testify against Fredericks in court,'' Brad Chilcoat said to Bobbi as they drove to the station.

''Why?''

''Because under oath I'd have to say he's dull.'' Chilcoat smiled. ''Imagine that, a dull rapist. Sounds painful.''

''You're gross.''

''Sorry.''

''Brad, do you think Randa might be interested in working with you on Saturday?'' Bobbi questioned carefully.

Chilcoat glanced at her as he drove. ''Sounds like you're not?''

''It's not that I'm not interested,'' Bobbi defended. ''It's that I have a chance to do something a little more interesting than babysitting a rapist.''

''Sounds like romance.'' Chilcoat smiled. ''Going sailing with Mr. Roberts again?''

''On a forty-two footer to Ensenada.'' Bobbi smiled.

''Okay,'' Chilcoat said. ''You want me to ask Randa?''

"Would you?"

"You'll owe me."

"Don't I always?"


"Jesus," Chilcoat said, as they walked into the detective squad room, "Shea's here."

"Isn't he supposed to be off IOD?" Bobbi questioned as they walked to the Homicide table.

"What the hell are you doing here?" Chilcoat said as they reached the desk where the broad-shouldered detective sat. His left arm was hanging in a sling. He ignored Chilcoat's question and looked at Bobbi. "Hi." He smiled. "You didn't stick around for me to say thanks yesterday."

"I wanted to," Bobbi answered, sitting down across from him. "But they wouldn't let me. How are you feeling?"

"Little stiff. He broke my collarbone. I'm wearing my first bra under all this." Shea smiled. "I'm glad you were there, Bobbi. You saved my life. It was a damned good piece of police work."

"If it wasn't for your thoughtfulness I wouldn't have been there."

"Trust me, not all my invitations turn into shootings," Shea assured her.

"Should be a rule," Chilcoat suggested. "No shooting on a first date."

"Shooting team told me they think you showed a lot of courage and compassion."

"I'm glad to hear that. They had me worried."

"They worry everybody. It's their job. I think you should be recommended for the Medal of Valor."

Chilcoat, who was standing and listening to the exchange, looked at Cliff Weldon, who sat at Shea's side. "Does all this mean they're going steady?"

"It means I owe her a dinner," Shea answered. "That is, if you don't mind cutting my steak for me?" he added, returning his look to Bobbi.

"I wouldn't mind at all," Bobbi assured him with a smile. She was surprised at the warmth Shea was showing.

"Saturday night?" he questioned.

"I'd love too, but I've already made plans."

"Some other time then?"

"Of course."

"Listen," Chilcoat interrupted, "I'd really like to stay for the second half of this meeting of the mutual admiration society, but I've got to see a girl about a stakeout."

"I'll catch up," Bobbi said to her partner.

"I doubt that, but I'll be in the Juvenile office anyway." He moved away.

Bobbi returned her attention to Dan Shea. "Shouldn't you be at home or someplace, resting?"

"It's not too bad."

"Have you had a chance to talk with Phillips?" Bobbi questioned.

Shea nodded. "We spent a couple hours with him this morning. Thanks to you he can still talk. Damned good shooting. Most cops would have emptied their gun into his pump."

"Thank you." Bobbi smiled. The compliment did much to restore her confidence. "I was worried."


The ritual had started earlier in the day just after his wife left for work. Dressed in jockey shorts, he sat down at his desk in the den and carefully drew a red circle around the date on the calendar. Just the thought of what lay ahead aroused him. During the drive into Los Angeles he had taken the stolen panties from beneath the seat of the car and inhaled his breath through them. A passing female motorist gave him a distasteful look.

Now at his desk in the office, with most of the other appraisers in the field, he took out the stolen picture of Bobbi Marshal and laid it in the open file in front of him. He studied the color Polaroid and savored the sense of anticipation that surged through him. The possibility that the police might, at that very moment, be outside waiting, watching, only added to his excitement. He moved a hand and ran a fingertip over the glossy surface of the picture as if he could touch her flesh. Labored breath rushed through his flared nostrils. She was reclining on her elbows on a beach towel. The string bikini covered little. The pageboy cut framed her face in a frozen, provocative smile. Soft shoulders gave way to melonlike breasts pulling the cups of her bikini tight. A soft crease ran horizontally across the top of her flat stomach, punctuated with a dime-sized navel. Her legs were long and tanned, and the swell of her calves excited him. He liked running his hands over their legs. He wet his lips and picked the picture up. Using a pair of scissors from the desk, he held the photo over the trash can and carefully cut it into indistinguishable slivers. He expected them to come for him after he raped her. There would be nothing for them to find. The calendar and the stolen undergarments were already in the trash. The picture of her was the last thing to go. They could search now. He'd laugh at them. He'd get away with it. He already had. He glanced at his watch. It was almost noon. In less than twelve hours he'd have her. He reached under the desk and squeezed his throbbing erection. He hoped he could wait that long.

Bobbi was going through a stack of crime reports at her desk when Brad Chilcoat returned from the Juvenile office. "Sorry," Chilcoat said, sitting down across from her. "Randa can't do it."

"Damn," Bobbi complained, feeling the weekend trip with Don slipping away.

Chilcoat could see the disappointment in her face. "This one meant a lot to you, huh?"

"Yeah, it was important," Bobbi admitted.

"Well, the day's not over," Chilcoat said to encourage her. "Let me ask around."

"I appreciate it."

"Chilcoat," the squadroom PA speaker called. "Line two-six."

Chilcoat punched a blinking light on the console and picked up the telephone. "This is Sergeant Chilcoat."

"Brad," the familiar voice of his wife said on the other end of the line, "it's me."

"Cathy!?" Chilcoat questioned with a look of surprise.

Bobbi pushed away from the desk. Chilcoat knew she was deliberately offering him privacy.

"How are you?" Cathy Chilcoat said in her husband's ear.

"Me? . . . Fine," Chilcoat answered awkwardly. "How about you?" He didn't know what else to say.

"Well, that's why I'm calling, actually," Cathy answered. "My mom and dad are up in Santa Barbara visiting Ray and Nancy and my sister is going to Las Vegas for the weekend."

"Yeah," Chilcoat said carefully, not knowing what to expect. He wasn't sure he really knew this woman as well as he once thought and he was being wary.

"And Judy has the flu. I wouldn't ask this if I didn't have to, Brad."

"Ask what?"

"I just got back from the doctor's. I pinched a nerve in my neck at jazzercize, or something. I don't know, but it's killing me. I can hardly walk. The doctor gave me a prescription and told me to go to bed."

She paused, waiting for her husband to say something. When he didn't, she went on.

"I need help with the girls, Brad. I know it's not your weekend, but could you . . ." Her voice fell away in a plea.

"Weekend?" Chilcoat said sarcastically. "Is that what you call that four-hour visit you allowed me last time?"

"Brad, I didn't call to fight with you. I can't. If you don't want to help me, just say so. I thought maybe you'd want to spend some time with the girls."

"You want me to take them over to my place?"

"Well, they were planning on having some friends over for a pajama party tonight. Could you come here?"

"I work 'til ten."

"I'm sure they'll be up much later than that."

"Okay," Chilcoat agreed.

"I appreciate it," Cathy said in his ear. "And . . ." She hesitated, then went on. "Could we keep this between you and me?"

"Oh, of course," Chilcoat replied. "Wouldn't want anyone to know I'm spending the night with my wife and kids."

Cathy hung up abruptly. Chilcoat replaced the telephone on the console. Bobbi returned to the desk and sat down. "Everything okay?"

Chilcoat gave her a sober look. "Sure."

The teletype that made it official was posted on the bulletin board in the Wilshire Division squad room during the lunch hour. Gilmore, a balding Robbery detective, was the first to spot it. "Jesus Christ," Gilmore blurted, "he's coming here."

"Don't believe it," a passing detective quipped. "They've been saying that for years."

"No, no," Gilmore said. "I mean Ballbusting Stone. They've made him our new captain."

Others were quick to gather around. "It's true. Holy shit!"

072888
APS OOL 400 500 600
LAPD AREA BROADCAST
1200 HRS
WIL/D LOS ANGELES POLICE DEPARTMENT

SPECIAL TRANSFER/EFFECTIVE IMMEDI-
    ATELY
STONE, JOHN W., CAPTAIN #13993
IS APPOINTED COMMANDER OF WILSHIRE DI-
    VISION DETECTIVES.

ATTN: ALL CONCERNED PERSONNEL
RE: OFFICE OF THE CHIEF OF POLICE
    JAMES PECK #4464
    CHIEF OF POLICE, LOS ANGELES

John Stone had been captain of the LAPD's Metro Division, a mobile strike force that was used strategically in the city's hot spots. Stone had a fierce reputation as a hardline disciplinarian, a trait required of any captain charged with managing Metro Division. It was obvious to the men staring at the announcement that the powers that governed the department from downtown Parker Center thought Wilshire Detectives needed a firm hand.

Captain Stone arrived shortly after the teletype. He took over George Westly's vacated office and summoned the three lieutenants assigned to the division's Detective Bureau. Stone was a sober man in his mid-fifties. He had dark curly hair and dark eyes. Aaron Stovich thought they looked cold. Lieutenant Stovich was with Lieutenants Mitchell and Radcliff when they sat down in the captain's office.

Stone closed his office door and sat down in the chair behind the desk. Stone's dark eyes searched the sober faces of the three lieutenants. They were not young men, and collectively they represented nearly seventy-five years of police experience.

"This office has been cleaned out," Stone began. "Everything that was George Westly's is gone. Now I'm going to do the same thing to the Detective Bureau."

The three lieutenants exchanged glances and shifted in their chairs.

"Wilshire Detectives is dirty," Stone continued. "Everyone knows Captain Westly was corrupt, so they think everyone that works here must be the same."

"That's bullshit," Lieutenant Mitchell protested sharply.

"It's not bullshit, lieutenant, it's reality. It's called 'reputation' and right now this division's reputation is in the sewer. If you don't agree I'll help you find a new job."

"You want a Detective Bureau full of yes men, is that it?" Mitchell challenged.

"You want me to ask you how to do it, lieutenant?" Stone countered with an icy stare. "You three helped George Westly run this division, didn't you? I don't want your advice. I want your cooperation. And your support. If you can't give it to me then get out now, or I'll throw you out later."

Lieutenant Mitchell looked to Stovich and Radcliff. Mitchell pushed to his feet. "Count me out," he said.

"Me, too," Radcliff said, following Mitchell's lead. They both looked to Stovich. He returned their look. It was devoid of any emotion.

"Aaron?" Mitchell questioned.

Stovich shook his head. "I've got work to finish here, Bill. Good luck to you."

"Good luck to me?" Mitchell huffed. "I think you're the one that's going to need it."

"Shut the door on your way out," Captain Stone suggested.

The two lieutenants stepped out of the office. Neither looked at their new commander, and Mitchell, the last out, deliberately left the door standing ajar.

Captain Stone pushed out of his chair and moved to close the door. "I'd like you to get me the files on all the current investigations, lieutenant, as well as the progress reports for the past six weeks. I'll spend the weekend reading. I'd like to meet again on Monday morning."

"Yes, sir," Stovich said, lifting himself out of his chair.

"Do you have any recommendations for replacements?" Stone questioned with a look at the office door.

"No, sir," Stovich answered.

"All right," Stone said, dismissing him. "I'd appreciate those reports as soon as possible."

Stovich moved for the door.

"Lieutenant," Stone said, pushing to his feet. "I saw

you coming out of IA this morning down at the Parker Center.''

Stovich paused at the door.

''Anything I should know about?'' Stone questioned.

''No, sir. Nothing that concerns you.''

# 16

# TOUCH OF FIRE

Bobbi was thinking about dousing the house with kerosene and throwing a match to it. In her mind it would be justified. Richard Fredericks had shattered the lives of nearly twenty women. He had inflicted pain that would never stop, wounds that would never heal, and it had cost him nothing. Now the bastard had cost Bobbi her weekend trip to Ensenada with Don Roberts. She and Chilcoat had spent the afternoon looking for someone willing to work in Bobbi's place. There were no takers. Don had called late in the afternoon. Bobbi was glad she had been away from her desk. She wasn't eager to tell him she couldn't go. She planned on calling him after they got off the stakeout at ten. By then he'd probably guess the answer and that would make the call easier.

Fredericks's car was sitting in the driveway of his home. It had been there when Bobbi and Chilcoat took the point at seven p.m. Collectively the stakeout team expected this to be the day. Eleven of Fredericks's rapes had been on Friday nights. But he was giving no sign that this Friday night was going to be anything other than dull. No one had yet said it, but a creeping doubt was beginning to set in. What if it wasn't him?

When Clair Fredericks failed to come home, the backup team was dispatched to check the Glendale Community Hospital where she worked. Her car was in the parking lot and she was still on duty.

"You know," Chilcoat said from the passenger's side

of the car where he sat slumped watching the Fredericks house, "if he doesn't go out tonight with his old lady still at work, people are going to say we're barking up the wrong rapist."

"It's got to be him," Bobbi argued, staring across the dark street at an illuminated window. "I can feel it."

"Last I heard there hadn't been any rapists convicted on feelings," Chilcoat answered.

"He'll do it," Bobbi said. "I just know it."

The two detectives had no way of knowing, but Richard Fredericks had left his home on Lakespur Drive shortly before seven p.m. Climbing over a back fence, he cut through a neighbor's back yard to the sidewalk on the adjoining block and casually walked away.

It was only nine blocks to the Burbank Airport. There Fredericks picked up the rental car he had reserved earlier in the day and drove off into the night.

At ten o'clock Bobbi and Chilcoat yielded the point to the next team. "Nothing is stirring," Chilcoat said into the portable radio. "Not even a mouse."

Bobbi drove the six blocks to the service station where Chilcoat had parked his jeep. When she swung in beside it and stopped, Chilcoat looked at her.

"See you in the morning."

"I can hardly wait," Bobbi answered.

Chilcoat opened his door to climb out. "Sorry Saturday didn't work out for you."

"It's like my philosophy teacher used to say," Bobbi answered sarcastically. "Life's a bitch, then you die."

"He must have been a retired policeman," Chilcoat said, as he climbed from the car. "Good night."

Bobbi's 240-Z growled and roared off into the night. The quiet hum of the car's engine, the warm leathery interior, and the stress of the past two days combined to engulf Bobbi in a cloud of fatigue. She literally ached for a day off. She could almost feel the warm sun on her skin as she stretched out on the hull of Don's boat. "Damn," she complained, knowing it would not be. She was now only seven hours from getting out of bed and returning for another three hours on the point. A call to Don, sorry, I can't go, and then into bed. Maybe a bath? No, a shower in the morning would do. She tried to remember how long she'd slept the night before. Two hours at the most. Don hadn't left until three. She was up again at five and was on the point at seven. It had been worth losing sleep over. She wondered if she and Don were in love. Time would tell. Don't rush, she cautioned. Don't hurry.

She wondered if Don really thought he had seduced her. The thought provoked a smile. It didn't matter. It wasn't likely Don Roberts was the kind of man who kept score. The Ensenada trip would have been so much fun. Dammit. She wondered if it was unladylike to want sex. She supposed not. No more unladylike than carrying a gun. Maybe, Bobbi thought, that was the disappointment. It wasn't that she was missing the boat trip. She was missing Don. She hoped the lovemaking had been as exciting for him as it was for her.

Finally Bobbi was turning west on Lindenhurst from Fairfax Avenue, where Stonehaven Towers stood. She stopped at the drive-up key lock for the subterranean garage and inserted her key. The iron gate across the entrance rattled and squeaked as it rolled aside. Bobbi pushed the car in gear and drove down into the gray artificial light of the wide garage. A set of headlamps appeared in her rearview mirror. A second car had driven in before the gate closed behind her. Bobbi watched the lights in the mirror as she drove across the garage toward her assigned space. The headlights swung to the left and disappeared down a row of parked cars. Bobbi wondered if it was Internal Affairs. No, she had Lieutenant Stovich's word that the surveillance had ended. Who then? Was it another tenant? Bobbi often followed other cars through the gate. Or were they the headlights of a clever burglar? Two condos had been hit in the past three months. She reached her space and pulled into it. Switching off the engine, she picked up her purse and climbed out. After locking her car Bobbi paused to listen. The cooling of the Datsun's engine was the only sound. The other car seemed to have vanished. Bobbi shouldered her purse and headed for the elevator.

Bobbi inserted her key into the elevator, twisted it, and waited. The movement behind her brought a sharp reaction as she whirled to face the man.

"Sorry," the man said, offering a friendly smile. "I didn't mean to frighten you." He was Bobbi's age and she had seen him in the building before. He drove a Porsche and lived on the eighth floor, she thought. She'd also seen him once by the pool.

"It's okay," Bobbi granted. "It's been one of those days."

The elevator arrived and they stepped inside. It was a small car, and Bobbi noticed that the man made no effort to divide the space fifty-fifty. He stood close as the car began its slow climb. Bobbi turned a shoulder to him and watched the floor numbers as they flashed on and off.

"My name's Jim," he said with Tic Tac breath. "The night's still young. Could I interest you in coming up for a neighborly drink?"

Bobbi offered a sober glance. "Like I said, Jim. It's been one of those days."

"I've got a little something upstairs that could put a spring in your step and a gleam in your eye," he said, leaning closer.

Bobbi took in a breath and looked at him. "What kind of business are you in?"

Jim shrugged. "Little of this, little of that. You know."

"I'm a cop," Bobbi announced. She wasn't in the mood for his John Travolta hustle. "You still wanna offer me a little something?"

Jim moved a step away from her. His aura of confidence slipped some. He forced a nervous grin. "I knew you were a cop. I was just putting you on."

The elevator chimed and stopped at the sixth floor.

Bobbi glanced at him as she stepped off. "Okay," she bluffed. "Give me a chance to freshen up and I'll be up. Say ten minutes?"

Jim looked alarmed. "Ah, yeah, sure. But make it a half hour, would you? I got a couple important calls to make."

The elevator doors closed and Jim was gone. Bobbi smiled as she moved down the carpeted hallway. Jim's bathroom toilet was about to get an overdose.

There were no lights on in the living room when Bobbi opened the door but the panorama of the city at night filled the room with a welcoming glow. She closed and locked the door behind her before she turned on the lamp at the end of the couch.

Bobbi stepped out of her shoes and slipped her jacket off. Tossing it to the couch, she pulled her blouse from the top of her skirt and unbuttoned it. Then reaching to the middle of her back, she unhooked her bra. She sighed with relief. She hated bras.

Moving down the dim hallway to the bedroom, Bobbi let the blouse slide off her shoulders into her hands. Then she slipped the bra off. The air was cool on her skin.

Stepping into the darkness of the bedroom, she reached for the light switch. Without a sound the man lunged from behind before her hand found the switch. Bobbi went stiff with an electric jolt of fear. A musty, foul-tasting glove covered her mouth and nose. A powerful arm went around her midsection, pinning her arms to her side. An instinctive scream rose in her throat, but it was little more than a muffled whimper against the glove.

The academy drills on attacks from behind were lost in her onrushing panic. Bobbi tried to find her footing and resist as she was pushed forward, but the man was big and powerful. He lifted her and they fell together onto the bed.

The gloved hand slid from Bobbi's mouth to the back of her head. The fingers spread and pushed down hard. The springs in the mattress groaned. Bobbi's lungs felt frozen with pain as they screamed for oxygen. The dry bedspread, pressing into her face, yielded nothing. The weight atop her was crushing and powerful. She twisted, pulled and kicked, but it was useless. She was in a death grip. The muscles and tendons in her neck were aflame with pain as she pushed up against the heavy gloved hand. The buzzing started first in her ears, but it spread quickly and cut deep into her brain like a sharp knife until it reached a deafening black roar. She was falling, falling. Just before she lost consciousness she remembered Lisa Cartwright's disheveled bed. Then there was no more.

He held her head in the spread even after she went limp. He knew she could be dangerous. None of the others had ever fought so hard. Finally he released her, watching for a reaction. There was none. He turned her head to the side. The tip of her tongue was sticking through her teeth. It was covered with blood and saliva. He pushed his weight off her and rolled her over. It was then he saw she was nude to the waist. Pulling off a glove, he reached and cupped her right breast in his hand. It was cool and supple. Bobbi moaned and a muscle spasm made her leg jump. The man jerked his hand from her breast and reached for the collection of panty hose and nylons he had readied at the foot of the bed.

Rolling Bobbi onto her stomach, he grabbed her limp wrists and bound them together behind her back. She was beginning to stir. Using another nylon, he tied a gag tight around her mouth. Bobbi coughed and made a gagging sound. Blood spilled from the corner of her mouth. He worked faster. Shaking a pillow out of its case, he tore the cloth into a strip and wrapped it around her head to cover her eyes. This face he didn't want covered. Then he pulled her to the edge of the bed and sat her up. Bobbi's head fell from one side to the other. She was sucking breath in through the wet gag across her mouth.

"Hello, Bobbi." Fredericks smiled. "You've been looking for me, haven't you? Well, guess who's here, Bobbi, and guess who's gonna get what she deserves."

He stood in front of her, looking down at her breasts. "You got great tits." He reached out and took one in his hand. The moment his hand touched her she kicked.

Blindfolded, she couldn't see and her bare foot missed its intended mark, brushing the outside of his left leg. Fredericks knew what the intent was. He drew back a fist and struck her hard in the stomach. Bobbi gasped and bent forward.

"Bad girl," Fredericks warned. "Don't do that." He slapped her hard along the side of the head and she fell to the floor at his feet. "Or I'll have to hurt you." He kicked her hard in the kidney with the toe of his shoe. Bobbi's body jerked in pain. "You understand me?"

Reaching down and grabbing Bobbi by the arm, he jerked her to her feet. She was weak, barely able to stand. Her breasts heaved and fell as breath hissed through the nylon gag. He took her by the neck just below the jaw and squeezed. Bobbi inched onto her toes as he lifted. "You try anything else, Bobbi," he warned, "I'll kill you."

He released her neck and moved his hands to her waistline. Unbuttoning her skirt he ran the zipper down. It fell away. "Beautiful," he said coarsely as he touched her nylon-covered hips. Then hooking a finger under each side of her panty hose he pulled them down.

"Lie down," he said softly, guiding her onto her back on the bed. There he rolled the panty hose slowly down each leg and pulled them away. Bobby lay naked and helpless before him. He leaned over her and planted a kiss softly in her pubic hair. Bobbi's legs were trembling.

Standing up, Fredericks pushed off his shoes and unbuckled his pants. They fell to the floor and he stepped out of them. He pushed his shorts down and kicked them away. Wearing a blue Christian Dior short-sleeved shirt and black socks, he climbed onto the bed, ready to mount her.

Bobbi's body was racked with pain. Her ear was aflame from the slap, and the kick in her side left her nauseated

and gagging as her stomach convulsed. The nylon gag tore
at her cheeks. She knew she was going to die. Oh, God,
help me, she screamed silently as she felt the bed move.
Then she felt the coarse hair of his legs against hers. He
was climbing atop her. Oh, God, please! His weight settled on her. His erection probed between her legs. Oh,
no! She tensed, trembled, gagged. The hair on his chest
scratched at her shoulders. She balled her hands as his soft
stomach covered her. He leaned close and licked at her
ear. His tongue was rough and wet, his breath foul. The
scent of his heavy aftershave and sweat added to the nausea. She felt him reach down to guide his erection to her.
"You're gonna love this," he said.

The telephone rang. Bobbi kicked and cried through the
gag. Oh, God, send someone. Help me. Help me! He let
his weight settle on her to hold her.

"Be still," he warned. "They're not coming, Bobbi.
No one's coming. I own you."

Bobbi gasped for breath. His weight and the gag were
suffocating her. The telephone continued to ring.

"You want me to tell them you're tied up?" He laughed
in her ear.

Bobbi felt the fight drain from her. It was as if she were
being pulled from her own body. She could feel him lowering himself to her. No, she gagged in a final futile protest, and then he was in her. "Oh, God, no."

He gave an animal cry as his body found hers.

Nine miles to the west, in slip four-thirty-six in Marina
del Rey Don Roberts stood in the main cabin of the forty-
two-foot *Compass Rose* with telephone in hand. He listened to the ring at the other end of the line. Four, five
times. Finally he gave up. "Dammit," he muttered. It
seemed Bobbi Marshal had made her decision. She loved
the police department more than anything, or anyone, else.
Don was disappointed. It was easy to imagine a life with
Bobbi Marshal. He had begun to think of them that way.
He thought she had, too. She was more independent than

he thought, maybe more than he wanted. That was part of her attraction. Early on it seemed manageable. Now he wasn't so sure. Better to find out now than later, he told himself, but it did little to ease his pain.

Brad Chilcoat arrived at the home of his estranged wife at ten-forty-five. After Bobbi dropped him off he drove first to his apartment in Echo Park where he showered and shaved.

When he arrived at his home twenty-five minutes later, he was wearing a shirt Cathy had bought him on their last anniversary, gray slacks, and a heavy splash of Chaps aftershave.

Cathy was in the comfortable family room when Brad let himself in with his key. The tape player was on with Cathy's favorite Lionel Richie album, and the lighting was soft. Cathy's hair was carefully combed and her makeup was fresh. She was wearing a belted white terrycloth robe.

"I thought I'd find you in bed," he said, surprised but not disappointed to find she was up.

"I almost called you," Cathy answered, sitting down on the couch where Chilcoat watched all his football games. He caught a quick glimpse of bare thigh as she crossed her legs beneath her.

"I'm feeling much better. I went out and sat in the Jacuzzi for a while. It really helped."

Chilcoat's already anxious heart raced even faster; he was certain that she was nude under the robe. This woman whom he had so quickly and eagerly betrayed now looked and smelled exciting. Sitting down on the end of the couch away from her, Chilcoat worried about being rejected.

"You have to be careful with these things," he said. "You overdo it and you'll wind up in a brace."

"I'll be careful," Cathy assured him with a fleeting smile. "Would you like something to drink?"

Chilcoat thanked the gods. It seemed he wasn't going to be dispatched into the night. "Yeah. That would be nice. It's been a long night."

"Would you mind fixing it yourself?"

He couldn't believe it, it was all falling into place. "Not at all," he said, pushing from the couch to cross to the wet bar. "Can I fix you one?"

"No, I shouldn't. Liquor and the prescription I'm taking might make me crazy."

"Just a small one," he urged. "It's a proven fact that alcohol relaxes muscles."

"All right. A small one."

Chilcoat stepped behind the bar and poured himself a double shot of brandy. He sipped it and then poured vodka and tonic into a second glass. "Girls upstairs?"

"Uh huh. Along with four others. They're calling every radio station in the Valley to make play requests."

"Here we go," he said, offering the drink to Cathy. He sat down on the couch again.

"Rather awkward to offer a toast in this situation, isn't it?" Cathy said, looking at her drink.

"Doesn't say anywhere we can't be friends," Chilcoat countered, extending his glass toward hers.

"I'll drink to that," Cathy agreed. As she reached to click her glass against his the neck of her robe parted to expose the shadow of her cleavage.

"To friendship," Chilcoat said and took a heavy drink. Cathy followed his lead.

"Oh, it's delicious." Cathy smiled. "I haven't had a drink in . . . well, it's been a long time. It tastes really good."

Chilcoat put his arm up on the back of the couch. It brought his hand close to her shoulder. Cathy didn't seem to notice. She took another swallow of her drink. "It was really nice of you to come over tonight," she said. "I know you must have had plans." She raised her arm and laid it atop Chilcoat's on the back of the couch. She touched his arm but he felt it immediately between his legs. The gap in her robe grew even wider. Chilcoat took another heavy drink from his glass.

"Tell me about work," Cathy said, squeezing his arm.

She seemed to be leaning closer. He wondered if he were imagining it. No, the arm on his was real and it was hot through the sleeve of his shirt. Cathy downed the remainder of her drink, throwing her head back as she drank.

"Ah, well, we're working on this . . . rape case," Chilcoat said awkwardly.

"Remember when we used to play rape?" Cathy giggled, reaching to set her empty glass on the cocktail table that sat in front of the couch. The part in her robe swept over the swell of her left breast. "And you'd tie me up?"

"That was before I became a policeman," Chilcoat reminded her.

"Right." Cathy smiled seductively. "You probably wouldn't enjoy tying me up naked anymore, would you?"

Chilcoat gulped down the remaining liquor in his glass and set it on the table. "Cathy," he said with a look at her, but she cut him short by reaching behind his neck and pulling his mouth to hers. She kissed him hungrily. Her hands raked his hair and back as her tongue searched his mouth. She moved close and molded herself to him. She was warm and ripe with the clean scent of chlorine from the Jacuzzi. Chilcoat responded eagerly. His hand massaged her leg through the terrycloth and then moved to find the part in the robe. Cathy sighed in his mouth as his hand found the inside of her thigh. He moved his kisses from her mouth down her neck, and into the open part in the robe between her breasts. Cathy moaned with passion as she leaned back on the couch to surrender. Chilcoat's mouth found a nipple and drew the breast into his mouth.

The family room's overhead light flashed on bright and brought a sharp reaction from both Cathy and Chilcoat as they bolted upright, straightening hair and clothing in the process.

"Daddy!" the two surprised twins said in unison from the mouth of the room, where they stood staring with four other little girls in pajamas.

"Hi, girls." Chilcoat smiled through clenched teeth.

"Mom," one of the twins said, "we wanna watch *Star Trek*. It's on HBO at eleven-thirty."

"Sure, honey," Cathy answered, pushing to her feet and adjusting the belt of her terrycloth robe. "Your dad was just leaving."

The sullen Chilcoat kissed his daughters as they took over the family room with the four other screeching girls. Cathy had already left the room with the empty drink glasses. Chilcoat gave the couch a final disappointed look and walked from the room.

The now sober Cathy walked with Chilcoat to the front door. She opened it and stepped outside. Chilcoat moved by her. Cathy glanced toward the family room and then pulled the door shut before she spoke to him. Her face was devoid of emotion. "I owe you an apology. I'm sorry. I don't know what came over me."

"I'm sorry, too, but for a different reason."

"I hope you don't think this has changed anything?"

Chilcoat studied Cathy's sober expression for a moment before he answered. "Like the song says, 'A kiss is just a kiss.' Good night, Cathy." He stepped to her and kissed her gently on the mouth. He intended it to be brief. Cathy changed that. She snaked her arms around his neck and held him. She lifted one of her legs and rubbed him with a knee.

They remained locked in their passionate embrace as Chilcoat guided them to the side garage door. He opened it and they moved into the darkness. He closed and locked the door behind them. When the lock clicked, Cathy pushed away from him and disappeared in the heavy shadows. Chilcoat's eyes and outstretched arms searched the darkness. All he could see was the faint outline of Cathy's BMW. "Cathy," he said to the darkness, and then she was in his arms. His hands found her. She was nude. "Oh," he moaned in the darkness.

After raping Bobbi once Dick Fredericks turned her onto her stomach and washed her with a warm washcloth. The agony became a blur of unending pain to Bobbi. She hung on the ragged edge of consciousness until he moved away from her. Was he gone? Oh, God, make him go. Let it end. Please, God, please. But then he was back putting something warm and wet between her legs. Bobbi wept.

Fredericks mounted her again and rode her doggie style until he was hard again. It didn't take long. He even thought she responded in that position, meeting his heavy thrusts. Yes, he was sure of it. She was enjoying it. They all did. He was sweating and breathing hard when he finished the second time. He gave a final thrust, grunted, and rolled aside.

The girl was breathing hard, too. Fredericks knew that was a good sign. He listened to Bobbi's raspy, gagged breath for a moment as he lay at her side. "You like that, don't you, baby? You want more?" He pushed off the bed and left the room.

Bobbi held her breath and prayed. She even tried to will him gone. She knew she couldn't tolerate more. She knew death was near. Oh, God, please, but then she heard him moving on the carpet. He was back.

He returned carrying Bobbi's purse. He turned on a small bedside lamp and sat down on the bed beside the bound and nude Bobbi. He rummaged in the purse. "Here it is." He smiled, lifting out the blue steel pistol. "Is this what you want, honey? A nice hard one."

Fredericks shifted on the bed and pulled Bobbi's legs apart. His breathing was rushed and shallow. He reached and ran the gun up along the inside of Bobbi's thigh.

Bobbi tensed when the barrel of the gun touched her. She knew instantly what is was. "No, oh, please, no," she moaned. "Oh, God, no."

"This is what you've always wanted, isn't it?" Fredericks pushed the barrel of the gun into her roughly. Bobbi arched her back and groaned. "I knew you'd love it," Fredericks snarled as he began to work the gun slowly back and forth.

# 17

# THE EYES OF A VICTIM

The man had left the room and returned several times before so Bobbi lay unmoving for a long time, but now the pain was becoming unbearable. It was as if she'd been violated by a white-hot iron. The pain combined with the growing numbness in her bound wrists forced her to move. Bobbi took a deep breath and rolled toward the edge of the bed. The sheet beneath her was wet and sticky. She searched with a foot and found the edge. She swung her feet to the floor and sat up. Immediately a roaring buzz filled her ears. Salty saliva flowed in her mouth and spilled out around the gag. Her head swam in a sea of black nausea. She gagged as her stomach retched. She nearly passed out as she awaited another stinging blow to the side of her head but it didn't come.

Bobbi sucked in slow, deliberate breaths to fight the panic that was swelling in her. She could feel something warm running down the inside of her upper thighs. It was a nightmare filled with indescribable pain and horror and she knew she'd never awake from it. He was gone but the oppressive vise of fear still held her in a breath-robbing icy grip. She had to get loose. She jerked and pulled on the tight loops of nylon that held her wrists, ignoring the pain. Slowly the stubborn material stretched and yielded. A wrist slipped free and Bobbi nearly fell from the bed. She sobbed as she pushed the blindfold up over her forehead. She squinted in the light from the small bedside lamp. The digital alarm clock read three-fifty a.m. She looked down between her legs. She was sitting in a pool of blood. Bobbi grimaced and closed her eyes. Her stomach convulsed and the bitter bile rose up into her throat. She pulled at the gag. It was too tight. She couldn't get it loose. She pushed to her feet and moved for the bathroom. She took several steps before she staggered and nearly fell. Her legs were shaking and weak. Resting a shoulder on the wall, she followed it to the bathroom. There, without turning on the light, she dug in a drawer for a pair of scissors. Finding them, she pushed the blade under the nylon gag and cut. It took several attempts but the gag finally fell away.

Bobbi rested her head on the cool countertop for a moment, sucking in breath. Then she raised her head and turned on the bathroom light. She stared in shock and disbelief at the image of the woman in the mirror. Her hair was disheveled and her eyes were two bloodshot red pools. Her lips were cracked and caked with dried blood. Her wrists were ringed with welts from the nylon restraints. Blue and purple bruises were forming where his fingers had squeezed her breasts, and the insides of her thighs were crimson with a combination of blood and body fluids. Bobbi gasped and turned away.

It was a few minutes after five a.m. when Brad Chilcoat stepped out of his estranged wife's home in Van Nuys. The deep purple of the night was beginning to yield to a softer blue in the east. A few unseen sparrows were already awake and chirping. The morning air was crisp and refreshing as he walked to his jeep in the driveway. Cathy was still sleeping when he left her side. They had moved from the garage to the bedroom after the girls retreated upstairs. There was little talk but it hadn't diminished their passion. Maybe the idea of words frightened them both. He knew things weren't like they used to be. They never would be. The hunger they shared had been more than physical. The passion that flowed was much more. It was the soul-deep, heartfelt emotion that only came with a shared and mature love. Although he'd slept little he felt better than he had in weeks.

Yesterday he was a man with serious problems and no hope. Now, as the new day dawned, he was still a man with serious problems, but now there was hope. Their problems hadn't disappeared simply because they made love. It would take effort, understanding, and change to put Humpty Dumpty back together but Brad Chilcoat knew that's what he wanted. Along with that came the realization that much of the problem was his and he would have to change. He hoped he could. He hoped Cathy would be willing to help.

Nine miles to the east, Detectives Webster and Lasski from Rampart Division sat in a nondescript van on the point watching the dark homes on Lakespur Drive. The Fredericks house was dark and quiet, as it had been when the two detectives came on duty an hour earlier. Two dew-covered automobiles sat parked in the driveway. "You see 'Miami Vice' last night?" Lasski asked his partner as he poured coffee from a thermos.

"Naw, my wife's sister came over. Brought her two pain-in-the-ass kids. One of the little bastards dropped jelly beans in my aquarium."

"Is that the sister that got the divorce?"

"Yeah, married a doctor. Six years later he runs off with a male nurse."

"You can't figure sex."

"Who wants to?"

"Look at Fredericks over there. Nice house. Nice neighborhood. Two cars. Good job. Wife's a nurse and he's a part-time rapist. You just can't figure it."

"Avoid a career in medicine, I'd say," Webster offered sarcastically.

The two detectives were not the only ones awake on Lakespur Drive. Clair Fredericks, her face turned away from the sleeping hulk of her husband, was staring into the darkness. She had found his note on the kitchen table when she came home at eleven.

Clair:
   I went bowling with Dave. Don't wait up.
                       Dick

Dick's car was in the driveway. Would he dare have a woman pick him up at home? She checked the hall closet. His bowling ball and shoes were gone. She bathed and went to bed. It wasn't until he climbed into bed at nearly four-thirty that she knew he was lying. He spent a long time in the bathroom with water running before he turned out the lights and eased himself into bed, hoping she was still asleep. Clair's nose recognized the odor of sweat. Not a light sweat from bowling but a heavy, salty sweat from exertion. It was mixed with the scent of perfume. Clair knew it wasn't hers. And there was another odor. It took a while but finally she recognized it. It was the light acid scent of sex. It wasn't long before the hulk beside her was snoring lightly. Clair knew the time had come. She would no longer be able to ignore it. Her husband was an unfaithful liar. She hated the idea of yet another divorce, but she also hated herself for lying quietly at his side, accepting the pain and humiliation. My God, there was no answer. Either way the pain would only grow worse. Either way she lost.

The closest Bobbi Marshal came to rational thought was the desire to clean herself. She'd been in the shower now for nearly an hour. The hot spray filled the room with billows of condensation. The wide bathroom mirror was clouded and streaked with droplets. Bobbi's skin was red from the hot water and the scrubbing but she couldn't stop. She had to get clean.

Post-rape fear and panic were syndromes Bobbi Marshal had learned to recognize, but never before had she experienced them from the inside. She had spent hundreds of hours in lecturing and individual counseling on the importance of post-rape conduct. The four basic rules were simple. Get safe, get help, get care, get support. But, as much as she thought she knew the victim's heart and psyche, she had never been touched by the fire. Now the experienced, court-qualified expert in sex crimes was just another frightened and battered woman. Statistically most rapes were quick, violent encounters. Bobbi's night of terror had lasted almost six hours. Six hours of pain, humiliation, and fear. Not only had she been violated by a brutal man but by the symbol of authority she'd carried for eight years, her own gun. The stained blue steel revolver still lay bloody and untouched on the sheets in the bedroom.

The rape had been psychological as well as physical. The confidence, self-esteem, and image as an independent single woman that Bobbi carried, along with her credibility as a cop, had been shattered. She'd been reduced to a helpless, panic-filled, whimpering animal hiding in a steam-filled shower, afraid to move because the man might have returned. She knew he was waiting. Waiting to cause more pain. Waiting to tie her up again. The fear rose and burst from Bobbi's open mouth in a desperate, agonizing scream.

A floor above, fifty-seven-year-old Doris Albert shook her sleeping husband. "Fred . . . Fred!"

"What?" The bald man pushed up on an elbow. "What's wrong?"

"Listen."

"I don't hear anything," he whispered.

"There was a woman screaming. Listen."

Fred Albert flopped down onto his pillow. "You don't leave me alone, there'll be a woman screaming in here. Go to sleep, Doris. You've had a dream."

"It was no dream. I heard it."

"Then call the police but don't bother me."

Doris waited and listened but there were no more screams.

* * *

At six-forty a.m. Brad Chilcoat arrived at the Arco Station where he and Bobbi had agreed to meet the night before. On the seat beside him were two cups of coffee and a bag of doughnuts from a nearby Winchell's. He was surprised that Bobbi hadn't yet arrived. She was always first. He considered it a good sign. Maybe his luck was changing. He picked up a copy of the morning *Times* from the seat and settled in to wait. He knew she'd arrive soon. He was eager to tell Bobbi about his night with Cathy. He wouldn't go into detail. He wouldn't have to. She'd see it.

After leafing through the paper Chilcoat checked his watch. Ten minutes had passed. Bobbi still hadn't arrived. He picked up the portable walkie-talkie from beneath the front seat and switched it on. "One-Zebra-thirty-three, this is seven-William-thirty-six."

"Go, thirty-six," the radio answered.

"Ah, I'm in the neighborhood. Anything stirring?"

"Female out of the suspect's house about twenty minutes ago to pick up the paper in the driveway. That's it."

"Roger," Chilcoat answered. "I've got a call to make. Then we'll take over the point."

"Hurry up, Ski's threatening to piss in my thermos."

Climbing from his jeep, Chilcoat walked to a public telephone booth at the corner of the service station's lot. He dropped in several coins and dialed Bobbi's number.

The water jetting from the shower was still hot, but the nude and battered Bobbi Marshal cowered shivering in a back corner of the glass enclosure. Convinced the man was waiting for her, she was frozen with fear. The telephone in the guest bedroom rang. Big Foot, on his departure, had torn out the telephones in the master bedroom and the kitchen but had missed the one in the guest bedroom. The telephone rang a second time. Bobbi caught the faint sound over the splash of the shower. It continued to ring. The man wasn't answering it. Maybe he was gone! Biting her lip until it bled, Bobbi twisted off the water. Her fingers were pasty white and wrinkled. Her sense of touch was gone. She held her breath and opened the shower door. The room was a cloud of condensation. Water dripped from everything. Bobbi stepped out.

She stood at the mouth of the open bathroom, listening to the telephone ring, too frightened to cross the hallway to the guest bedroom. What if he were there waiting? It could be a trick. No, she told herself. He was gone. Someone was calling. Someone could help. She darted across the carpeted hallway and into the guest room.

Brad Chilcoat listened to the telephone ring one more time and then hung up. He was convinced Bobbi was on her way.

Bobbi grabbed up the telephone on its last ring. Water ran from her matted hair and her arm. "Hello," she cried into the receiver. The steady electronic hum of the dial tone answered her. "Hello," she repeated desperately. "Please answer me." The dial tone continued to hum. Bobbi hung up the telephone and sank to the floor beside the bed weeping. "Help me, please. Someone help me."

Brad Chilcoat took over the point at seven a.m. as scheduled. Alone and not wanting to draw Dick Fredericks's attention, he parked the jeep facing away from the house and watched it in his rearview mirror. He was confident his partner would arrive soon, and then together they could pick a new spot. At seven-thirty he still thought there was a chance she might come. At eight o'clock the hope was giving way to annoyance. The thought that Bobbi might have gone with Don Roberts to Ensenada was becoming a distinct possibility. The remaining two hours of the quiet Saturday morning dragged by and Chilcoat was relieved by the next team at ten o'clock. He drove away angry.

There were a lot of things you could do as a policeman, and you could get away with most of them, if you were careful, but at the top of the unwritten yet golden police rules was, "I will never screw my partner." Brad Chilcoat felt that he had just been screwed. Bobbi wasn't home and she had failed to show up for duty. There was only one answer. She'd set sail for Ensenada. She had become what most male cops claimed all policewomen were: unreliable. Worse was the fact that she had done it without telling him. He was disappointed, angry, and hurt. He had put his ass, perhaps even his life, on the line by taking the point this morning by himself. He vowed he wouldn't do it again. If she failed to show this evening, and he was certain she would, then it had to be reported. "Shit," Chilcoat cursed and struck the hard plastic of the steering wheel.

The midday sun and time were both working to bring calm to Bobbi Marshal's emotional storm. It was ten-fifteen when she first looked at the clock. Now she knew who had called. It was Brad. She had missed the morning stakeout. My God, he might be on his way over! She had to clean herself up. She had to think of an excuse. She was sick. That was it. It was even true. She couldn't tell him she'd been raped. She could never tell anyone that. Even the thought of it brought on a new rush of pain and guilt.

Bobbi grimaced as she wrapped the bloodied gun in a towel and carried it into the bathroom. There she sat it carefully on the floor of the shower, turned the water on, and let it run. Returning to the bedroom, she gathered the soiled sheets into a ball and took them to the washer that sat behind slatted doors in the kitchen. She dumped soap and bleach in and turned the machine on. It felt good to be doing something. Next she hid the end of the frayed wire for the telephone that had been pulled from the kitchen wall. Unless someone tried to use it it would never be discovered.

Hurrying down the hallway, Bobbi returned to the bedroom and pulled the spread up over the bed and smoothed it. The fact that the room no longer looked like the scene of a rape helped. Taking a bottle of perfume from the dresser top, she sprayed the air with it.

The gun on the shower floor was clean when Bobbi turned off the water. She picked it up and toweled it dry.

Her hand shook when she stood at the mirror and tried to put on eye makeup. The lipstick pencil was equally as uncooperative.

Makeup finally complete, Bobbi stepped into a pair of slacks and a pullover sweater. When she was dressed she paused to study her image in the mirror. It was as if she hadn't seen herself before. Her hair was disheveled and styleless. Her makeup was a series of unblending smears. She looked and felt like a weary whore. She lowered her head to the countertop and cried.

The spartan apartment had become a symbol of Brad Chilcoat's loneliness, and he spent as little time there as possible, but he was there now, waiting. Waiting for Cathy to call. Waiting for her to ask him to come home. He knew she'd call. At least that was how he felt when he arrived there shortly before eleven. Now it was almost two and he was still waiting. Oh, God, make her call, he pleaded silently. He was sitting on the floor watching the Braves battle the Dodgers on the small black and white TV Dan Shea had loaned him. It was a beautiful day outside and he longed to enjoy it, but he had little money to do anything and he was afraid if he was away from the phone he'd miss Cathy's call. He closed his eyes and willed it as hard as he could. Call, Cathy, call. Call me, dammit. The telephone rang. He sat startled for a moment and then sprang at it. "Hello," he said, grabbing the receiver.

"Sergeant Chilcoat?" a male voice questioned.

"Yeah," Chilcoat said, making no attempt to hide the disappointment in his voice.

"Phil Epstein from the detective desk," the voice announced. Chilcoat knew the man. He was from one of the Wilshire Burglary teams and he obviously had weekend duty. "I just got a call from Bobbi Marshal. She's reporting off sick. Said she won't be able to make the stakeout tonight."

"Did you get the number she was calling from?" Chilcoat questioned.

"I didn't ask for it. She said she was sick," the detective answered defensively. "I just assumed she was calling from home. I did ask why she wasn't calling you direct. She said she lost your new number. I offered to look it up for her but she asked me to call. Shit, I didn't think anything of it."

"And there was no need to," Chilcoat said, trying to cover his anger. "I'm just pissed because the Dodgers are losing."

"No problem. They've had a year of it, haven't they?"

"Yeah. Thanks, Epstein." Chilcoat hung up. He silently damned Bobbi Marshal. If she was sick, why hadn't she answered her telephone? Chilcoat knew the answer. It was because Bobbi wasn't home. He knew he could prove her a liar by picking up the phone and dialing her number. He had the urge to do it, but if he did he was duty-bound not only to report her but to confront her as well. He had no appetite for that. The disappointment was tough enough. Their partnership was probably in its final days anyway. He had hoped it would end on an upbeat note, but given the circumstances that possibility was now gone. He'd go to Lieutenant Stovich Monday morning and tell him it was time. Stovich wouldn't ask questions. No one would be surprised. The thoughts made him very sad. He wondered if it were unmanly for an LAPD detective to cry. The crowd roared on the TV set. It was the final out. The Dodgers had lost.

Bobbi took three Darvon tablets for the burning pain. The tablets were from an old prescription her dentist had written. She knew she had to calm down, regain control. If she didn't the secret would be out. Detective Bobbi Marshal had been raped. Raped? Why didn't she fight? Why didn't she call the police? There were too many whys for Bobbi to answer. It wasn't that she didn't want to report the rape. It was just too late, she rationalized. If she had only changed the lock on the door. If she had only called as soon as he left. If she had only reached the telephone when Brad called. If only she had stayed at the bank!

Somehow the afternoon disappeared. The shadows of early evening brought on the fear of night. What if the man came back? Bobbi barricaded the front door with an overstuffed chair from the living room. The dead bolt lock had a safety button, and once it was depressed a key could no longer open it from outside. After turning on all the lights in every room she sat down on the couch, gun in hand, and watched the door.

Bobbi allowed cautious thoughts as she wondered who the man was. It was obvious he wasn't Dick Fredericks. How could it be? Even now Fredericks was being watched, followed. How could he elude the police, track her down, rape her, and return undetected? Fredericks had been Bobbi's discovery and she was wrong. The mistake had been costly. She agonized over a way to tell Brad Chilcoat they were following the wrong man, but how? How could she convince him without revealing her own rape? She did not doubt it was Big Foot. She could still hear his voice. "You've been looking for me, haven't you?" His breath was foul and he reeked of heavy aftershave. It was Big Foot, and she was the tragic proof.

The telephone in the guest bedroom rang. "Brad," Bobbi said and hurried down the hallway. She had no idea what she was going to say to him but she was eager to hear a familiar voice. "Hello," she blurted, pressing the receiver to her face. It was almost a plea.

"Bobbi, it's Mom. Are you all right?"

"Mom . . . I . . . yes, I'm okay."

"You sound strange. Have you been crying?"

"I . . . I was just on my way out . . . to work."

"Oh, that's too bad. Your father and I had to drive in to the Petersons' in Westwood. We're going to stop for dinner on the way home. I thought maybe you'd like to join us."

"I wish I could, but . . ."

"Can you come out tomorrow?"

"I'm not sure, Mom."

"Give me a call tomorrow. In the morning."

"I will, Mom. I have to go now."

The flame in her insides seemed to be spreading. Bobbi took another three Darvon before returning to the couch and her vigil of the front door. She had been awake for thirty-nine hours. Sleep overcame her quickly.

Bobbi awoke with a start. Her eyes went first to the door. It was still secure with the chair sitting in front of it. The room was bright with sunlight. She looked to the clock on the kitchen wall. It was ten minutes after one. Bobbi laid the gun aside and pushed off the couch. The missing blocks of time were still leaving her bewildered but stiff arms and legs told her she'd been on the couch a long while. Her head was fuzzy with the drug hangover. The pain still burned between her legs and her ribs were sore when she stretched. And she still felt dirty. Her mouth was dry and foul-tasting. She moved down the hall to the bathroom.

The shower was long and hot but Bobbi was beginning to realize the unclean feeling could not be washed away with water. Leaving the shower, she quickly toweled herself dry, avoiding a look in the mirror, and dressed. She blow-dried her hair but made no effort with makeup.

She moved the chair from the door and back to its original position but she kept the dead bolt locked and the safety chain in place. She spent the afternoon cleaning. She vacuumed and dusted, cleaned the windows, washed the sheets a second time, and cleaned and oiled her gun. When she finished, the pain in her insides was even worse. Bobbi knew she needed help.

It was nearly six-thirty when she sat down on the bed in the guest bedroom. She picked up the telephone and dialed the number with a trembling finger. When he answered, Bobbi sobbed. "Don, can you come over? I need help. I've been raped."

# 18

# PROBABLE CAUSE

"My God, Bobbi," Don Roberts said when he arrived. "We've got to get you to a hospital."

"No. No, I can't," Bobbi pleaded as she clung to him and sobbed.

Don reluctantly agreed, but after making a brief phone call he drove Bobbi to a client's home in Westwood. The man was a professor at UCLA's School of Medicine. His wife, a soft-spoken redhead in her mid-forties, was a gynecologist.

Bobbi wept as Don spoke softly with the two. She tried not to cry, she wanted to stop, but her body still wasn't hers. Finally the woman slipped an arm around Bobbi's shoulder and led her into a back bedroom of the comfortable home.

After the examination Don drove to a nearby pharmacy and filled several prescriptions. Bobbi's lacerations and contusions were dressed with a soothing ointment, and she was given several injections of antibiotics as well as an antidepressant. The effect was dramatic and immediate. Bobbi could feel the veil being lifted. With its passing came an awareness of thirst and hunger.

Elizabeth, the sensitive redhead, sat with Bobbi in the kitchen as an almond-eyed Mexican maid brought Bobbi apple juice and a cup of hot soup. "Rape, unlike other physical trauma, sometimes wounds the spirit as well as the body," the woman warned. "Be careful, Bobbi. It's easy to let it get out of control. Keep in mind you're still the same person you were before. This man didn't take anything from you. Don't let him cause you any more pain. You're a healthy young woman. Put this behind you and go on.''

The woman made Bobbi take two more capsules after the soup was gone. ''Continue to take these as directed. I'll give you my card. I want you to come into my office on Wednesday. And I think you should report this to the police.''

Bobbi waited until they drove away before she said anything to Don. ''You didn't tell them I was a policewoman?''

''It didn't seem important.''

They slept in the living room. Don sat on the couch, his feet propped on the coffee table. Bobbi, her head in his lap, lay beside him. The drugs and the exhaustion combined to give her a deep, dreamless sleep. She awoke early at first light. Easing off the couch, she allowed Don to sleep while she made coffee and got ready for work.

The reality of the rape seemed distant and dreamlike, and as long as she didn't dwell on it the trembling, fear, and shame were controllable. She felt an incredible sense of loss. She wasn't sure of what, but the painful ache was nonetheless real. Maybe it was the realization that her life would never be the same again. She now understood the pain she'd seen in Lisa Cartwright's eyes.

Bobbi put extra effort and time into her makeup and hair. She was depending on it to hide her pain. She selected a long-sleeved, high-necked sweater to hide the bruises. When she finally finished dressing, she checked her image in the bathroom mirror. The pleasing reflection reinforced the thought that she might get away with it. She had to.

''Good morning.'' Don smiled when Bobbi returned to the kitchen. He was sitting at the counter drinking a cup of coffee. ''You look nice.''

''Thank you.'' Bobbi smiled, pouring herself a cup of

coffee and adding more to his. Don's face and neck were blue with the stubble of his beard and his hair was in need of a comb. Bobbi had never seen him like this, and somehow it made her feel closer to him.

"Would you like me to drive you in this morning?" Don questioned.

"No," Bobbi answered. "If you did that they'd know something was wrong."

Don seemed surprised by her answer. "You are going to report this, aren't you?"

Bobbi sat her cup down. "Don, do you know what you're asking?"

Don scratched at the stubble on his neck. "I'm not asking. I guess I was expecting."

His suggestion had her heart racing and a wave of panic engulfed her. "I need . . . I need time to think," she defended. It was less than convincing.

Don pushed away from the counter and walked around it to Bobbi. He took her by the shoulders and looked into her eyes. "Bobbi, you have friends. They'll want to help, just like I did. But they can't unless you let them. Don't try to keep this thing inside. Don't be his victim again."

"It's too late," Bobbi said, averting her eyes. They were rimmed with tears. "There's nothing to be gained now. It's just too late."

Don released her. "I've got court this morning. Van Nuys Civil. I don't know what courtroom, but if you need anything call my office. They'll know where I am."

Bobbi walked with him to the door. "I appreciate everything you've done." There was a chill in her voice.

"We'll get through this, Bobbi," Don assured her, slipping his jacket on.

"*We* didn't get raped, Don. I did."

Don kissed her lightly on the cheek and left.

Captain John Stone was in his office at Wilshire Detectives early. He had spent the weekend studying the paper image of the division. It was hard to pinpoint what it was the division was doing wrong, yet slowly but surely the tip of the iceberg had emerged. They had lost their edge. They were going through the motions. Wilshire Detectives had become a paper tiger. If crime increased, instead of an aggressive police action, all that showed was an increase in the flow of paper. George Westly hadn't been the commander of Wilshire Detectives. He had been their administrator. John Stone was determined that would change. Wilshire Detectives was about to get a stiff kick in its paper ass.

One by one the senior detectives in the bureau were summoned to the captain's office. John Stone was building a fire under each one and hoping it would spread to the others.

Only Lieutenants Mitchell and Radcliff were excluded. They were busy cleaning out their desks. Both were being transferred to Property Division, the LAPD's equivalent of Siberia.

"Tell me about Big Foot," Captain Stone ordered when Aaron Stovich took his turn in the hot seat.

Lieutenant Stovich laid out the case history, going chronologically over Big Foot's nineteen known rapes. He carefully built the profile of the rapist and his victims, adding bits and pieces of the evidence just as they had been gathered, leading eventually to the identification of Richard Fredericks. It was as if he'd investigated each crime himself.

"Who made the connection to Fredericks?" Captain Stone interjected.

"Marshal."

"The same Marshal that's involved in the Chilcoat lawsuit?"

"The same."

"Lieutenant," the captain said, pushing back in his chair, "you've had eight detectives on this stakeout, round the clock, for five full days. All we've got is eight people tied up and a truckload of overtime chits. To cover a stakeout like this properly you need at least twice as many men and we don't have them. We're up to our tombstones in gang murders and robberies but we're busy babysitting a rapist, and only doing it half ass.''

"What do you suggest we do, captain? Let the sonofabitch do it again?''

"No, what I suggest you do is go and arrest the sonofabitch.''

"Arrest him?''

"You're pulling punches, lieutenant. You know Fredericks is guilty. You've convinced me he's guilty. Now it's up to the DA and the courts. What the hell are you waiting for, Polaroids of him humping his next victim? Bring him in.''

Bobbi had reported for duty at eight and was at her desk in the squad room, thumbing through the reports that had come in over the weekend. She saw Lieutenant Stovich when he came out of the captain's office. He walked directly to her. "Chilcoat still out on the point?''

Bobbi nodded. "Until ten o'clock. He's with Evon Hughes from Hollywood.''

"Get on the radio. Tell 'im to arrest Fredericks and bring him in.''

Bobbi's heart swelled into her throat. She felt the blood draining from her face.

"You okay?'' Stovich questioned, seeing Bobbi's reaction.

Fredericks wasn't Big Foot. How could she tell them? A thousand frightening images flashed through her mind. "I . . . it's the flu. I had a tough weekend.''

"Uh huh. Anyway, the old man's pulled the plug on the stakeout. He said we can't justify the OT and manpower so we're gonna go with what we've got.''

Bobbi nodded. She couldn't speak.

Brad Chilcoat was slouched behind the wheel of the unmarked car, staring across the street at the office front of Image Market Appraisals. Once again they had followed Dick Fredericks from his home in Burbank to the office on West Pico Boulevard, and Chilcoat was pissed. Pissed at a rapist who wouldn't rape, pissed at an estranged wife who wouldn't call him, pissed at a partner who'd lied to him about being off sick, and pissed at the blond policewoman beside him who wouldn't shut up. The blond was younger than Chilcoat, mid-twenties he guessed, and all she talked about was movies, and what a hunk Tom Cruise was. "Did you see *The Color of Money?*" the blond pressed, cutting through the wall Chilcoat was trying to build.

"The color of money? Yeah, it's green."

"I'm talking about Cruise and Newman." The blond was annoyed with his ignorance.

"I thought you were talking about the color of money?"

"Seven-William-thirty-six," Bobbi's familiar voice said over the radio concealed in the detective car's glove box. "This is seven-William-ninety, come in."

The blond propped open the glove box, but Chilcoat reached across her. "I'll get it," he answered, keying the mike. "This is William-thirty-six. Go ahead, ninety." He was glad to hear Bobbi's voice. He was hoping she'd admit to her lie and apologize. Hell, even he made mistakes now and then. He had decided to be big about it. He knew how compelling love could be. Although she still deserved a good ass chewing.

"William-thirty-six, the lieutenant advises you arrest Fredericks and bring him to the station."

"Jesus," Chilcoat said soberly.

"William-thirty-six, do you copy?"

"Roger. Arrest Fredericks and bring him in. I copy." Then he added, "Ah, ninety, have a black-and-white meet us here for backup."

"Roger. Stand by."

Bobbi tried to return to her desk but the salty taste in her mouth warned her not to. She hurried down the hall and to the restroom. She barely made it into the stall before the fear turned her stomach inside out. She was still kneeling and retching when Dorothy Pettigrew, the black senior detective from Juvenile, walked in. "Bobbi, are you all right?"

"It's the flu," she lied.

She stayed in the restroom for nearly an hour, taking several more of the Valium the red-haired doctor had given her. She felt the waves of fear ease some, but when she held a hand up it trembled.

Lieutenant Stovich; Dan Shea, his arm still in a sling; a blond policewoman; and several uniformed officers were standing in a group near the interrogation rooms when Bobbi returned to the squad room. "He's here," the lieutenant said as Bobbi reached them.

"He's really a pussycat." The blond policewoman smiled. "Would you like to meet him?"

Bobbi opened her mouth but there were no words. The heavy scent of a familiar aftershave hanging in the air had reached her.

"Let's take a look from number three," Lieutenant Stovich suggested. "Chilcoat's in there with him."

The small, dark room was separated from the interrogation room by a large, dim, glass window. On the other side were Dick Fredericks and Brad Chilcoat. A microphone in the other room delivered their filtered conversation to the viewing room. Bobbi was thankful for the darkness. She reached out and supported herself with a hand to the wall. Dan Shea and the lieutenant seemed not to notice.

"Don't I have the right to make a telephone call?" Dick Fredericks said. Bobbi recognized the voice instantly. Her head swam and she feared she was going to faint. She staggered. Dan Shea saw and grabbed her.

"Let's get her outside," Stovich urged.

Dan Shea drove Bobbi home. The lieutenant didn't even seem suspicious. The flu story and reporting off sick on the weekend were serving her well.

Bobbi pushed the safety lock and put the chain in place

on the door before lying down on the couch. She was still trembling. The lie was closing in and suffocating her. The fear that they were soon going to find out was robbing her of rational thought. It was only a matter of time before Brad Chilcoat would catch Big Foot in the snare of his own lies. Bobbi could almost hear Fredericks confessing to the rape. He'd want to. Confessing, no matter the cost, was a chance to brag. "Yeah, I did it. I raped her. I raped her with her own gun." Bobbi's heart pounded in her ears. Her eyes welled with tears. Captain Stone would soon know the truth. The arrest of Judge Unger, Cathy Chilcoat's lawsuit, the shooting of Delbert Phillips, and now the cover-up of her own rape. He wouldn't have to search for reasons. Bobbi had given him many. She knew they would come before the day was over. Maybe it would be Lieutenant Stovich and Captain Stone. Perhaps a team from Internal Affairs. She wasn't sure who, it didn't matter, all she knew was that they'd come.

The one thing that really did matter to Bobbi Marshal was her career, and that had been shattered. Everything of value, everything that mattered was gone. What Bobbi hadn't destroyed herself, Richard Fredericks had. She could see nothing ahead, and then the thought came to her. The Valium in her purse. A handful of the tablets would bring relief. Peace, escape. There would be no questions. No shame.

Bobbi lifted herself off the couch, picked up her purse, and walked to the kitchen. She considered writing a note, but the cloud of despair in her mind wouldn't allow her to think of what to put in it. Wouldn't her death say enough? Standing at the sink, she lifted the prescription vial from her purse.

Holding the plastic vial in her trembling hands, Bobbi struggled with the safety cap. She depressed it and turned. The stubborn cap refused to come off. She twisted harder with all of her strength. The cap popped open with a crack and the vial fell into the sink. Bobbi grabbed at it, but only four tablets remained. The others disappeared down through the black rubber mouth of the garbage disposal. Bobbi flung away the vial in anger. With tears running down her face, she took two of the remaining tablets and returned to the couch. Even her attempt at suicide had ended in failure.

Thirty-six hours had passed since Bobbi Marshal's night of terror, and the depression she was experiencing was normal. Bobbi had often warned others of it, yet she was blind to the symptoms in herself.

The two Valium Bobbi took at the station, combined with the two she swallowed in the kitchen, took her back to the couch and kept her there. She was thinking of the bank when sleep overtook her.

Richard Fredericks surprised Detective Sergeant Chilcoat when he agreed to a consent search of his office, automobile, and home. The three searches took over four hours. Fredericks remained calm, cool, and cooperative as he was transported from one location to another. "Hey, I'm as eager to get this cleared up as you are," he told Lieutenant Stovich. The two of them sat in the living room of Fredericks's home while the Sex teams systematically searched the house. They found nothing.

Fredericks was finally booked into jail at Parker Center late in the afternoon. He was charged with nineteen counts of 261 P.C.: forcible rape. Bail was set at seventy-five thousand dollars. Fredericks was no longer smiling.

They met in an eighteenth-floor conference room in the Criminal Courts Building, for the filing of the criminal complaints. There were five detectives: Criminalist Wade Morris from SID; Rose Ann Douglas, head of Trials; Edward Solomon, head of the DA's Criminal Complaints Division; and a secretary from the DA's office, who took everything down in machine shorthand. Chilcoat, representing the Sex teams, started the presentation with a detailed overview. When Chilcoat finished, Wade Morris gave a detailed accounting of the evidence and how it could be linked to Richard Fredericks. The conference ended at five-forty-five. It was Rose Ann Douglas who made the suggestion. "Gentlemen, you've given us a great deal to consider. We'd like some time to study the case before we make any decisions."

"Decisions?" Chilcoat questioned. He was worried at the suggestion of a delay. "What's to decide other than how many years the sonofabitch gets?"

"Sergeant." Rose Ann Douglas smiled, to squelch his fears. "You didn't investigate these crimes in a single day. All we're asking is an opportunity to study the reports before we decide on a course of action."

"How long are you talking about?" a detective from Rampart Division asked.

Rose Ann's smile was still holding. "By noon tomorrow."

The thump on the door jolted Bobbi awake. The sedatives were making her head feel oversized and her neck wobbly. She sat up. The shadows in the room told her it was late. She was stiff and the bruises on her ribs and breasts ached. The thump on the door sounded again. Bobbi wet her lips. They had finally come. She wiped at the grogginess and pushed off the couch. Her mouth was dry and she felt wrinkled and soiled. The door chime rang. Bobbi stepped to the viewer in the door and peered out. She expected to see a sober duo from Internal Affairs or perhaps Captain Stone and Lieutenant Stovich. She saw neither. It was Brad Chilcoat. Bobbi quickly unchained and unlocked the door.

"You look like death warmed over," Chilcoat said when Bobbi opened the door.

"Nice to see you, too," she said as he stepped inside.

Chilcoat sat down in the chair Bobbi had used to block the door after the rape. She sat on the couch across from him.

"I came by to say I'm sorry," Chilcoat said as he studied Bobbi.

"To say you're sorry?"

"Yeah." Chilcoat leaned his elbows to his knees. "When you didn't show Saturday morning, I got really pissed. I just knew you went to Ensenada with Don Roberts."

"I wish I had," Bobbi said, pushing off her shoes and folding her legs onto the couch.

"Sorry I missed you at the station this morning. How are you feeling?"

"Better," Bobbi answered, but he didn't look as if he believed her.

"You need anything? Maybe some chicken soup? There's a Jewish deli right over on Wilshire."

"No, but thanks for offering."

"We filed on Big Foot this afternoon," Chilcoat told her.

Bobbi's heart raced with fear. She was afraid she wouldn't be able to maintain her composure and talk about the man. When she didn't respond, Chilcoat continued. "They're gonna give us the answer tomorrow. You know the DA's office can't decide what day it is without four meetings. When they call I'm going to ask that his bail be revoked."

"He's out?" Bobbi blurted.

"Could be. I don't know. We put seventy-five thousand on him but all he needs is ten percent of that. He owns a house. He won't have any trouble coming up with it."

Bobbi was hyperventilating and she was close to being physically ill. "Brad, I'd like to talk but I don't feel very good."

Chilcoat was immediately on his feet. "Don't worry about work. Just take it easy and get over this thing."

"I will," Bobbi said, pushing off the couch.

"I'd kiss you good-night but I don't want your germs. Get well. I miss your face."

Bobbi locked and chained the door behind him. Her heart was pounding. My God, she thought, he could be out. He could come back.

* * *

Clair Fredericks was surprised to find her husband's car wasn't in the driveway when she arrived home from work. Dick was an avid baseball fan, and seldom missed a game on TV on Monday night. She sensed there was trouble. When Clair opened the front door she heard the telephone. She noticed that the cushions on the couch had been pulled out and pushed back. A drawer on a hutch in the dining room was standing open a quarter of an inch, and the chairs around the dining room table had all been moved. It frightened her. She knew someone had been in the house. She picked up the telephone on the kitchen counter. "Hello." Her voice was tense.

"Clair, where in the hell have you been?" It was her husband.

"I had to work overtime an hour. Richard, someone's been in our house."

"Yeah, I know. It was the police."

"The police! Richard, where are you?"

He avoided a direct answer. "Clair, I need you to go to my desk and find the deed to the house."

"The deed to the house! Why?"

"Because I need it and twenty-five hundred dollars from our savings for a bondsman."

"A bondsman! Richard, what's wrong?"

"There's nothing to worry about. It's all a mistake. I'm going to sue their asses off."

"Richard," she demanded, "where are you?"

"I'm in jail."

"Oh, my God!"

"Listen to me, Clair. You need to find the trust deed to the house and twenty-five hundred dollars in cash. Take both of those to a bondsman. Tell him—"

"Richard, it's after six. The banks have been closed for three hours."

"Sonofabitch, maybe your mother has it."

"Richard, she doesn't keep that kind of cash."

"Well, goddammit, you've got to get it somewhere."

Clair's eyes were rimmed with tears. "Richard, what have you done?"

"I haven't done anything, Clair. Nothing. It's all a mistake."

"What were you arrested for?"

"I'm going to sue them for every goddamned penny they have. They'll be a bunch of sorry bastards when I'm through with them."

"Richard, what have you been arrested for?" Clair demanded.

The line was silent for an awkward moment. Clair could hear her husband's breathing, and then he answered in a cold, single word. "Rape."

# 19

# JUSTICE DEFERRED

Brad Chilcoat drove toward his apartment in Echo Park after leaving Bobbi, but the farther he drove the more he dreaded the idea of being there. He had spent hours on Saturday and Sunday waiting for Cathy to call and ask him to come home. After their shared passion of Friday night, Saturday and Sunday had been painfully quiet. What the hell was wrong with her? He stopped at the next pay phone to make a call.

"Dan," Chilcoat said into the receiver, "it's Brad. Hey, listen, my TV just went tits up. Care for a little company? I can bring a couple of six packs. Great, see ya in twenty minutes."

They sat in Dan Shea's comfortable family room and watched the Giants battle the Mets. Two other Homicide cops were there too, but they left shortly after the game ended. "I'm hungry," Shea said, heading for the kitchen. "You want some cold beef?"

"Beef?" Chilcoat answered. "I'm not sure I remember what it tastes like."

Chilcoat sat at a bar in the kitchen while Shea got out a package of sliced beef, swiss cheese, rolls, and an assortment of spreads. "How long are you going to stay in the apartment?" Shea questioned. "I was planning on a little remodeling."

"I thought I was going to get to go home this weekend," Chilcoat said, sampling a piece of the cheese, "but Cathy never called."

Shea paused and looked at Chilcoat. "What do you mean, she never called?"

"Well, Friday night Cathy was having a problem with her neck. She asked me to come over and help with the girls. I went over and we wound up in bed. It was great. I spent the night. I had to work Saturday morning. She never called to invite me back. Never a fuckin' word. It's like it never happened, and I know she wanted it just as much as I did."

Shea had been listening intently. "You know, Brad, sometimes you're such an asshole you should be required to carry a warning sign."

"Me! An asshole? What the hell are you talking about?"

Shea reached in the back pocket of his jeans and pulled out his badge case. He flipped it open in front of Chilcoat's face. "You know what this is?"

"It's a badge."

"It's also a crotch opener. Fifty percent of the women you show it to are going to lie down and open their legs." He returned the badge to his pocket. "Most of us that carry a badge don't abuse that fact."

"Don't point that at me," Chilcoat defended.

"How many women have you seduced without telling them you were a cop first?"

Chilcoat was silent.

"You've been screwing camp followers, Brad. You don't get a trophy for that, and if you're lucky you won't get AIDS either. What the hell is it you're trying to prove?"

"I'm not trying to prove anything."

"You've still got a chance. That's more than some of us have. I've been down that road. I called home one night. Told Julia I had to work. She wanted me to come home. Kim was making her debut in a fifth-grade play. Getting in the pants of a record clerk was more important to me. When I came home at one o'clock in the morning, the Highway Patrol was waiting in front of the house. Julia and Kim were dead. You've got to quit thinking with your dick, Brad. You said you waited all weekend for Cathy to call you. Why in the hell should she call you? Would you be calling her if she was the one who'd gone out and screwed half of L.A. County? You'll be goddamned lucky if she ever takes you back. Crawl if you have to, Brad. Your family's worth it.''

Bobbi packed a bag and drove to her parents' home in San Marino. The thought of spending the night alone when Richard Fredericks could be released on bail was impossible. Her father was at a lodge meeting when she arrived. She shared a cup of coffee with her mother, who thankfully didn't ask any questions. Then she soaked in the bathtub and went to bed early. The comfort and familiarity of the house and her old room brought back a sense of security and peace she hungered for. She was lying on the edge of sleep, wondering what her life would have been like if she hadn't become a police officer, when the tall silhouette of her father stepped quietly into the room. He crossed to the side of the bed and looked down at her. Bobbi couldn't see his face in the shadows. John Marshal sat down on the edge of the bed. He took one of Bobbi's hands and cupped it in his big, powerful hands. "Your mother told me you were here. I just wanted to come up and say good night." His voice was a whisper.

"I'm glad you did," Bobbi answered. She felt a sudden surge of emotion choking her. She was thankful for the darkness.

"Everything okay, kiddo?" the authoritative silhouette questioned.

"It's been a little tough out lately."

John Marshal massaged his daughter's hand. "I've never told you this since you left the bank, but I'm very proud of you, and if you ever want to come back, you just let me know."

"Thanks, Dad."

"Do you need any money?"

"No, I'm okay. I just needed a night away from it all. A night at home."

The silhouette nodded. "During the recession of the seventies when I thought we were going to lose the banks, I told your mother I had to work one night and drove over to your grandfather's house in Oak Glen. He must have been in his late eighties then. Not likely he even knew why I was there, but I was frightened. I walked around the old house, sat beside him for a while. It helped. Made me realize fear is a lot more imagined than it is real. I don't know what kind of problems you're having, but I want you to know I'll do anything I can to help you. You also need to know that things are never as bad as you think they are. Fear can be a terrible thing. Don't let it make decisions for you, kiddo. Take it from an old man who's lived a lot of years."

Bobbi sat up to hug her father. She kissed him on the cheek. "I love you, Dad." A tear spilled down her cheek to his, disappearing into the stubble of his beard, but the old man said nothing.

Bobbi left her parents' home early. Once on the south-bound Pasadena Freeway, sandwiched among the hundreds of other cars, Bobbi no longer felt the paranoia of a rape victim. It wasn't likely that many of the motorists were enjoying the rush-hour drive, but Bobbi Marshal was.

The idea had come to Bobbi after her father's visit to her bedroom. It was time to put the fear behind her. Richard Fredericks had been arrested and jailed as Big Foot. If he hadn't confessed to any of the other rapes, why would he ever confess to hers? If he hadn't confessed yesterday it was likely he never would. And even if he did, and included Bobbi among his list of victims, she could now shrug and deny it as the fantasy of a man with serious mental problems. Reason also told her she wasn't cheating justice. Would Fredericks's prison sentence be greater for twenty rapes than it would for nineteen? Not likely. No, there was nothing to be gained by admitting to the rape. It would remain a secret. With Fredericks in jail, and Bobbi not involved in his arrest, it wasn't likely she'd ever have to see him, not even in a courtroom. Things were working out after all. Justice was at hand. The means were not all that important after all. The fear could be managed. It had to be.

In downtown Los Angeles, District Attorney Raymond Bendicci was already in his office on the eighteenth floor of the Criminal Courts Building.

Rose Ann Douglas and Ed Solomon had stayed late with the district attorney the night before, going over the Big Foot case the police had presented to them. After a lengthy discussion of the case, the district attorney had asked for their professional opinion on the odds of a successful prosecution and conviction. Ed Solomon had seen it as sixty-forty in favor of a conviction. "Juries hate rapists," he said. "They'll convict him."

"I agree, juries hate rapists," Rose Ann Douglas had said. "But first we have to prove beyond a reasonable doubt that Richard Fredericks is Big Foot. It's true that the police have brought us a preponderance of circumstantial evidence. We can prove he wears the same size shoe as the rapist. We can prove he's of the same blood type. We can prove he has the same color and texture of hair, both pubic and scalp. We can prove he had access to the victims' homes, but of all the nineteen women we can put on the stand not one of them can point a finger at Richard Fredericks and say, 'That's the man.' A point the defense is not likely to miss. I give it fifty-fifty."

The district attorney thanked the two and dismissed them. "I'll let you know my decision in the morning."

The fact was he'd already made it. With nineteen victims the trial could last six or eight months, or longer, well into the election. Not bad if they were assured of a conviction, but the consequences could be disastrous if they lost. Thus, the only possible decision was to reject the case. Send it back to the police for further investigation. The district attorney knew recycled cases seldom resulted in filings. The accused, once aware of the police efforts, covered their tracks, and most usually fled to other jurisdictions. The fact that Richard Fredericks might rape again was not among the district attorney's considerations. His job, he rationalized, was to prosecute, not to worry about how the police did their job.

Brad Chilcoat was at the Sex team's desk in the squad room when Bobbi arrived. Chilcoat looked in a sullen mood. He hardly glanced up from a report when Bobbi sat down across from him. "Good morning," she offered.

He glanced up. "Feeling better, huh?"

"Much," Bobbi answered.

Chilcoat pushed the report aside and gave Bobbi his attention. "The city attorney called. I have a meeting with him at nine."

"About Cathy's lawsuit?"

"What else?" Chilcoat glanced at his watch and pushed out of his chair. "I've gotta go. I'll get back as soon as I can," Chilcoat promised.

"Good luck," Bobbi offered, and he was gone.

"Where's Chilcoat going?" Lieutenant Stovich said as he reached the Sex team's desk. He looked angry. His cigar had been chewed down to a stub.

"City attorney called him in for a meeting about Cathy's lawsuit," Bobbi answered.

"Short straw goes to you then," Stovich said soberly. "The DA's office just called. Big Foot's a reject. Insufficient evidence. He's in Central Jail. Go do a five-ten release."

Bobbi was stunned. "A reject! He's walking out the door?"

"It's not my decision. It's the DA's. Have the five-ten on my desk by noon." Stovich turned and walked away.

Bobbi's hands trembled as she searched through the case folders on the desk. Her mind was a rush of panicky thoughts and she could hardly breathe. She willed herself calm. She had to stay in control. She had to get through this crisis. She'd made it through the others. She could make it through this one. She found the arrest report and the five-ten arrest disposition form. She stuffed the reports into her purse and headed for the door.

She drove the streets randomly for nearly an hour trying to think. The man had robbed her and nineteen other innocent women of their self-esteem. He had reduced them from successful, independent professionals to a band of helpless, frightened neurotics, and he was about to get away with it. The greatest irony was that she, his latest victim, had been commissioned to unleash the beast, to set him free. The decision had been made by those who had never seen him. Their skin had never crawled under his touch. They had never lain bound and naked before him. They had never smelled his foul breath. They had never suffered the indescribable violation of his sweaty flesh. They had never known the fear.

It was knowing that she would have to face him that gave the idea form. Fredericks would relish the knowledge that she had not reported him. What was it a victim had once said to her through a mask of tears? Reporting the rape was worse than being raped. No, the pain didn't always end with the departure of the rapist. For many it was only the beginning. Fredericks would know he was the victor. Bobbi Marshal setting him free would tell him that he had not only raped twenty women and got away with it, he had raped justice as well. But Bobbi Marshal had a plan. Her fear had turned to anger.

Bobbi showed her ID card to a khaki-clad officer behind a heavy wire mesh before he pushed the button on the electric lock. The metal door to Parker Center's Central Jail swung open and Bobbi walked down the spartan gray corridor. Her heels clicking on the cement floor made the only sound in the reinforced silence.

NO WEAPONS BEYOND THIS POINT, a sign warned at the end of the gray corridor. Bobbi took the thirty-eight pistol from her purse and placed it in one of the lockers along the wall. She dropped the key in her purse and pushed the button on the wall for the elevator that would take her to the second-floor felony section.

The elevator was large, cold, and slow. When the doors opened on the second floor, Bobbi stepped off and walked to the jail's booking counter. A heavy-set jailor looked up from a newspaper.

"I've got a five-ten release for Fredericks," Bobbi said through the wire mesh. She glanced at the paper she carried. "Booking number six-one-three-seven-seven-four-two." She slid the form under the wire to the jailor. "I'd like to see him before his release."

The jailor gave the five-ten a cursory once-over and then keyed a nearby intercom. "Hey, Phil, wrap up Fredericks, R., booking seven-seven-four-two. He's out on a five-ten. Detective's here to see 'im. Send 'im up to interrogation two."

"Fredericks, R.," a Latin voice answered on the intercom from somewhere deep in the bowels of the cell blocks. "Seven-seven-four-two, over easy, and on his way."

The jailor glanced at Bobbi. "You know where the interrogation rooms are?"

"Yes."

He signed the two copies of the five-ten. He returned one to Bobbi and kept the other.

"Skirt in for interrogation!" another jailor shouted before buzzing Bobbi through a heavy metal door. It clanged shut behind her.

The small interrogation room was lined with once white acoustical block, now yellowed with age and nicotine. The floor was gritty and dotted with cigarette butts. The air was stale and thick with the odor of sweat. Bobbi sat down in one of two chairs at the small wooden table. She was tense and her breath was rushed, but she was in control. This time the surprise was going to be Fredericks's. She savored the thought of making him squirm. She crossed her legs, adjusted her skirt, and waited.

It wasn't long before Bobbi heard footfalls in the corridor outside the room. They approached the door and stopped. "Fredericks is here," a Latin voice called as the jailor knocked on the door and then opened it.

Bobbi saw Fredericks flinch with shock when he saw her. He tensed and balled his fists. Bobbi held an unemotional, sober expression as she studied his face. He quickly averted his eyes. Bobbi knew she would have to be strong if her plan was going to work.

"Sit down," the broad-shouldered Mexican officer ordered. A hand on Fredericks's shoulder pushed him to the chair across the table from Bobbi.

"I'll be at the end of the hall," the dark-eyed officer said to Bobbi. It was more a warning for Fredericks. He pulled the door shut and was gone.

Fredericks's darting eyes roamed the room. They looked everywhere but at Bobbi.

Bobbi wet her lips and began. "Richard, I'm Detective Bobbi Marshal. I work the Sex team at Wilshire Division. I wasn't there when you were brought in yesterday." Her tone was deliberately measured, even.

He allowed his eyes to find her. They were the nervous eyes of an animal. They frightened Bobbi, but she gripped the edge of her chair, held his look, and went on. "I'm bringing you good news." She forced a convincing businesslike smile. "You're being released."

"My wife got my bail?" Fredericks said, straightening in his chair.

"No. Bail won't be necessary," Bobbi explained with a glance at the five-ten form lying on the table between them. "The district attorney has reviewed your case and decided there's insufficient evidence to take you to trial."

"You mean they can't prove anything?" Fredericks asked cautiously.

"Basically that's it," Bobbi granted.

Now he allowed himself to smile as he pushed back and relaxed in the chair. "Nobody said anything?"

"Nobody," Bobbi assured him. "And as soon as we finish here, you're free to go."

"I told the other detective I have nothing to say. That's

my right." His tone was becoming more confident. It was as if the power and authority was shifting from one side of the small table to the other.

"Consider this off the record," Bobbi said, toying with the open collar of her blouse. Her polished nails found the top button and played with it. Fredricks was watching. "I was just curious as to how you feel about being accused of rape?"

"I feel they were wrong," he answered flatly.

"Wouldn't you be flattered to be accused of seducing nineteen women?"

"Nineteen? There could be more." He had taken the bait. "They say not everyone reports it."

"Yes, I've heard that." Bobbi shifted in her chair, re-crossing her legs slowly after moving them from beneath the table. She saw his eyes glance to her nylon-covered calves. "Why do you suppose that is?"

Fredericks shrugged. "I suppose some enjoy it."

"Bondage and intercourse with a restrained sexual partner can be stimulating for both male and female . . . so I've heard," Bobbi said, forcing a bashful smile.

"Have you ever done it?" Fredericks challenged in a near whisper.

Bobbi raised her eyes to his. "Have you?" she whispered in reply.

Fredericks shifted in his chair and cleared his throat. "What is this, some kind of trap?"

"Trap?" Bobbi said innocently. "For it to be a trap I'd have to be one of your victims."

Fredericks's jaw tightened as he looked to her. She held his look. "Let's say you did rape me," Bobbi suggested. He swallowed hard. "The only way it could be criminal was if I complained. If I were to ever admit I enjoyed it . . . or if I invited you back, there would be no chance of prosecution."

Fredericks was breathing hard now. She could hear his labored breath.

"Do you understand what I'm saying to you?" Bobbi added.

Fredericks pushed back in his chair and wiped at the perspiration that beaded on his chin. "I don't have anything else to say." He sniffed.

"All right," Bobbi agreed, moving her legs back under the table. "Let me verify a few items and we'll be finished." Her knee brushed his and Fredericks jumped as if he'd been touched by a live wire. "Sorry." Bobbi smiled.

She turned the five-ten report to her and dug in her purse for a pen. "I don't know about you, but every time I come into this jail I feel like I need a bath." She ran a hand down from her neck and over her breasts in a washing motion. Fredericks swallowed again as he watched. "When I get home I'm going to get out of these clothes and into the tub. I don't think I'll put anything on until I wake up in the morning. Tuesdays are the one night I have free." She paused for a moment and held his look. "If you know what I mean?" Bobbi clicked the pen she lifted from her purse. "Is your correct date of birth, eleven-eighteen-fifty-one?"

"Yeah," he answered.

"And you're six-foot-two-inches tall?"

"Yeah."

Bobbi could feel Fredericks's eyes on her as she wrote. "And you still live at fourteen-oh-six Lakespur Drive, Burbank?"

"Yeah."

Bobbi clicked the pen and looked at him. "I guess that's it." She folded the report and pushed it into her purse. Standing, she shouldered her purse. "Maybe we'll run into each other again some time."

"You never know," Fredericks answered.

"True." Bobbi smiled seductively. "You just never know." She moved to the door and stepped out.

# 20

# MARSHAL LAW

Leaving the jail, Bobbi went immediately to the restroom on the ground floor of Parker Center. She washed her hands, again and again. She was once more on the brink of being physically ill. She had been repulsed by the sight and smell of Fredericks, and only an angry determination saved her from losing control. She had to hold on. She had to get through the day. She needed to work, to think, to do something to escape the panic that kept returning to haunt her.

The plan was simple and just, Bobbi thought as she drove west on Wilshire Boulevard. Dick Fredericks would come to her condo and she would kill him. Even a polygraph test wouldn't shake her story. Yes, I was in fear of my life. The conclusion would be obvious. He had seen her on television. They had talked in the jail. The bastard had come to rape her. He got what he deserved. Even if the truth did come out, that this was his second visit, the shooting would still be justified. Perhaps even more so. No one would blame her. She had already shot one man. It wasn't that difficult. Anger. That was it, keep the anger. What was the line from the poem, "Do not go gentle." That's what she had to watch. "Do not go gentle," she said aloud.

Bobbi's mind kept returning to the jail interrogation room. Was she convincing? Did Fredericks believe her? He had asked if it were a trap. He was suspicious. Yes, but he was also an egomaniac. He would want to believe it was true. He would want to come back. He would want to believe she wanted him. She fought the urge to pray that he would. This was between Bobbi Marshal and Dick Fredericks. She didn't need anyone's help. Not even God's.

It was late morning, and the squad room was almost deserted. The arrival of Captain John Stone seemed to be spurring more detectives from behind their desks. Bobbi glanced at Lieutenant Stovich's desk as she came into the room. The lieutenant was there, engrossed in paperwork. Bobbi walked to his desk and dropped the five-ten form into his basket. The lieutenant glanced up at her. "Fredericks have anything to say?"

"No."

"I talked to the Surveillance unit. They're working on a couple of bank bandits. As soon as they bag 'im they'll give us a hand with Big Foot."

"Unless something else takes priority," Bobbi suggested.

"Reality is, money is more important than virtue," Stovich said.

"Someday Fredericks will run into a piece of reality," Bobbi said coolly.

"You did what you could," Stovich said. From him it was a compliment. "Don't lose any sleep over it. I called Burbank PD, told them what we had. Maybe if nothing else, we've saved someone else from getting raped."

"Maybe," Bobbi agreed and walked away.

Brad Chilcoat's stomach was in an angry knot when he left the city attorney's Civil Division. If the captain from the department's legal liaison office hadn't been there, he would have told them all to go to hell and walked out ten minutes after the meeting started.

The volume of material they had gathered on him and Cathy was impressive. The intimate details they revealed were shocking. Loan applications, telephone bills listing multi-unit messages and long distance numbers, medical records, dental records, bills from the hotel where they last vacationed, character statements from friends and neighbors, credit card records, and school records that were seventeen years old.

Three senior deputies were assigned to handle the case. Their strategy emerged early. They were trying to paint Cathy Chilcoat as a gold digger, an unloving wife who had led her busy, devoted husband into an abyss of debt and now wanted more. Millions more—thus the lawsuit.

"You're all full of shit," Chilcoat barked, bolting to his feet when he could listen to no more. "The next sonofabitch that insults my wife is going to get his ass kicked."

The three city attorneys fell silent. One ashen-faced man cowered. The LAPD captain looked angry but he didn't challenge Chilcoat.

"I'll tell you who the goddamned gold digger is," Chilcoat spat at them. "It's the fuckin' police department. They're the ones that took everything I had. They're the ones that promised me they'd be faithful until death. They're the ones that came between me and my family. They're the ones that make me work sixty hours a week. They're the ones that call me in the middle of the night and made me work on my tenth anniversary. And they're the ones that should pay."

After Chilcoat stormed out the three city attorneys conferred. The bottom line of the confidential memo they drafted to the carrier of the city's liability insurance: "The overt hostility and bias on the part of the husband of the Plantiff makes the likelihood of a successful defense against the lawsuit remote. We recommend the prompt pursuit of an out-of-court settlement."

Cathy Chilcoat was wearing a pair of faded five-year-old jeans, a Mickey Mouse sweatshirt, and a fine mist of Navajo Sinclair Latex Interior Wall Paint. She was painting the hall bathroom. Cathy's blond hair wore streaks of Navajo paint and her red nails were dotted with pinpoints of white paint. She was nearly finished. She paused when she heard the noise in the front hallway. Was it her mother?

She wasn't supposed to arrive until the middle of the afternoon. It was the cat, Cathy concluded. She worked the roller in the paint tray and reached for the ceiling. Ceilings were a bitch. After fifteen minutes of it her neck was hurting, and the wet roller felt like a wet cement block. Again she heard the thump in the hallway. Cathy paused and set the paint roller in the tray. "Tabby," she threatened, "I'm going to kick your feline butt."

Stepping out of the bathroom into the fresh air, Cathy sniffed. The inside of her nose felt like paint, and her lashes kept sticking together. She rubbed her nose with the back of her hand and moved down the hallway to the entryway. She was shocked to find a ragged pile of men's shirts, pants, wire hangers, shoes, and fishing gear. She gasped just as Brad appeared in the open front door with an armload of pillows, sheets, and a pair of black rubber wading boots. He tossed it atop the pile on the floor and looked at Cathy. "I'm home, Cathy," he announced boldly. "And come hell or high water, I'm never leaving again. This is where I belong. This is my house and you're my wife. I was wrong. I'll tell you, I'll tell anybody." He turned to the open door, leaned out, and shouted, *"I was wrong!"* He turned back to the shocked Cathy. "I love you, Cathy. I'm dying without you. Please forgive me. Give me another chance. I'll do anything. I've changed. I'll be a good husband. I need you."

A well of emotion rose inside Cathy. She closed her eyes, bit her lip, and sank to her knees as a sob choked from her lips. She covered her face with her hands. Chilcoat stepped quickly over the pile, getting a foot tangled in fishing line. He knelt in front of Cathy and drew her into his arms. "Don't cry, baby. It's all over. It's all going to be okay. I'm going to take good care of you. Don't cry." Her arms came up and went around his neck to hold him. "Don't cry, baby," he sobbed through his own tears as he pulled her tighter against him.

Later Cathy was in the master bathroom recovering from the shock of her husband's return as she cleaned the paint from her hands and nails. Brad put away his clothes and fishing gear, then rolled up his sleeves and went to work finishing the painting in the hall bathroom. Cathy could hear him whistling. The sound was comforting. The telephone rang. "I got it," Chilcoat called. "I want the world to know I'm back and that I love you."

A moment later Chilcoat called from the hall, "Cathy, it's for you."

Cathy crossed the bedroom and sat down on the bed to pick up the telephone. "Hello."

"Cathy, its Greg Downing." It was her attorney. He sounded alarmed. "Who was that man? It sounded like your husband."

"It was."

"Oh, God, Cathy," Downing said. "You've got to get him out of there!"

"Greg, what's wrong?"

"Cathy, please just get him the hell out of the house."

"I'm not going to do anything until you tell me why."

"I just finished talking with Taylor Fox. He's the senior claims rep for Occidental Insurance. They carry the city's liability package. The city is offering you seven hundred and fifty thousand dollars to settle out of court."

Cathy didn't respond.

"Cathy," the man went on, "that's the better part of a million dollars."

Now she answered. "I know how much it is, Greg."

"If they even suspected your husband was there, they would accuse us of fraud and immediately withdraw the offer."

Cathy raised a hand to cover her eyes. "I don't know how to tell you this, Greg, but Brad's home to stay."

"Cathy, now listen to me. It's important you don't make an emotional decision. This money could—"

"Greg," Cathy interrupted, "I said my husband is home to stay. Tell them it's over. I'm not for sale." She hung up.

"Thanks," Brad Chilcoat said from the doorway.

Cathy looked at her husband and smiled. "I hope you're worth it."

"The bathroom's done." Chilcoat grinned, rolling down a sleeve. "Consider us even."

"Do you have to go back to work?" Cathy questioned.

"Yeah, but I'm not in a hurry."

"Good." Cathy smiled, lying back on the bed.


Dick Fredericks was splashing on a heavy dose of after-shave in the bathroom when his wife came into the bedroom. Clair glanced at him, noticing the fresh shirt and slacks. "Are you going out?" She seemed surprised.

Fredericks examined his image in the bathroom mirror. He ran a hand back over his hair to smooth it before he answered. "I've got to get out for a while. Maybe go down to the bowling alley." He looked at Clair. "After spending the night in jail I need a little space. I won't be too late."

"Richard," Clair cautioned, "I don't think this is wise. Not after what happened."

"What happened?" he challenged sharply. "Some ass-hole made a serious mistake. That's what happened."

"We need to talk, Richard."

"We can talk tomorrow."

"We're running out of tomorrows, Richard. I don't know how much more of this I can take."

He turned out the bathroom light and brushed by her. "If your going to leave me, finish the laundry first, would you?"

"You bastard, you're going to regret this, I know what you're doing," Clair shouted after him. Her only answer was a door slamming shut.

# 21

# DEATH DOTH PART

"Chilcoat," Lieutenant Stovich called from his desk, "take a message for Marshal on two-six."

Chilcoat punched the blinking button on the telephone console and picked it up. "This is Sergeant Chilcoat. I'm Detective Marshal's partner. May I help you?"

"Perhaps, sergeant. My name's Don Roberts. I'm a friend of Bobbi's. I've been trying to get in touch with her for a couple of days. She hasn't been at home and I've left messages at the station, but she hasn't returned my calls."

"I'm sorry you missed her. She left here maybe an hour ago."

"I called her at home. She doesn't answer."

Chilcoat was reading the worry in the man's voice. "Do you have a reason to be worried about her?"

Don didn't answer.

The silence was an answer for Chilcoat. "I don't know what's going on between you two, but if you've done anything to hurt her, Roberts, I'm going to take it very personal."

"It's nothing like that," he assured him.

"Then what is it?" Chilcoat pressed.

"I don't know that I have the right to tell you. I was hoping Bobbi would."

"If it concerns Bobbi's well-being," Chilcoat answered, "and if you're really concerned, and I can help, you're obligated to tell me."

"All right," Don said soberly. "She was raped."

"What!" Chilcoat blurted into the telephone. He was stunned. "When . . . who did this?" he questioned.

"I don't think she knows. He was waiting when she came home Friday night. He tied her up. I don't think she even saw his face."

"Oh, God, it was Big Foot."

"What was that?"

"Nothing. Listen, Roberts, let me see if I can get in touch with her. Where are you?"

"At my office."

"I'll tell her you called," Chilcoat promised, "and you were right in telling me."

Chilcoat hung up the telephone. His emotions were scrambled. That sonofabitch. How did he do it? Were they following the wrong man? My God! Bobbi had been sent to release him. Was it Fredericks? She'd been raped Friday night. He grabbed at a stack of reports on his desk and dug through them wildly. He found the copy of the five-ten release form. He looked at it then grabbed up the telephone. His hand trembled as he dialed the number. "Ring, you sonofabitch," he growled impatiently into the receiver.

Finally a woman's voice answered. "Hello."

"Mrs. Fredericks?" Chilcoat questioned.

"Yes."

"Mrs. Fredericks, this is Detective Sergeant Chilcoat from Wilshire Division. Is your husband home?"

"No, he's out. Is there a problem?"

Chilcoat could hear the apprehension in the woman's voice. "Could you tell me if he was home last Friday night?"

"He's in trouble again, isn't he?"

"Friday night, Mrs. Fredericks. It's very important."

"I worked until eleven," she answered. "I found a note when I came home. It said he went bowling."

"Was his car there?" Chilcoat asked, knowing that it was. He and Bobbi had followed Fredericks home from work on Friday night. The car was still in the driveway when they were relieved at ten p.m.

"Yes. He said he went with friends," Clair Fredericks answered. "He came in late."

"Thank you, Mrs. Fredericks." Chilcoat wanted to hang up.

"Sergeant," Clair said, "do you know where my husband is?"

"I'm sorry. No, I don't."

"It's him, isn't it, sergeant. He's a rapist."

"Mrs. Fredericks, I can't discuss it now." Chilcoat hung up. His heart was pounding in his ears. Bobbi had been raped by Big Foot on Friday night and then forced to release him from jail on Tuesday morning. She had never said a word. Now he was out on the street and Bobbi had gone home sick. The idea finally crystallized. Bobbi was planning to kill him. "My God," Chilcoat breathed as it hit him. He looked across the room. "Lieutenant!"

When she first arrived home Bobbi feared the man might already be there, waiting. Gun in hand, she had moved carefully from room to room. Now she sat in the dark living room, hidden in the shadows, waiting.

A soft light was on in the master bedroom, and the light was on in the bathroom with the door standing slightly ajar. She had filled the tub with hot water and bath oil. Its inviting aroma had drifted throughout the rooms. A touch of FM music in the bedroom added a final convincing touch. As soon as the man stepped into the dark condo, Bobbi was betting his eyes would go to the light spilling from the hallway. He would hear the music in the bedroom, detect the aroma of the bath oil, and, like a moth to a flame, be drawn down the hallway. Bobbi would stand, take careful aim between his shoulder blades, and call his name. He would turn, and in three seconds of fire and thunder it would be over. He would be dead, killed with the gun he had once held in his own hand as he violated her with it.

Sitting in the dark, with a gun in her lap, waiting to kill a man, was not her idea of a fun evening. But there were no options left. There was no other way now. The district attorney had made his decision. The shattered lives of nineteen women weren't enough reason to try Richard Fredericks in court. Whose rights had been violated? For those who had tasted the pain of his assault, even death seemed to fall short of a just punishment. It wasn't a matter of her taking the law into her own hands. The law had abandoned those nineteen women. In the absence of law it was the survival of the fittest. Winners wrote the history of the world. Bobbi Marshal wasn't about to let Richard Fredericks turn her into a loser.

The thought of the others brought Bobbi her first twinge of guilt. Nineteen other women had had the courage to do what she had failed to—call the police. Yes, but they weren't police officers. They didn't know how difficult it was to work in the macho world of cops. Add an admission of rape and it became impossible. Bobbi tried to recapture the anger that smothered her reason, but it kept eluding her. She was a hypocrite. She could call herself a cop but she no longer deserved to be one. The word cop didn't fit with failing to report crimes or setting a trap to kill a man. The moment she made the decision she had crossed the line. She knew she'd never be able to live with the guilt. A day or two after the shooting she'd voluntarily resign. Other cops had resigned after shootings. This would be her second in less than a week. No, no one would question it. Working at the bank wouldn't be that bad. It was difficult seeing herself as anything other than a cop. Time would change that. At least she hoped it would.

A shadow broke the strip of light at the bottom of the front door. A jolt of fear shot through Bobbi, stopping her breath. Someone was standing outside the door. Was it him? She moved the smooth surface of the gun in her palm. It was warm from her touch. My God, what if it was Don? Maybe it was he who called earlier. Now he had come over. What would she tell him? Maybe this was best. Maybe the killing was a bad idea. NO! Don't lose it. Do not go gentle. She curled her finger around the trigger. It was Fredericks. It had to be him. Don would have rung the bell by now. It was Fredericks, and he deserved what he was going to get.

The shadow moved. Bobbi was staring so hard her eyes ached. She forced herself to take a breath. She prayed he wouldn't hear. Her heart was pounding and her mouth was cotton-dry. What if he saw her? What if he ran? What if he saw the gun and went to the police? Oh, God, help me. She could feel the gun becoming slippery in her sweaty hands.

The shadow outside the door moved again. A key clicked in the lock. Bobbi's breath stopped. Her throat was aflame and her heart felt as if it were about to burst. A muscle began to dance in her leg. The gun felt like a slippery fish in her clammy hands.

The dead bolt on the door gave a crisp metallic snap as it opened. Bobbi sat paralyzed with fear, unable to move. She knew he would see her. The door would swing open and he would find her. He was going to rape her again.

Bobbi's mouth moved as the door inched open allowing in light from the hallway, but her voice was gone. She watched in terror as the familiar silhouette of Richard Fredericks stepped into the darkness of the room and quietly closed the door.

Eleven blocks away a detective car raced west on Wilshire Boulevard. Chilcoat was behind the wheel. Lieutenant Stovich was on the passenger's side. "Clear on the right," Stovich shouted as Chilcoat slowed for a red traffic light at Hauser Boulevard. Chilcoat laid on the horn and shot through the intersection. He swung the car to the curb lane and regained speed. The slower traffic swept by in a blur.

Stonehaven Towers looked quiet and peaceful when the detective car pulled to an abrupt stop in front. The two men scrambled out and ran up the steps to the double glass doors that lead into the illuminated lobby. Chilcoat grabbed the door. It was locked. He shook it and kicked at it in frustration. "Shit!"

Lieutenant Stovich moved to a row of brass call buttons with a recessed speaker. He punched six or eight buttons without reading names. "Yes," an irritated male voice answered from the speaker.

"Police, open the door," Stovich ordered.

"How do I know you're the police?"

"It's an emergency, open the goddamned door!"

Chilcoat was pulling on the door when the electric lock buzzed. It swung open and the two men hurried inside.

"What floor?" Stovich said as Chilcoat stabbed at the elevator call button.

"Six."

The elevator chimed. The doors parted. The two men stepped inside. Chilcoat pushed the floor number and the car began its climb. An instrumental version of "Moon River" drifted from an overhead speaker. Somehow it seemed to add to the elevator's slowness. "Come on, come on," Chilcoat willed impatiently. Finally the car stopped and the doors opened. "This way," he said.

The carpeted floor cushioned their footfalls as they ran down the hallway to Bobbi's door. Chilcoat pounded on the door and pushed the bell. "Bobbi," he called frantically. "Bobbi, open the door." He tried the knob. It was locked.

"Maybe we should kick it in," Stovich suggested.

Chilcoat hammered on the door with his fist. "Bobbi, open the door."

The lock clicked. Chilcoat stepped back. The door opened. The light from the hallway illuminated Bobbi's tear-streaked face. The blue steel revolver hung in a hand at her side. Bobbi looked to the two men. "He's in the hallway."

Chilcoat pushed by and moved inside. Light from the bathroom spilled into the hallway to reveal the form of the man lying facedown on the floor. "Oh, no," Chilcoat breathed. It wasn't until he stepped over him that he saw Fredericks's hands were locked behind his back with handcuffs. Chilcoat reached and flipped a light switch in the hallway. Fredericks was staring up at him. "I know." Chilcoat smiled down at him. "Someone made a mistake."

Bobbi and Lieutenant Stovich stood at the mouth of the hallway. The lieutenant had an arm around her shoulder. "I couldn't do it," Bobbi whispered. "I wanted to, but I just couldn't."

Lieutenant Stovich stayed with Bobbi while Chilcoat took the handcuffed Fredericks down to the lobby to be picked up by a black-and-white. Bobbi, calmer now, washed her hands, freshened her makeup, and sprayed on cologne to overcome the feeling of being dirty again. She joined the lieutenant at the kitchen bar. "I'm ready to give a statement."

"I wish I could say you don't have to," Stovich said.

"I was looking for an easy way out," Bobbi confessed. "I finally realized there are none."

Dan Shea sat in the interrogation room with Bobbi. He knew only that the man had been arrested at Bobbi's condo, and if he had any interest in the details, Bobbi couldn't see it. He wasn't there to ask questions. He had bought each of them a Diet Coke and now they were sitting and talking about carpets. It felt good to talk and think about something other than rape and death, but Bobbi knew it wouldn't be more than a brief reprieve. Soon her rape and the attempt at revenge would be common knowledge. Bobbi was sorry it was over. She had sometimes allowed herself to wonder how her career would end. She hadn't expected this. Her career, like the reality of justice, was turning out to be a disappointment. She felt very melancholy. She was going to miss men like Dan Shea.

"I'm here because Sergeant Chilcoat called me," Clair Fredericks told the uniformed officer at the reception desk in the station's front lobby.

"Okay," the officer said, coming from behind the desk, "come with me." The young officer led Clair down the hallway and into the detective squad room. There were several detectives and uniformed officers clustered near the Homicide table. "Wait here," the officer instructed Clair. He walked to the group. He recognized one of the detectives as Cliff Weldon from Homicide.

"Pardon me, Detective Weldon."

"Yeah."

"The lady over there claims Sergeant Chilcoat called her. Something about a rape."

Weldon glanced at the woman. "Just what we need, another walk-in victim. Chilcoat's in with the old man. Sit her down over at the Sex team's desk."

"Right."

The desk officer walked to the Sex team table. Bobbi's shoulder bag sat on the center of the desk. The officer picked it up and set it on the floor. Then, with a wave to Clair, "Ma'am, over here please."

Clair crossed to him. "Have a seat. Sergeant Chilcoat will be with you in a couple of minutes."

"Thank you," Clair said meekly and sat down.

The sober Captain John Stone sat in his office with Lieutenant Stovich and Chilcoat, listening as Chilcoat told what little he knew of his partner's rape. When he finished, the captain picked up a cup of coffee on his desk and tasted it. His mouth was dry. The coffee was cold and bitter. "Well," Stone said, clearing his throat, "if I understand correctly, Marshal's now willing to make a statement about her rape."

"Yes," Chilcoat answered.

"And she's willing to go to court?"

"Yes."

"What about the lack of vaginal slides," Stone questioned. "How will you prove a rape ever occurred?"

"Bobbi's rape was four days ago. So we don't have slides but we can use testimony from the doctor she saw on Sun-

day. She also has bruises all over her body. She'll allow
SID to take pictures,'' Chilcoat explained. ''We've got her
testimony and the nylons he used to tie her up with, and
the grand prize is the key the sonofabitch used to get into
her condo tonight. Big Foot used a key every time.''

''Okay,'' the captain agreed. ''But we're still hamstrung
on this thing. We've got enought evidence to prosecute the
bastard, but if we put him in jail tonight we're going to
have to deal with the fact she lured him back there. You
and I know it was to kill him, but the defense will say she
invited him back the second time because she also invited
him there the first time . . . and then our case turns to dog
piss.''

''How do we overcome it?'' Lieutenant Stovich asked,
taking the unlit cigar from his mouth.

''We let Fredericks walk tonight. Kick his ass out on
the street. In the morning you take Marshal to the DA's
office. Have her make a detailed statement. File the criminal complaint and get an arrest warrant.''

''Do you know how difficult it's going to be to turn this
sonofabitch loose?'' Chilcoat complained.

''You got a better idea?'' Captain Stone countered.

''No.''

''Where's Bobbi?'' Lieutenant Stovich questioned.

''Interrogation room two with Dan Shea.''

''Let's get her out of there before we cut Fredericks
loose. Have Shea take her down the hall to the coffee
room.''

Chilcoat nodded and pushed from his chair.

''How is she?'' the captain questioned.

''How would you be?'' Chilcoat answered.

Clair Fredericks watched as the detective came out of
the office and walked to one of the three doors along the
wall close to her seat. When the door opened she glimpsed
a woman and a man sitting inside. When the door opened
a second time the two men and the woman came out. The
young brunette looked shaken. She moved by Clair, fol-

lowing the two men to the hallway, where they disappeared. Clair was still staring after them when the scent reached her. The brunette's perfume sent an electric jolt surging through Clair. It was the smell her husband had brought home on his body last Friday night. The heavy weight of the realization settled over her. There had been no mistake. Richard was what she hadn't even allowed herself to think, a rapist! The panties hidden under the seat of his car, the circles on the calendar, the lies about where he was, the humiliating efforts at making love to her. It all became painfully clear. She was closing her eyes when she saw the gun in an open purse at her feet.

She had her hand over her face when the man touched her shoulder. "Mrs. Fredericks?"

Clair raised her head. It was the detective she'd seen earlier. She brushed away a tear. "Yes."

"It wasn't necessary for you to come in," Chilcoat said.

"I . . . I needed to know what was wrong."

"Your husband's been arrested."

"What for?" she questioned apprehensively.

"He was in a woman's apartment but we're going to release him."

Clair stiffened some as she remembered her husband's words. "I'm going down to the bowling alley. I won't be late." She took a deep breath to steady herself and looked up into Chilcoat's face. "Is my husband a rapist?"

"I can't answer that."

"But can't you see I need to know?" Clair pleaded, tears streaming down her cheeks. "He's lied to me. I have a right to know. I'm his wife. Can't you see what this is doing to me?"

"Yes, ma'am, I know. And I'm sorry, but I still can't discuss it with you." Chilcoat turned his back and moved to the door of one of the interview rooms. Clair knew her husband was waiting in there and she didn't want to see him. She didn't want to hear his lies. Why couldn't they keep him? Why couldn't they help her? Why couldn't they understand what he was doing to her? Damn him. Goddamn him. Clair's pain flashed to an angry rage when she heard his sarcastic laugh. "She told you she set me up, right? Just like the first time. I don't have to rape anyone. I can get plenty of pussy."

Clair looked up through a veil of tears as he stepped from the interview room. Fredericks stopped when he saw her. He realized she'd heard his boasting. "Who in the hell asked you to come here?" he demanded.

The words stung. Clair lowered her head to escape his anger and again saw the gun in the purse. She grabbed it without hesitation. Raising the blue steel pistol, Clair pushed to her feet. She aimed the gun with two shaky hands. "No more," she screamed. "No more."

"Lady, don't," Chilcoat pleaded with an outstretched hand.

"Jesus Christ," Cliff Weldon said as he dived for cover.

Captain Stone jerked open the door of his office.

"Clair," Dick Fredericks said, reaching toward her. "Put the gun down."

The gun exploded and Fredericks's left eye disappeared. A flap of hair and scalp sprang from the back of his head, peppering the wall and Brad Chilcoat with bits of blood and brain.

When he didn't fall, Clair fired a second time. The second bullet punched a dark, pencil-sized hole in the middle of his forehead. Blood jetted from his ear. He staggered backward, his head bobbing. He bumped into the wall and slid down, leaving a red swath of blood on the tan plaster.

Clair followed the fallen form with the gun. She was about to fire again when Chilcoat lunged. He grabbed the woman's hands and pushed the barrel of the gun high. It exploded. Plaster rained down over them. Chilcoat twisted and wrenched the gun from her hands as a uniformed officer grabbed her from behind and took her quickly to the floor with a choke hold.

Chilcoat leaned on a nearby desk, wiping the blood from his face. His ears were ringing from the concussion of the shots. He was breathing hard. "Jesus," he muttered softly.

Others quickly gathered around the body. A cloud of blue smoke hung in the air. It was rich with the acidy smell of burned powder.

"Is he dead?" a young officer asked as if afraid of the answer. No one answered him.

"Get the woman down the hall into the holding tank." It was Captain Stone. "Weldon, get us an ambulance. Lieutenant, I want the name and serial number of everybody in the room and nobody leaves. Chilcoat, you hang on to that gun. Where in the hell's Shea?"

"Right here," Shea answered from the door to the hallway. Bobbi was at his side. She was staring at the body on the floor and the blood that pooled around its head. A few feet away she saw her open purse on the floor. Now she knew whose gun the woman had used. She felt her stomach tightening.

"You got a homicide to handle, sergeant. Let's get started."

"Yes, sir."

The captain looked at Bobbi. "Marshal, did you see any of this?"

"No, sir," Bobbi answered soberly.

"Then get out of here."

Bobbi turned and walked away.

# EPILOGUE

Don Roberts called shortly after the black-and-white dropped Bobbi off at home. He wanted to come over but Bobbi made excuses. Yes, she was fine. Yes, she was busy. She gave him a maybe on Friday night for dinner. How could she tell him what had happened? She wasn't sure she understood it herself. Maybe it was as simple as the conversation she'd heard in the watch commander's office minutes afterward. "Hey, what happened in the squad room?"

"Nothing. Some asshole got shot."

Cop justice, or fate? She didn't know. Maybe they were one and the same.

Bobbi took a bath, did her nails, and fought the urge to call the station. Damn Captain Stone. Her partner was there. Dan Shea was there. She had a right to be there. Would any of them be there if it wasn't for her? The answer to that, she knew, was the reason she wasn't there. It was over, and she already missed it.

She turned the news on at eleven. The report from the scene was brief. The reporter was standing in front of Wilshire Station for his forty-second segment. "Police are refusing to identify the slain suspect until next of kin are notified, but they have stated the man was in custody for the investigation of rape. We've learned from an informed source that the police suspect he may have been the brutal rapist the police were calling 'Big Foot.' The irony in this shooting is that the suspect was shot by his wife. The shooting, as we said earlier, took place in the station. Police are not saying how the woman managed to carry the gun in undetected. We'll have more details as they become available. Back to you at the studio, Joan.''

Bobbi curled up on the couch in the living room. Waiting to fall asleep, she thought about Clair Fredericks. Clair had done what Bobbi couldn't. Bobbi pitied her. She understood Clair's pain. Maybe, Bobbi thought, after a while she would visit her. She wasn't sure what she would say, but she knew it was important the woman know someone cared.

Except for the small hole in the door of interrogation room three and the pencil-sized hole in the ceiling, the squad room looked normal. It was full of its usual morning chatter, busier perhaps, with talk of the shooting.

Although Bobbi had been the catalyst for the shooting death of Richard Fredericks, the Detective Bureau seemed casual about their interest in her. There were a few questions when she first arrived. ''Is it true Big Foot came into your apartment?''

''Where were you when she shot him?''

''In the coffee room.'' In their eyes that made Bobbi as much a spectator as they were and the questions quickly ceased.

Bobbi noticed Dan Shea and Cliff Weldon weren't at their desks. Neither was Lieutenant Stovich. When eight o'clock came and Brad Chilcoat didn't appear, she guessed that he, like the others, was at home asleep. No doubt the shooting investigation took most of the night.

She was surprised when the door to the captain's office opened and Lieutenant Stovich and Brad Chilcoat came out. Both men looked haggard. It was obvious neither had had any sleep. Stovich went to his desk and Chilcoat walked to where Bobbi sat at the Sex team table. His shirt was dotted with what looked like pinpoints of dried blood. ''Bobbi,'' Chilcoat said, sinking into the chair across from her, ''the skipper wants to see you.''

"You've been here all night?" Bobbi questioned.

"Yeah." Chilcoat nodded. "Cathy's probably at home working on a new lawsuit."

"I'm sorry, Brad."

"Hey, no sweat." He smiled. "I got a real bang out of it."

Bobbi pushed out of her chair. "Any idea what he wants?"

"Not often do captains confide in me."

Bobbi noticed Captain Stone's face was dark with beard when she was escorted in by his adjutant. "Sit down, Marshal," the captain said. "Did you get some rest?"

"Yes, sir."

"You've got friends in this division, Marshal. As a matter of fact, they kept me up most of the night talking about you."

"I don't know what to say, sir."

"They pointed out that no matter how much we try we'll never know the horror that you've been through. Never."

Bobbi didn't respond.

"I've only been in the division a short time, Marshal, but I've seen you do good work while under a great deal of stress. I hate to lose people just because they make mistakes."

Bobbi remained tense and silent.

"Cops are always being forced to make decisions, most of them under stress, so it's not surprising that sometimes we make mistakes. I can accept a mistake when it's admitted, and honest. You've admitted yours. Isn't that correct?"

"Yes, sir."

"The man who raped you is dead. You, me, Sergeant Chilcoat, and Lieutenant Stovich are the only ones in the department that know about your rape. That correct?"

"Yes, sir."

"Is there anyone else we need to worry about?"

"No, sir."

"What you've suffered, Marshal, is a rare and exceptional problem. Exceptional problems sometimes call for exceptional solutions. I don't have to tell you what you've done wrong. You know. I can only warn that it would never be tolerated again. Each of us at one time or another needs help in our careers, so don't think what I'm about to propose is charity or sympathy. You're probably a better cop now than you were a week ago. Good cops are hard to find, and I think you're a good cop, Marshal. If you can pull it together, I'd like you to stay."

"I . . . I'd like that, too, sir." Bobbi's voice was little more than a whisper.

"Then in my opinion it serves no purpose to report your rape. With your agreement, we'll consider the matter closed, forgotten."

"I . . . I agree," Bobbi stammered. "You won't regret this, sir."

"All right then, get out of here and get back to work."

"Yes, sir." Bobbi pushed out of her chair. Her heart was racing with excitement. She moved for the door, paused, looked back at the captain. "Thank you, captain."

"For what?"


Bobbi brushed a tear from her eye as she closed the door to the captain's office behind her. She thought her heart was going to burst. She wanted to shout, laugh, cry, but she did nothing other than walk back to her desk. Chilcoat was waiting. There were tears in Bobbi's eyes when she reached him.

"Thanks," she managed with effort.

Chilcoat smiled.

# POLICE THRILLERS
## "THE ACKNOWLEDGED MASTER" *Newsweek*
# ED McBAIN

POISON                                    70030-1/$3.95US/$4.95Can
"Sums up the hot-wire style that has kept McBain ahead of the
competition for three decades."            *Philadelphia Inquirer*

EIGHT BLACK HORSES                        70029-8/$3.95US/$4.95Can
A series of bizarre clues signals the return of the Deaf Man—
who this time intends to exact his full measure of revenge.

LIGHTNING                                 69974-5/$3.95US/$4.95Can
The compelling new novel in the 87th Precinct series, where
the dedicated men and women who wear the gold badge push
themselves to the limit of danger.

ICE                                       67108-5/$3.95US/$5.50Can
"In the rough and raunchy world of the 87th Precinct…a half-
dozen murders—including a magnificent piece of street
justice—keep nerves jangling."            *Philadelphia Inquirer*

DOLL                          70082-4/$3.50 US/$4.50 Can

THE MUGGER                    70081-6/$3.50 US/$4.50 Can

HE WHO HESITATES              70084-0/$3.50 US/$4.50 Can

KILLER'S CHOICE               70083-2/$3.50 US/$4.50 Can

BREAD                         70368-8/$3.50 US/$4.50 Can

80 MILLION EYES               70367-X/$3.50 US/$4.50 Can

HAIL TO THE CHIEF             70370-X/$3.50 US/$4.50 Can

LONG TIME NO SEE              70369-6/$3.50 US/$4.50 Can

DOORS                         70371-8/$3.50 US/$4.50 Can

WHERE THERE'S SMOKE           70372-6/$3.50 US/$4.50 Can